I0654493

The Streets Made Me 3

Lock Down Publications and Ca$h
Presents

The Streets Made Me 3

A Novel by *Larry D. Wright*

Lock Down Publications
P.O. Box 944
Stockbridge, Ga 30281

Copyright 2020 by Larry D. Wright
The Streets Made Me 3

All rights reserved. No part of this book may be reproduced in any form or by electronic or mechanical means, including information storage and retrieval systems without permission in writing from the publisher, except by a reviewer who may quote brief passages in review.
First Edition September 2021
Printed in the United States of America

This is a work of fiction. Names, characters, places, and incidents either are products of the author's imagination or are used fictitiously. Any similarity to actual events or locales or persons, living or dead, is entirely coincidental.

Lock Down Publications
Like our page on Facebook: Lock Down Publications @
www.facebook.com/lockdownpublications.ldp
Book interior design by: **Shawn Walker**
Edited by: **Lashonda Johnson**

Larry D. Wright

Stay Connected with Us!

Text **LOCKDOWN** to 22828 to stay up-to-date with new releases, sneak peaks, contests and more...

Thank you!

Submission Guideline.

Submit the first three chapters of your completed manuscript to ldpsubmissions@gmail.com, subject line: Your book's title. The manuscript must be in a .doc file and sent as an attachment. Document should be in Times New Roman, double spaced and in size 12 font. Also, provide your synopsis and full contact information. If sending multiple submissions, they must each be in a separate email.

Have a story but no way to send it electronically? You can still submit to LDP/Ca$h Presents. Send in the first three chapters, written or typed, of your completed manuscript to:

LDP: Submissions Dept
P.O. Box 944
Stockbridge, Ga 30281

DO NOT send original manuscript. Must be a duplicate.

Provide your synopsis and a cover letter containing your full contact information.

Thanks for considering LDP and Ca$h Presents.

Dedication:

Especially for my son, Jeshurun Wright, and all the other victims of the deadly opioid crisis.

Acknowledgments

I'm hungry for success and plan to eat off this book game by any means necessary. Despite my relentless ambition, my compelling stories would remain caged in my head without the dedicated team working behind the scenes. Big shout-out to my project manager, Adriannah Beckham. You came through in the ninth inning and hit a home run when the haters tried to derail this project. Sincere thanks to Ca$h, Shawn Walker, my editor, my graphics arts team, and the entire Lock Down Publications roster. We the best!

Bless up to Wink, my biggest fan. Cassie, big sis! Tasha lil' sis! Steven, baby bro! Dana Goodnight, Roscoe, Jaishawn Stoudemire, Jimmy Henchmen, Freeway Rick, Lala the Clown, Sonia Mack, Lady Boss. Courtney Williams, that bullet was meant for me. J-Dub, you owe me. I took the charge, plus that Fed Ex package was short ten pounds. Much love to all those who have touched my life and influenced my writing. Baller Belly Empire 'till death do us or the feds unglue us. God is amazing!

About the Author

Hard-hitting and unapologetic are adjectives that describe the writing style of crime novelist Larry D. Wright. A native of Los Angeles, California, Mr. Wright uses his real-life experiences and vivid imagination to weave provocative tales of love, betrayal, revenge, and redemption. "I strive to make my characters raw, realistic, and relatable," insists the talented story teller.

Mr. Wright is signed to Lock Down Publications and continues to find success with his action-packed crime series, "The Streets Made Me." His future projects include more novels, Street Lit Magazine, a web series, and a podcast titled, Late Night with Larry Wright. "I plan on using my passion for literature and technology to build a lucrative multimedia empire," Mr. Wright reveals.

"I'm not a perfect man. My reputation of being ruthless, unfor-giving, and relentless proceeds me." ~J. Prince~

Larry D. Wright

Chapter 1

God Forgives: I Don't

It was a perfect night for a homicide—hot, humid, and unusually quiet. Darkness gripped the city of Los Angeles like O.J.'s glove. Najee's heart thumped in his chest as he parked on Mulholland Drive and tucked his burner into the small of his back. He exited the vehicle slowly and allowed his eyes to become acclimated with his surroundings before merging with the shadows. Black jeans, black Timbs, and a black hoodie camouflaged his movements.

He proceeded with caution, his target was a formidable opponent, beautiful, wealthy, and extremely treacherous. Angela Rodriguez was a major drug distributor and a sicario for the nation's deadliest criminal enterprise. She murdered her unsuspecting victims by sneaking up behind them and wrapping piano wire tightly around their necks. The FBI began calling the lethal strangulation technique the Spanish Guillotine.

For the past several months the cocaine diva had been Najee's coke connect, lover, and mortal enemy. The latter was the reason adrenaline surged through his trigger finger. He breached Angela's security system and hid behind the tall hedges lining the cobblestone driveway of her Hollywood Hills mansion. As always, he fully understood that he was going to the morgue if he got shot or to the Feds if he got caught. It was that simple.

There are no fairytale endings for those who embark on a life of crime, therefore, relying on one's instincts becomes essential. Paranoia becomes a welcomed companion, an asset so to speak. It helps your spider senses tingle and keeps your edges razor sharp because the moment you stop looking over your shoulder or forget that skepticism is the best defense mechanism, *Bada Boom-Bada Bing*! It's a wrap, game over!

Najee could feel death around the corner. Its long tentacles gripped his throat, squeezing, constricting, pushing him closer to the inevitable. So far, however, he had evaded the grave, eluded the law, and outwitted his enemies.

11

He crouched low behind the row of thick bushes and racked a Teflon slug into his blicky. He was patient, professional, and prepared to post up all night if need be. As he waited, a sense of accomplishment swept through him. Just under an hour ago, he had avenged his loved ones by murdering Benzo Al, the powerful and equally ruthless leader of Los Cinco Diablos.

Revenge is best served cold, but it was hot .45 slugs that gave Najee retribution and caused Benzo Al's early demise. He murked the Mexican kingpin slowly and methodically, enjoying each bullet just as a hungry wolf savors its prey, yet Najee wasn't a mindless killing machine. There was a method to his madness and a noble cause behind his savagery.

As Najee adjusted into a more comfortable position, he contemplated the origins of his war with the cartel. Los Cinco Diablos, also known as The Five Devils, used murder, intimidation, and an elaborate network of drug tunnels to strong-arm their way to the top. Their members were unapologetic, unpredictable, and utterly unrepentant.

On Benzo Al's orders, Los Cinco Diablos soldiers murdered Najee's parents, raped his fiancé, and kidnapped his son. Living up to their barbaric reputation, Angela personally cut off the child's thumb and promised to deliver a body part each day until there was nothing left to bury except his dick. Such heinous crimes deserved an equivalent punishment, so as far as Najee was concerned, the murders thus far were warranted, absolutely necessary, and sheer poetic justice. Killing Angela and robbing her stash house would be equally enjoyable.

An unmarked squad car eased through the nine-foot black iron gate and stopped inches away from Najee's hiding spot. He ducked low and gripped the butt of his gun. Angela sat in the passenger seat. Distress crisscrossed her features. It had been a long day. Special Agent John Sullivan, a slippery third-generation cop, sat behind the wheel. A condescending smirk creased the corners of his lips. Najee wanted to stand up and drill both of them, but he had ten million reasons not to. Instead, he leaned forward and caught snippets of their conversation.

"How much did the Committee pay you to sell out and help me escape?" Angela inquired.

The Committee was the five Los Cinco Diablos board members.

The smug look on Agent Sullivan's face deepened. "Actually, they didn't pay me to help you escape."

"Wha—what do you mean?" Angela stuttered. Her hand reached for the door handle.

Agent Sullivan quickly jabbed her in the ribs with his gun. "You and Benzo Al were standing in the way of a lucrative merger with the Nogales Cartel," he explained. "So, the Committee put a green light on both of you."

The revelation floored Angela. Agent Sullivan aimed the tool at her melon and applied pressure on the blue steel trigger. Angela had no delusions about the game. She knew this day would come. No fairytale endings. She closed her eyes and whispered a prayer to Malverde.

Bang! Bang!

A flock of frightened pigeons flew from the trees. A dog barked in the distance.

Angela opened her eyes and screamed. The grotesque pink and red gash in Agent Sullivan's head oozed thick fluid. Blood splattered on the left side of her face. Chunks of brain and skull fragments splashed into her mouth. She gagged and spit the salty pulp and bits of bone onto the floor mat.

Najee reached through the shattered window, popped the locks, and pulled Angela out by her ponytail.

"Move, bitch!" he ordered and shoved her toward the house.

Angela stumbled and broke one of her Ferragamo heels. Najee was the last person she wanted to see, yet she was relieved to be alive.

As she limped up the cobblestone walkway, she asked, "Why did you kill Agent Sullivan? I thought the two of you had an understanding," she spoke clear English with a hint of her Mexican heritage.

Najee jammed his gun against Angela's spine and pushed her forward. "Don't play stupid," he warned.

They both knew Agent Sullivan was a crooked cop who sold his soul and services to the highest bidder. No cartel operated without corrupt officials who accepted la mordida, *the bite*, which is street slang for bribes. Najee marched onward and punched in the six digits to disarm the house alarm.

Angela was surprised that he knew her security code. She needed to stall for time, so she began asking questions. "How long have you been planning this?"

"Toda mi vida. All of my life." Najee enjoyed the shocked look on Angela's face when she discovered he spoke Spanish, but the question was the distraction she desperately needed.

Najee foolishly forced her into the domed ceiling living room without frisking her for a weapon. He looked around cautiously to make sure they were alone, then steered Angela toward the mysterious locked door on the first floor. She never allowed him into that part of the mansion, so he was positive the room held her safe.

"No more questions! Stop bumpin' yo' gums and open this fuckin' door," his tone was serious and determined.

He kept his strap pressed firmly against Angela's backbone and watched her closely as she slid a key into the lock and twisted the brass doorknob. He nudged the door open with the toe of his Timberland boot and cautiously followed her inside. His eyes quickly swept across the room. Infant clothing hung in the walk-in closet and a cherry wood baby crib sat in the corner where he expected the safe to be. Confusion tangled his mind into a tight knot.

"You have a baby?" he managed to utter.

Angela smiled and proudly rubbed her growing belly. "I will in about seven months."

Najee caught a case of the bubble guts. He intuitively knew the baby belonged to him. He and Angela did not make love, they made lust. Their sex was rough, passionate, and unprotected. On many nights Angela would lock her thick legs around his back and beg him to cum deep inside of her. He did so willingly over and over again.

14

Her deception fueled his rage.

"You told me you were on the pill! I should blast yo' triflin' ass for lying to me!" He aimed the ratchet at her chest.

Unperturbed by the threat, Angela stepped close to Najee. Her luscious lips were next to his. The gun barrel was only inches away from her nipples. She seductively caressed the scar on the side of his face. The fresh knife wound was courtesy of Benzo Al.

"I hate you," she began. "But I love you so much more, papi. What's even crazier is that I'm sad for you, too—" She paused, and a single tear rolled down her right cheek. She wiped it away with the back of her hand and continued, "You're like the twilight. You're suspended between darkness and light. The darkness representing evil, the light symbolizing good. Remember I told you that one day you would have to choose a side? Well, today is that day. Either you kill me or let me go."

Najee's trigger finger trembled. He was a man who lived by gangster principles. Killing a child went against every code he stood for.

Angela knew this and used it to her advantage.

"Put the gun down, Najee. You can't kill me."

Chic! Chic!

Nella appeared from seemingly nowhere and chambered a slug into her Glock 40.

"But I can, bitch!"

She kept the heat trained on Angela as she informed Najee that Detective Brooks had a plane and new passports waiting for them at a private airstrip in Bakersfield.

"Let me shoot this cartel tramp so we can bounce."

Najee lowered his gun with a deep sigh. His shoulders sagged under the weight of his mistake.

"I can't let you shoot her." He took a step toward Nella.

Nella took a step back.

"Why?" she quizzed.

She couldn't comprehend why he wanted to spare Angela's life after all the pain and loss the Diablos had caused. Something wasn't right.

Angela threw coals on the kindling fire.

"Tell her what you know in your heart, Najee. Tell her I'm pregnant with your baby."

"Your baby?" Nella asked.

The freckles on her redbone skin seemed to darken when she frowned. Tension swelled in her veins, and her heart pounded. She was hurt but wasn't going to give the other woman the satisfaction of seeing her cry.

"I thought you loved me?"

Najee faced Nella and gazed lovingly into her eyes.

"I do love you. Angela don't mean shit to me. I was just doing what I had to do in order to get to Benzo Al," he confessed.

Nella's heart softened, but her eyes hardened.

"Then prove it. Shoot this bitch! Not for me. Do it because she's going to teach that baby to hate you. One day he'll be in your nightmares, the next he'll be at your front door with a gun."

Angela saw an opportunity to make her move. As Nella and Najee argued, she eased her pistol from the small of her back.

Najee contemplated Nella's words. She was probably right, but he didn't want the blood of a child on his hands.

He positioned himself between Nella and Angela and said, "If that's my fate, then so be it, but I can't murder my own seed."

"Then I will."

"I won't let you."

Nella raised her gun.

Najee raised his gun.

Angela raised her gun.

Chapter 2

All or Nothing or Nothing At All

"Watch out!" Angela screamed and shoved Najee and Nella out of harm's way.

Blocka! Blocka! Blocka!

A young-looking Mexican man in black, military fatigues squeezed off three rounds. The APC ammo missed their target.

Angela kneeled on one knee and aired him out with her .380. Two slugs penetrated his chest. He dropped with a thud.

Nella and Najee recovered just as two more young shooters stood in the doorway. The baby-faced assassins were fit, reckless, and armed with Remington AR-15s. The *N* insignias on their military fatigues identified them as Nogales Cartel operatives. Unfortunately, youth and ignorance run parallel. The inexperienced gunmen left themselves exposed.

A Nogales Cartel soldier stepped inside the bedroom. Najee aimed his burner center mass and double-tapped the trigger. Two Teflon slugs ripped through his intestines and kidney. The third gunman raised the muzzle of his AR. Nella swung the .40 caliber in his direction, aimed, realized she couldn't get off a clean shot, so she took cover just as the gunman squeezed off a three-round burst. Angela came off her knees blasting. She struck the young cartel soldier in the neck. The bullet sliced through his trachea. Blood squirted from his jugular vein.

As quickly as the shooting started, it ended. One of the downed gunmen gargled blood and chanted in Spanish. Najee stood over him and pointed his banger at the assailant's dome.

"Wait, don't shoot! Let him finish," Angela pleaded.

"Why, what is he saying?"

"He's praying to Malverde, the patron saint of narcos."

Unimpressed, Nella walked up to the mangled body and drove two bullets into his face.

"Fuck him and you!" she declared and mean mugged Angela.

Angela rolled her eyes.

"Your shade don't faze me, bitch!"

"I got cho' bitch right here," Nella rebutted and turned her gun sideways gangster style.

Najee stepped between the beefing women.

"Yo, y'all chill the fuck out! If we survive this shit, y'all can kill each other then, but we gotta stick together for now." He looked both women in the eyes to make sure they understood.

The women mumbled their displeasure but complied.

"Angela, what's crackin'? Why is the Nogales Cartel on your heels?"

"You tell me. You're the one who made a deal with the devil."

"With the death of Benzo Al, the merger should be secure, right?"

"Wrong! You got played. There was never gonna be a merger. Men like El Feo don't share their throne. It's all or nothing or nothing at all."

The power suddenly went out, and the room got pitch black. Angela swept the curtains aside and looked out of the window.

"Aww, shit!"

Four similarly dressed assassins ran across the front lawn. She heard one of them giving orders. Angela kicked off her heels and tucked her gun in the front of her jeans.

"We have more company. Quick, follow me."

Nella and Najee looked at each other indecisively and then reluctantly followed Angela into the bathroom. They arrived in time to watch her bend over the tub, turn the hot water valve counterclockwise and lift the stainless-steel faucet. A locking mechanism clicked open. She raised the fiberglass tub like the hood of a car. A rusty ladder led down into the city's sewerage system. Najee was impressed by the cartel's ingenuity and criminal savvy.

Authorities believed that Los Cinco Diablos were the architects of a number of sophisticated tunnels scattered across Mexico, Texas, Arizona, and California. The clandestine tunnels were used to smuggle fugitives, money, drugs, and other illegal cargo. It was rumored that the engineers who designed and constructed the underground passages were murdered when the project was complete so that their locations would remain a secret.

Conspiring whispers came from the hallway. The leader issued orders in Spanish. "¡Traemelo, ahora! Bring them to me, now!"

Angela climbed onto the rusty ladder.

"Hurry, we gotta roll out!" The damp metal felt cold under her bare feet.

Najee helped Nella descend the ladder, and then he followed. Moving too quickly, his foot slipped on the last rung, and he landed in a puddle of sewer water. A Nogales Cartel soldier appeared in the opening. His mistake cost him his life. Nella drilled him with three shots to the torso. He grunted and fell backward. His comrades wisely hesitated before descending the ladder.

The cylindrical-shaped tunnel was low, perhaps five feet high, green mold grew on the concrete walls. The murky, ankle-high sewage water smelled like urine and mildew. A faint, circular ray of light trickled in from a drain cover located the distance of a football field to the west. Angela, Najee, and Nella ducked low and ran in that direction. They were followed by automatic gunfire. A .223 bullet nicked Angela's ear and knocked a chunk out of the cement. Nella swiveled around, aimed, emptied her clip, and kept running without breaking her stride. The gunman fell face first and splashed in the sewage water.

At the end of the tunnel, the women stopped and stared at each other. Angela touched her ear, then examined the blood on her fingers before expressing her gratitude.

"I saved your life, and you saved mine. Now we're even, bitch."

"Like I said, hoe, I got cho' bitch right here."

Nella knew her clip was empty, but she taunted Angela anyhow by aiming the .40 at her face and pulling the trigger.

Click! Click!

Najee shook his head realizing he was in for a lifetime of baby mama drama.

"Y'all stop sizing each other up and watch my back while I push open this drain cover."

19

They needed to move quickly. The sounds of Spanish-speaking men and boots splashing in water approached from the rear.

Nella looked up. They were under the source of light. The brown manhole cover was adjacent to another ladder. Najee climbed up first. He pushed upward on the heavy, steel cover until it came ajar and then used his fingers to pry it all the way open. He slid the cover to the right and stuck his head out of the opening. The manhole was in the middle of a side street. Najee was greeted by fresh air, streetlights, and the buzz of evening traffic traveling on the intersecting thoroughfare.

Having a sense of urgency, he used his upper body strength to climb out of the round opening, then assisted Angela and Nella. They made it out just as the remaining Nogales pistoleros appeared under them. Najee popped off four shots to provide cover fire as Angela and Nella slid the manhole cover in place.

They were happy to be alive, however, their elation was short-lived. Two black GMC Yukons swooped up followed by a black sprinter van and high beam headlights blinded the trio. Men with black ski masks and assault weapons equipped with Tricon infrared beams jumped out of the first SUV and surrounded Najee, Nella, and Angela. Red dots appeared on their foreheads.

"Manos arriba," a masked man ordered them to put their hands in the air.

A second man confiscated their guns.

Najee noticed the letter N tatted on his wrist in Old English.

A handsome, chiseled-faced Latino man rolled down the back window of the second SUV. He had the athletic physique of an underwear model and the rugged good looks of a villain in a Quentin Tarantino movie. The top three buttons of his blue and yellow Versace shirt were open revealing a smooth, muscular chest and a Malverde medallion hanging from a thin gold chain. He was a narcos. His gold Rolex glistened like the fire in his captivating eyes. His entire persona exuded wealth, power, and danger.

He exhibited his authority by snapping his fingers. His men immediately grabbed Angela and placed a black burlap bag over her head. She struggled to escape, but the men were too strong and determined. Najee rushed forward to assist her but was slugged in the gut with the stiff stock of an assault rifle. He folded over and fell to the ground.

The masked men slung Angela into the side door of the sprinter van and smashed off. The two SUVs followed closely behind.

As Najee peeled himself off the pavement, Angela's words did somersaults in his mind, all or nothing or nothing at all.

Nella noticed the haunted look on Najee's face, and asked, "Who the hell was that?"

"That was El Feo, the Ugly One!"

Larry D. Wright

Chapter 3

Absolute Power

"Salud." Julio 'El Feo' Estrada Jr. held up a shot glass of Cuervo and toasted his men to another job well done.

The men returned the salutation, drained the tequila, and disbursed, leaving the boss and his bodyguard, Gustavo alone at Metro Tire World in Boyle Heights.

The tire shop was a front for the Nogales Cartel. It was a place where they stashed money and drugs. The bodyguard bolted the front door and stood at the entrance with his muscular, tatted arms folded across his wide chest.

El Feo remained in the corner office with the lights out. He lounged in a leather recliner with his legs crossed. The carrot-orange embers on the end of his cigar grew brighter with every puff. Inhale, exhale—gray plumes of smoke oozed from each nostril. The tire shop was hot and oppressive, but there was a cool determination about his demeanor.

From the large window in his office, he could see Angela. Hemp rope bound her to a chair, plastic security ties restrained her wrists and fear gripped her soul. She had good reason to be afraid. She knew El Feo well. He had a penchant for extortion, vicious assaults, drug trafficking, torture, and of course, murder. He shared the number one spot within the Nogales criminal syndicate. He had cheated, intimidated, and killed his way to that prestigious position.

At the beginning of the decade-long war with Los Cinco Diablos, his father, Señor Julio Estrada was kidnapped in Juarez, Mexico. The family patiently and optimistically waited for a ransom request; none came. The bloated body was discovered in a cemetery near Nogales with his hands and feet cut off. El Feo retaliated by beheading three Los Cinco Diablos soldiers. The decaying head of Ramón Vega was found in his daughter's backpack with his dick stuffed down his throat. The heads of the other cartel operatives were never recovered, but their decapitated bodies were found sitting upright in the pews of a Catholic church.

Many more murders and mutilations followed, and the streets ceased calling him Baby Face. His charm and good looks were an illusion. It was his gruesome acts of terror that earned him the name El Feo, the Ugly One. Lose a shipment or come up short, and he'd force you to watch as he doused your kids with gasoline and set them on fire while they were still alive. Become a rat, and he'd cut your tongue out first then force you to watch the entire family go up in flames.

There used to be strict codes against murdering women and children, but with the new generation, sacred traditions were disregarded. The elders within the Nogales Cartel tolerated his sadistic conduct. He was a necessary evil. With ruthless enemies such as the Sinaloas, Los Cinco Diablos, and the Gulf Cartel, fear was a prerequisite to obtaining and retaining absolute power. There was, however, one board member who disapproved of El Feo's unconscionable antics, but even though they shared the top spot since the death of Pablo Estrada, he was a relic of the past, an old man filled with nostalgic memories of how things used to be.

El Feo thought about his grandfather, Enrique Estrada, as he crushed the tip of his cigar in an ashtray. Surprisingly, Enrique discouraged a merger with Los Cinco Diablos. The old man's adamant objections and Benzo Al's outright rejection derailed his bid to peacefully take over the Diablos drug corridors into the United States. Now he had to take their lucrative drug routes by force, a hostile corporate takeover, and Angela would be the first executive on the chopping block.

Angela watched El Feo approach her. He walked with the egotistical confidence of a man who was connected, respected, and believed he was untouchable.

He kneeled in front of Angela.

"Buenas noches, señorita. We meet again."

His eyes took in her sexy lips, golden-brown skin, and thick thighs. Her phat monkey caused a camel toe in her tight Emilio Pucci jeans. Even in distress, she was a bad bitch.

"So sad all this beauty has to go to waste," El Feo commented. "All you and Benzo Al had to do was give us your drug tunnels and routes through the Rio Grande."

Angela raised a skeptical eyebrow.

"*Give?* Don't you mean share our smuggling resources? You were never serious about a merger, were you? The marijuana trade is essentially dead, so you want to steal our coca business and the Sinaloa Cartel's heroin market, don't you?"

El Feo had a guilty look on his face like a cat caught with bird feathers in his mouth.

"You were always a smart chica, Angela. I can use you on my team," he offered while rubbing his hand up her thick thighs.

Angela rejected his proposal and spit in his face. "I'd rather die on my feet than live on my knees."

If El Feo was caught off guard, he didn't let it show.

"Have it your way." He wiped the spit off the bridge of his nose and licked his middle finger.

His lips curled into a smile, but Angela saw a dark veil fall over his eyes. The smile hardened, and El Feo lurched forward and smacked her with the back of his hand. The blunt blow left a purple bruise on Angela's right cheek and blood trickled into her mouth. She trembled inside but put up a brave and resilient front.

In her world, it was an honor to die with dignity and cowardice to beg for your life. "Let's get it over with, pendejo. Kill me if you have the balls."

El Feo placed a black toolbox on a nearby workbench, unbuttoned his diamond cufflinks, and slowly rolled up his sleeves.

"Kill you? I can't kill you yet," he admitted.

Angela began to second guess the green light on her life. *One of the board members must want me alive,* she thought and threw a verbal jab.

"Still taking orders from El Padrino like a bitch, huh?"

"The old man doesn't know you're here," he said over his shoulder while lifting the silver clasp on the toolbox. "I can't kill you because that will be too easy. I'm gonna make you suffer."

"Pablo Estrada suffered. I twisted a sharp piano wire around his neck and choked him until he pissed on himself," she boasted.

"Wait, you think this is about revenge?" He turned to her and laughed. It was the demented laugh of a psychopath. Imagine the Joker at Def Comedy Jam. "My uncle was in the way. I was planning on killing him myself, but you beat me to it. Thanks for the favor, but this isn't about revenge. It's about my pleasure and your pain. It's about the location of your drug tunnels."

El Feo turned back to the black box and rubbed the stubble on his chin as he contemplated which tool to select. "Ah, here we go!"

He retrieved a pair of rubber-grip pliers and approached Angela. Her eyes widened. El Feo's handsome features darkened, and his gaze landed on her big toe. He stooped down, pinched the edge of her polished toenail between the pliers, and viciously peeled it backward. The bloody toenail ripped away from the skin and popped up like the silver tab on a soda can. Angela screamed in agony. The pain was excruciating, and this was only the beginning.

El Feo eyed her other big toe and grinned sadistically.

"I'm gonna start at your feet and work my way up to your eyeballs! Are you ready to tell me about the tunnels?"

"Fuck you!" Angela screamed and spit in El Feo's face again.

Chapter 4

Business Is Business

Detective Brooks had a *fuck you* scowl on his grill as he strolled into Palermo's with Najee close behind. The sign out front might as well have said, *No Cops or Blacks Allowed.*

"Where's Carmine?" Detective Brooks asked the bartender as he made a beeline to the kitchen.

"Hey, you can't go back there!" the bartender protested and grabbed the baseball bat he kept under the bar.

Detective Brooks and Najee ignored the warning and kept mobbin' toward the back of the Italian restaurant. They went through the kitchen and into the storage area. Carmine's oversized bodyguard stood in front of his office door.

Detective Brooks leaned over and whispered to Najee, "Let me do the talkin'," he suggested. "And don't make any sudden moves."

Carmine's bodyguard, Fat Tony reached for the iron in his shoulder holster but realized it was Detective Brooks. The one thing the mob didn't do was kill cops. It brought too much unnecessary heat.

"What the hell are you doing here without an invite, Brooks?" Fat Tony questioned. His chest was as wide as a refrigerator, and his heart was just as cold.

Detective Brooks was all business.

"Step aside, Tony, I need a word with your boss."

"Make an appointment," Fat Tony advised. He noticed Najee, and his frown deepened. "Who is this friggin' moulie?"

Najee took off and slammed his fist into Fat Tony's gut. He followed with a stiff left hook to the ribcage, knocking the wind out of the big man and driving him to one knee. The bigger they are, the harder they fall.

The guy with the bat came rushing forward. Najee lifted the bottom of his hoodie and revealed a banger with duct tape wrapped around the grip. The SIG Sauer was big and intimidating like a schoolyard bully.

"This ain't what chu' want," he declared, stopping the would-be tough guy in his tracks.

Fat Tony reached for his piece, but Detective Brooks already had the drop on him. He pressed the steel against the back of Fat Tony's dome.

"Don't do it!"

Fat Tony didn't do it.

Detective Brooks turned to Najee and stated, "I thought I said don't make any sudden moves!"

Najee shrugged his shoulders. He wasn't good at following orders.

Detective Brooks confiscated Fat Tony's weapon.

"I'll take that."

He shoved the Smith and Wesson down the front of his pants, grabbed Fat Tony by the collar, and escorted him into the office at gunpoint.

Carmine's office turned out to be a dark, smoke-filled card room. A red lightbulb gave the room a funkadelic vibe. Four middle-aged, distinguished Italian men sat around a poker table playing cards. Velour tracksuits, gold chains, and gray chest hair made them look like mobsters from an episode of the Sopranos.

Carmine was down on poker chips, but it didn't matter. He was the boss. As the head of the Salerno Borgata, he got a piece of everybody's action, so he was technically gambling with their money.

Despite the intrusion, Carmine kept his poise. A cherry lollypop made his right cheek bulge. He fanned his cards out and grumbled at another shitty hand. "What brings you to this side of town, Brooks?"

"I need information." Nothing went down in L.A. without Carmine hearing about it.

"What do I look like, Alexa?"

"No," Detective Brooks played along. "But you do look like a man who wants to keep making money off that nice little thing you got going on at the San Pedro docks. I wonder what would happen if somebody told Sergeant Baker a shipment of counterfeit goods was coming in from China on Wednesday? You remember Sergeant

Baker, don't you? He's that greedy son of a bitch who runs Vice in the Harbor Division."

Carmine got the point. This was a shake-down. "What do you need to know."

"The Nogales Cartel snatched somebody important to my friend," Detective Brooks stressed the word friend as he nodded toward Najee who had his back against the wall and his eyes on the Italian mobsters. "And we want her back—in one piece."

"Fugget about it. I don't do business with those wetbacks. They're pushing uncut synthetic opioids, and bodies are dropping everywhere. Pretty soon, there won't be any addicts to sell to."

"Listen to me, Carmine, a woman got kidnapped by a dangerous man. I need the name of somebody who knows where she's at or the next time I come back; I'll be with some of my old friends from the LAPD. And trust me, they won't be looking for garlic meatballs!"

"Don't threaten me!" Carmine's voice rose. "We go too far back. Your name is in that little black book of mine, which means I got as much dirt on you as you got on me."

It was true. When Detective Brooks worked the beat in Hollywood, he collected a thick envelope every week. In exchange, he looked the other way as the Salerno family pushed boy, coke, meth, and women up and down Sunset Boulevard.

This was different, though. This wasn't one of those times to look away. "Don't test me, Carmine. You have a lot more to lose than I do," Detective Brooks cautioned.

Carmine didn't appreciate getting shook down like a two-bit corner boy, but he understood how important this must be to Detective Brooks. "Geez, you're bustin' my balls. I'll put my guys on it. If they find anything, I'll hit your line."

"Thanks, I owe you one," Detective Brooks said and gave Fat Tony his gun back.

Carmine folded his shitty hand and tossed the cards on the poker table. "Fugget about it. No hard feelings. Business is business, just don't come around here again without going through the proper channels, capisce?"

Later that night Najee got a call. It was Detective Brooks. He had a name.

"Carmine's people came through. The guy we're looking for is Omar Cruz."

"How connected is he?"

"He moves a shit load of pills and H for the Nogales Cartel. I did some digging and found out he operates out of a rundown building in Inglewood."

"Does he roll with a crew?"

"No heavy hitters, just your typical thugs, drug dealer friends, and female groupies. Carmine gave us the green light to lean on him as hard as we need to as long as there's no blowback on them. What do you wanna do?"

Najee looked over at his beautiful black queen sleeping peacefully. Nella was a level up from other women. She was smart, street-savvy, and had exquisite tastes and expensive shopping habits. Maintaining her lavish lifestyle took money, lots of it. Even before she met Najee, she was in her own lane and runnin' up a check. Najee merely found a diamond in the rough and polished it. He loved her over everything. She was his Earth. He was trying to stay on the sidewalk, but the streets were calling. He knew what he had to do. It was what he was born to do—kill.

"Let's go to work," Najee replied as he slipped on his kicks, grabbed his bulletproof vest, and put a pair of wooden Santería beads around his neck. He had taken them off Benzo Al's dead body with hopes they would bring him good fortune and longevity. "Text me the address. I'll meet you there with the tools."

***

Omar Cruz snuck into America to do construction work but found that slangin' yay and extorting other drug dealers was easier and a lot more lucrative than laying shingles on a hot roof. The game had been good to him and his crew. They had the fly whips, the bad bitches, and expendable money to blow on whatever the fuck they chose, but when you're playing deep in them streets, life could go from sugar to shit in a matter of minutes.

That's all the time it took for Najee to slide on Omar, but he too had to move with caution. He sat behind the wheel of his triple black Dodge Challenger Demon scoping out Omar's building. Getting in would be easy. Getting out was a different story.

"It's now or never," he told Detective Brooks and pulled a black hockey mask over his face.

The unlikely duo exited the vehicle under the cloak of darkness, dashed across the street, and crept to the second floor of the old apartment building. Najee knocked on Omar's door, careful not to bang too hard like the one-time.

"¿Quién es? Who is it?" Omar asked.

"Es Jose," Najee replied with the most common Hispanic name he could think of.

"Jose, really?" Detective Brooks asked in a hushed tone. "How stereotypical."

Najee shrugged with a smile.

"My bad!"

There was movement on the other side of the door. Najee's tactic worked. Omar held his piece-of-shit .38 Revolver down by his leg as he unbolted three deadlocks and opened the door slightly. A brass chain kept it from opening all the way. When Omar peeked through the crack, Najee stepped back, lifted his right foot, and kicked in the door. It crashed open and hung on one hinge like a broken jaw.

Detective Brooks went through first. He still moved good for a retired cop. Omar tried to get up off his back, but Detective Brooks drove a boot into his face, knocking him down again. Blood and snot gushed from his nose.

Detective Brooks put his foot on Omar's chest, aimed a Steyr machine pistol at his forehead, and warned, "Move and I'll make sure you have a closed casket!"

Omar didn't move, but one of his goons did. He stood up from the kitchen table and pumped a shell into his Mossberg, that's as far as he got. Najee swung the K in his direction and fanned him down.

Bullet fragments slammed into his neck, right below his earlobe. Another bullet hit him in the left cheek, the third knocked his brains out through his mouth, chunks of it jiggled on the kitchen table like pink Jello. He fell face-first onto a pile of Ziploc bags filled with M-30 pills that were made to look and mimic Oxytocin. Smaller baggies stamped with a black, 4H spider web logo and filled with Fentanyl were scattered all over the small, humid apartment.

The gunshots brought unwanted attention. Nosey neighbors peeked out of their doors.

"Snatch up ol' boy and let's bounce," Najee told Detective Brooks.

Outside in the hallway, Najee spotted a small, Mexican kid in a pissy diaper with a runny nose and dried buggers caked over his top lip. Najee picked the kid up, put him in the house, and closed the door. He did so just in time. Two slugs pierced the drywall where the kid was standing.

Najee took a knee and let off cover fire. Detective Brooks held Omar by the collar and kept the Steyr pressed against his neck. They knew better than to retreat into Omar's apartment. It was a death trap. Instead, Detective Brooks used Omar as a human shield, as he and Najee advanced forward blasting.

The goons at the bottom of the staircase returned fired with something beasty. Eight rounds struck Omar causing his body to do the Harlem Shake. The others missed their target and punched holes the size of lemons in an apartment door.

Detective Brooks shoved Omar in the back, and his bullet-riddled body tumbled down the staircase. His heavy weight knocked the two goons down like bowling pins. One of the goons recovered quickly, got up, and ran.

"Don't let him get away!" Najee shouted.

Detective Brooks looked at Najee like he was crazy.

"You want me to chase him? Yeah, right! I'm twice your age!"

He had a point; Najee took off after the runner.

"Don't do nothin' stupid, like kill him. We need him alive," Detective Brooks reminded, but it was too late. It was already going down.

Najee ran downstairs, into the lobby. As he reached the glass entry door, he saw a shadowy figure on the other side and was greeted by gunfire. He quickly dropped to his stomach; glass shattered around him. From the position on his belly, Najee emptied the clip, causing the runner's body to twist and turn. He staggered a few steps, smearing blood on a row of parked cars until he succumbed to his injuries and melted on the sidewalk like a popsicle on a hot Sunday.

Najee heard a single gunshot and trotted back to Detective Brooks. He rounded the corner and saw the last goon sliding down the wall leaving a streak of blood. He died in a seated position with legs stretched out in front of him and his chin slumped against his chest. His eyes stared ahead into the afterlife. A small red dot decorated the center of his forehead, but the back of his skull was split open to the white meat.

"Damn!" Najee cringed at the gruesome head wound. "Did he talk?"

"He didn't know where El Feo is keeping Angela, but he did know where El Feo is keeping his money!"

"I can work with that." Najee left the building and peeled off in his Challenger. He had to get back to wifey and seed.

Larry D. Wright

Chapter 5

Thug Passion

"Gimme some of that good dick, papi!"

Nella scooted to the edge of the bed and watched Najee leaning coolly against the bedroom door smoking a blunt. Her hand slipped under the elastic of her Victoria's Secret panties and her middle finger dipped deep into her wet pussy.

Najee extinguished the Garcia Vega, walked over to Nella, and removed her hand from her panties. He replaced it with his own, inserted his index finger, and rubbed her G-spot.

A low moan escaped Nella's lips, "Put it in me, daddy."

Najee winked at his wifey as he sucked the sweet juices off his finger.

"Patience, mami!" he reprimanded while pulling his hoodie over his head.

Tattoos and penitentiary muscles rippled under his wife beater and the Vanilla scented candles made his dark skin glow.

"At least let me taste it. It's mine!" Nella unfastened his Versace Medusa belt buckle, unzipped his jeans, and pulled his dick out of his boxer briefs.

It was hard and chocolate like the rest of his body. The shaft was eight inches long and so thick her fingers didn't touch when she gripped him. Her petite hand formed a C as she squeezed the base. A clear drop of pre-cum seeped from the big, circumcised head. Desiring to suck the skin off his throbbing pole, she opened her sexy lips into the shape of an O and took the first four inches into her warm mouth.

"Damn, baby girl, that throat feels good," Najee groaned.

He enjoyed watching the top of her head bob up and down. She was trying to swallow all of him. Spit drooled from the corners of her lips. She moaned and took him further into her mouth, determined to deep throat that magic stick. Her eyes watered as the head slid past her tonsils and her nose pressed against his curly pubic hair. She gagged, came up for air, deep throated him again, choked, and reluctantly released him. A long string of spit stretched between her bottom lip and his saliva-coated cock. She used it as a lubricant and pumped his love muscle up and down.

Wanting to prolong his orgasm, Najee took a step back. "You can taste this dick later but first I want to please you," he said smoothly.

Even his foreplay technique had swag. Unlike other men who started at the top of a woman's body and worked their way down, Najee drove a woman crazy with anticipation by starting at the bottom and slowly working his way up. Tonight, was no exception. He gently held one of Nella's pretty feet and placed ten delicate kisses on each of her toes. Electric volts shot from the soles of her feet to her erect nipples. He gazed into her eyes and licked his lips like LL Cool J before nibbling, teasing, and finally sucking on her pinky toe. Nella couldn't wait until that same mouth did the same thing to her throbbing clit.

Holding one of her sexy legs in the air, he planted ten sweet kisses on her ankles, twenty kisses on her calf muscle, and thirty kisses on her kneecap. He repeated the process on the other leg. Nella squirmed and her thick thighs fell open. Najee's dick grew another inch looking at her phat monkey. It poked out of her panties in 3D. He held her sexy, light-skinned legs wide apart and used his tongue to spell *I Love You* in cursive on her right thigh, and then he spelled *Until Infinity* on the left. Heat came from her juice box, making the crotch of her panties moist.

Next, he used his teeth to slowly peel down her sexy panties. Nella giggled and raised her big booty to assist him. Spreading the lips of her shaved pussy open, he ran his tongue up and down her slit fifty times, teasing, tasting, and savoring before flicking her clit one hundred times in small circles. Nella held the back of Najee's head, lifted her hips off the bed, and pushed her pussy against his mouth. Using one hand, he reached up and twirled her nipples.

He wet the long, middle finger of his other hand and worked it into her tight asshole. Meanwhile, his mouth kept sucking her clit and licking the lining out of her honey hole for the next twenty minutes. Finally, Nella's body tensed up, and she exploded on his tongue and chin.

"Fuck me!" she panted barely above a whisper.

He rolled her onto her shoulders, placed two pillows under her big, soft ass, and pushed the wide head of his dick into her small opening. He stroked slowly and stretched her pink pussy walls until he was balls deep.

"Can I beat it up, my Nefertiti?"

"Yes, my Pharaoh!"

Having his queen's permission, Najee placed Nella's thick legs over his shoulders and pounded in and out of her tight cunt. The force of his thrusts made her titties flop and drove the headboard into the wall. He drilled into her deeper, harder, and faster.

Nella yelled, "Oohhh, right there, Bae! You finna make me cum!"

Najee pulled his dick out, shoved it back in, and pulled it out again making Nella skeet cum. Her feminine nectar gushed onto his thighs and wet the sheets.

"Still wanna taste this dick, lil' mama?" Najee asked out of breath.

"Yeah, daddy!" Nella panted.

Najee maneuvered Nella so that her head was hanging off the side of the bed. He stood over her, and she looked up at his balls as he pushed his wet, sloppy dick into her mouth. He tea bagged her throat while Nella played with her pussy. It wasn't long before his sperm shot off like rounds from a machine gun. Najee moaned loudly. His throbbing pole was so deep down her throat she didn't taste the first three blasts of cum. She managed to catch the fourth and swallowed just as the fifth and sixth jet of thick cum squirted into her mouth. She swallowed that and sucked on the sensitive head trying to siphon out more.

Just as she drained him dry their baby began crying. Najee's smile beamed brightly.

"See, you woke the baby up with all that moaning. Told you, you couldn't handle this dick," he teased. "I'm gonna run-up in that big ol' booty next."

Nella giggled. "Boy, bye! You can't handle all this ass!"

Najee slipped on his boxer briefs and rushed into the baby's room. Nella pulled Najee's wife-beater over her head and made it to the room just as Najee was changing his son's diaper. She leaned against the door frame and watched the first-time father in action. He was a good man who was constantly placed in bad predicaments. The bullet marks on his body were just surface wounds. Nella worried about the scars on his soul.

"Where did you learn how to change diapers so good?" She walked in and hugged him from behind.

Najee finished his handy work and scooped his son into his arms.

"You already know my step-pops was a pimp and my mother used to do her thing. Anyhow, over the years, Boulevard had women who had children. I was the oldest, so I would babysit when they hit the track."

Nella followed him into the kitchen. Now that the baby was carefully cradled in his arm like a football, Najee heated a bottle of Good Start formula and dabbed a few drops on his inner wrist to check the temperature.

Nella was impressed with his parental skills.

"He wakes up every night at the same time. I think he inherited your bad dreams."

Lil' Najee was already as complicated as his father. Najee was light illuminating darkness, but his attentiveness to his son made her think of Angela and the baby she was carrying. A jolt of jealousy shot through her.

Sensing her mood change, Najee pulled Nella into his other arm. It felt good having his family together for the first time.

"What's wrong, Ma? Holler at me." His invitation received no reply, so he pushed harder. "I'm your man, baby girl, you can talk to me about anything."

Nella took a deep breath and sighed.

"What about Angela?" There, she said it.

"What about her?"

Angela was a subject Najee wanted to avoid, but he knew this conversation was inevitable.

Nella turned to face Najee.

"When Los Cinco Diablos took our son, I had no doubt that you would bring him home and make those responsible pay with their lives. And I have no doubt that you'll go to war for Angela's baby, too. I was just wondering when you were gonna leave us again?" She finished and pried the baby from his arms.

"Wait!" Najee stopped her from leaving and pulled her close to his chest. "The people who snatched Angela could've simply murked all of us, but they chose to take Angela alive. Do you know why?" He lifted Nella's chin with a finger and looked into her eyes to make sure he had her full attention. "That cat El Feo is a sick muthafucka! He's gonna torture her first, and if she's lucky, she'll be dead when he set her on fire. I gotta find her before that happens!"

"How do you plan on doing that?"

"Every man has a weakness. Mine is my family. El Feo's weakness is his money."

"You plan on hitting his stash houses?"

"Not all of them, just the main one—" He paused and gazed at his son's missing thumb.

He promised to make Angela pay for what she did. Anger boiled in his heart, but the baby slept peacefully, oblivious to the chaotic world he inherited.

"Look, Bae, this shit might get ugly. So, I want you to take Lil' Najee over to Detective Brooks' house. He'll be safe over there."

Nella fell against Najee's muscular chest. She knew Najee didn't love Angela, but she had warned him numerous times that his obsession with revenge was going to ruin him and destroy their relationship. Her prediction was coming to fruition.

A bad feeling rumbled in her gut, and against better judgment, she suppressed her woman's intuition. She knew what type of life Najee led when she first met him. He kept it one hundred about who he was and what he did. When they fell in love, he tried to shield her from his occupation, but she wanted to be part of his world and vowed to be his ride-or-die chick. She was determined to live up to that obligation.

"Follow this." She pointed at his heart. "And use this." She rubbed his smooth bald head. "You can't outgun them, but you can outsmart them, and you need the help of someone who's just as crazy as you. Got anybody in mind?"

Najee's answer came easily.

"The Deacon!"

Chapter 6

Stay Schemin'

The Deacon took a toke off a finger-sized joint, held the sativa in his lungs, thumped the ashes in the ashtray, and exhaled all in one seamless motion. He was smooth, but beneath his docile demeanor lay a dark, demented, and deranged soul.

"Run that by me again, mon!" His Kingston roots were confirmed by his thick, Caribbean accent.

Najee retrieved a crumpled map from the center console of Nella's Bentley and unfolded it across the steering wheel. "The Nogales Cartel has a stash house right here." He tapped a predominantly Chicano community in East Los Angeles. "It's the main hub for all of their Southern California money drops. Once a month they prep the dough and transport it to Mexico. Like I said, all we gotta do is—"

The Deacon held up his hand to interrupt.

"I got that part, Soulja Boi. Rerun the part about exchanging the money for Angela."

Najee stared straight forward. The sun hid behind dark clouds, and a drizzle pelted the windshield. The Deacon was like a big brother to him, but the Deacon was also a consummate professional. Najee knew he would have questions, lots of them. He took a breath and got straight to the point.

"The Nogales Cartel snatched Angela, bruh."

"Good for dem. Saves us some bullets." He took another puff off the joint and held the THC in his chest.

"She's pregnant, my nigga."

"So!" The Deacon shrugged his broad shoulders.

"The baby is mine," Najee revealed.

"Wha—what?" The Deacon choked on the news, hacked, and coughed up white smoke.

Najee patted his back.

"You alright, cuz?"

The Deacon stubbed out the joint, swiped his long dreads out of his face, and turned to Najee. He possessed a scowl that could bend iron.

"Are you shittin' me? You got Angela pregnant? The same Angela that tried to kill you a couple of days ago?" he asked in disbelief.

Najee nodded.

"The fuck was you thinkin', mon?" He gave Najee a big brother slap on the back of his head.

"I was caught up in the life and thinking like Sinatra," he admitted. "You already know how the Nogales Cartel get down, so I don't have to tell you what they're probably doing to her as we speak. I have no choice, bruh. I have to save her, but I can't do it alone. I need you in the trenches with me."

The Deacon sat in silence considering Najee's sincere plea. The murder game was calling him again. Despite his best efforts, he couldn't outrun what he had become. He found sanctuary in the church, but truthfully, he was a mercenary, a hired gun.

The blood of a killer flowed through his arteries. It had been that way when he trained Al-Shabaab fundamentalist in Mogadishu near the Somalian border and remained that way when he formed the Kill Squad with the Bishop, the Pope, and the Alter Boy.

They convinced themselves that they were God's angels of death cleansing the world of evil. The other members of his crew met violent and untimely deaths. The Deacon was the last disciple standing, and after each homicide, quoting a Biblical scripture was his ritualistic way of purging his sins.

After what seemed like an eternity, the Deacon's lips parted. His teeth were yellow, but his smile was bright.

"Yeah, mon, I'm in. Run that plan by me again."

"My man!" Najee's mood lightened, and he and the Deacon shook up. "As I was saying, all they do is count racks up in that bitch. I'm talking between five or ten mill tickets every fourth Friday of the month."

"Whew!" the Deacon whistled. "That's a lot of bread, which means it's probably protected by a lot of guns. We can't kick in the front door, Soulja Boi. Dem bum bloodclot Mexicans will murda us good."

"You right, bruh. That's the beauty of this move. We're not going in. We're gonna wait until the money comes out."

The Deacon removed an engraved silver case from his breast pocket, selected another fat joint, lit it, inhaled, exhaled, and said, "I'm listening."

The Deacon offered Najee the joint but he kindly declined. Although they were scheming on a come up, he felt it was especially sinister to smoke loud on holy ground. They were in the parking lot of Mount Nevaeh church. Nevaeh is heaven spelled backward, but some of hell's worse attended Sunday service there.

Najee resumed laying out his plot.

"It's too risky to use gang members, hardened criminals, or drug dealers to move the gwap. I'm sure the cartel has a few border patrol officers on the payroll, but there are too many local PD, Highway Patrolmen, State Troopers, and ICE agents between here and San Ysidro."

"That's true. So, how do they get the money out of the country undetected?"

"They hire ordinary citizens as mules—women, college students, elderly couples—you feel me? This reduces the chances of the transport vehicle getting jammed up by them peoples, and luckily for us, it makes the smash and grab that much easier."

The Deacon's grin widened, displaying two rows of tobacco-stained teeth.

"Respect, mon. How did you get all this intel?"

"Detective Brooks, he's the ex-cop that gave me the four-one-one on Benzo Al's spots. Check this out." Najee got out of the car and the Deacon followed.

Najee carefully surveyed his surroundings, looking left then right before opening the trunk. A young, blonde-haired UCLA student lay curled up in the fetal position. His mouth, wrists, and ankles were bound with duct tape. His eyes widened in horror when he saw Najee and the taller, deadlier Rastafarian hovering over him.

The Deacon had smooth, dark skin the color of motor oil and bloodshot red eyes. Standing at 6'3, he was fit for his fifty years. Thick, lustrous dreads rested on the shoulders of his black Michael Kors suit. The jacket hugged his athletic frame. The two street legends stared down at the vic. Light rain and the gold cross atop the church's tall white steeple made the duo appear more menacing.

"Who's the Yankee?" the Deacon inquired.

"He's the Nogales Cartel mule. He's supposed to take the dough to Puerto Nuevo. That's a small fishing village south of Tijuana. A lot of white boys go down there to fish for halibut and tuna."

"That's the perfect cover story."

"Fa' sho'," Najee agreed and slammed the trunk shut. "By the way, I'm a real nigga, so you already know I'm not giving back all the money!"

Again, the Deacon's grin broadened.

"Bless up! Much respect!" He expressed his approval with a firm handshake and shoulder bump. "You said dem make a run to Mexico once a month. When is the next drop?"

It was Najee's turn to smile. "Tonight!"

***

East L.A. - Nogales Cartel Stronghold

"Ay, homes, it's going down ésta noche. Tonight! I need you to be on point. No fuck ups, entiendes?" Domingo, a major drug distributor and El Feo's number two man grumbled through the satellite phone from his location in Nogales, Mexico.

Felix, a short Mexican with a rotund belly, thick black mustache, and short hair that was slicked to the back, turned down the volume of the soccer game.

"I'm on it, ese. I got it covered, homes." Felix was in charge of logistics for the Nogales Cartel's East Los Angeles stash house.

East Los Angeles, or East Los as it is commonly referred to by the locals, is a predominantly Latino barrio located in the shadows of the city's tall, majestic skyscrapers. It's not uncommon to see

44

innocent Hispanic children playing in the same front yard as chickens or hardworking entrepreneurs on the corner selling homemade tamales.

Unfortunately, they share the same turf with predatory drug dealers and violent gang members. The tumultuous combination has snuffed out the hopes and aspirations of a generation of dreamers. It was here, deep in the bowels of one of the most dangerous and underserved neighborhoods in the nation, that the Nogales Cartel claimed as their U.S. headquarters.

The board members recognized that poverty and despair made the impoverished community a perfect breeding ground for young, loyal, fearless, and often time, expendable soldiers. Felix was one of them. Recruited more for his brawn than his brain, Felix assured Domingo that he was on point, then leisurely went back to cheering the fútbul game while scoffing down a plate of fríjoles.

Two heavily armed cartel pistoleros stood guard by the steel-reinforced front door. Their dark eyes were focused, and their bald heads were constantly on the swivel. Tattoos and Bushmaster AR-15 assault rifles added to their sinister appearance.

Three Latina women huddled around a long kitchen table preparing large boxes of currency for shipment to Mexico. Unlike the movies, they were not beautiful and naked. They were middle-aged, heavy-set illegal immigrants selected for their thoroughness and ability to be discreet.

They moved quickly and methodically like Santa's Elves in an Amazon distribution center. The first woman on the assembly line separated the cash by denomination—twenties, fifties, and hundred stacks. She rubber banded them into large bricks, pushed them to the second woman, and retrieved another trash bag full of cash.

The second woman placed a large brick of rubber-banded hundred-dollar bills into a clear plastic bag and then carefully sat the bag on a digital scale. There was too much money to count by hand. At this level of the game, criminal enterprises weighed their illegal currency.

The second woman glanced at the scale, it read one pound. She wrote $48,000 in a leather-bound notebook and then proceeded to weigh a thick block of twenty-dollar bills. One pound of twenties contains four hundred and eighty bills. The second woman placed the loot into a plastic bag, wrote $9,600 in the ledger, and pushed the bundles toward the third woman.

The third woman heat-sealed each plastic bag with a commercial grade vacuum sealer and placed the one-pound bricks of money into a cardboard box. This process went on for the next two hours.

A portion of the proceeds would find its way into the greasy palms of corrupt police and government officials, but the bulk of the money would go into the coffers of the narcotráficantes.

The third woman taped up the last cardboard box, stacked it on top of a waist-high row of similar boxes, and reported to Felix, "The dinero is ready."

"What's the count?" Felix examined the rows of boxes stacked against the wall then glanced at the face of his Patek. The gringo driver was late.

"Cinco punto cinco millón."

Five-point five million, not bad for a slow month, thought Felix. This was all profit. The mid-level dealers and the corner boys had already taken their cut.

"Muy bien, señora. Good job!"

"Grácias. What do you want us to do with the ones, fives, and tens?"

Felix looked at his watch again. Timing was everything, and El Feo didn't tolerate fuck ups. The deep rumble of a truck's engine caught his attention. He rushed to the window, parted the blinds, and looked outside. The ghetto streets seemed darker, grimier than usual. A bad feeling suddenly punched Felix in the stomach.

"Take the fetti to the chapel mañana and ask Father Francesco to pray for our souls."

Chapter 7

Chess Not Checkers

"Pray for your soul, cabrón!" an angry voice yelled from the front porch of the Nogales Cartel stash house followed by the haunting sound of a brass demon being racked into an automatic weapon.

A rapid succession of thunderous gunfire pierced the tranquility of the night.

Knocka! Knocka! Knocka!

Najee and the Deacon dodged the polymer tip bullets, took offensive positions, and returned fire.

Blam! Blam! Blam!

Casper and Flaco, the two tatted-up pistoleros who were guarding the stash house, retaliated with more hot slugs. Najee and the Deacon retreated and took cover behind an old Ford F-150. Najee crouched low with his back against the front tire. The Deacon balanced on one knee near the bed of the truck. He peaked around the rear bumper but quickly brought his head back just as AR shells peppered the side of the pickup.

"I thought this was supposed to be easy," the Deacon shouted over the gunfire.

Ignoring the comment, Najee fumbled with a new magazine and finally managed to slam the thirty-round banana clip into the bottom of his Draco, chamber a round, and squeeze off.

The bullets missed Felix by inches. He attempted to get into the driver's side of a white Chevy Silverado parked in the driveway. A 20' Sea Ray fishing boat was attached to its hitch. The hull of the boat was loaded with bricks of vacuumed sealed cash.

The Deacon spotted Felix trying to escape. Moving stealthy, he slid under the F-150. Lying flat on his stomach, he finger-fucked the trigger. Hot lead ripped through Felix's Achilles, damaging the tendon connecting the heel with the calf muscle. He hopped on one leg, stumbled, and fell face-first on the front lawn.

The Deacon pressed his right eyeball against the Vortex sniper scope, aimed, smiled, and squeezed.

"Blessed be the Lord my Rock who trains my hands for war, and my fingers for battle," he chanted Psalms 144:1 after confirming the kill.

Felix's body jerked from the impact; dark blood squirted out of his carotid artery. The petrified college student witnessed the carnage, panicked, and bolted up the block.

Casper and Flaco wisely split up. Casper found shelter on the side of the stash house. Flaco dashed to the rear of the Silverado. This maneuver gave them a tactical advantage. Increasing their odds, as reinforcements swerved around the corner in a blue '64 Impala. The four Hispanic passengers gripped fully-autos with hundred round drums. The low rider screeched to a halt in front of the stash house.

The driver spotted Casper.

"Where are they?"

"Right here, muthafucka!" Najee stepped from behind the truck. A black Jason hockey mask hid his face.

He held the stick waist level and started blasting. The driver caught one to the dome, leaving him slumped over the steering wheel. A mist of blood sprayed the headrest.

Najee's muzzle flash gave away his position. The remaining Nogales Cartel hitters exited the low rider, stood in the middle of the street, and let off. Empty bullet shells clinked off the asphalt. Najee dove behind the F-150 just as armor-piercing ammo ripped through the metal leaving holes the size of golf balls.

Najee and The Deacon were out manned and out gunned. It was only a matter of time before the inexperienced, yet relentless gunmen decided to flank them.

"I thought jah had this all planned out, Soulja Boi?" The Deacon scoffed impatiently while reaching into his jacket for a fresh clip.

"Just hold tight, bruh. This is part of the plan."

"Oh, really!" The Deacon said sarcastically, then came over the bed of the truck, sprayed slugs in the direction of the stash house, and ducked back into position.

The wail of police sirens blared in the near distance, red and blue flashing lights illuminated the dark sky.

Casper feared the consequences of being captured. "Rapido! Let's go, ese!"

"What about the fetti?"

"Leave it. This fuck up is on Felix, not us."

"El Feo ain't gonna see it that way," Flaco insisted.

The police sirens got closer.

"Haz lo que Te digo. Do as I say. Let's go!" Casper ordered more forcefully.

He knew if they were detained they would be questioned, deported, and ultimately executed by the Mexican Federal Judicial Police.

Casper snatched the dead man out of the driver's seat and got behind the bloody steering wheel. Flaco and the surviving cartel hitters quickly piled into the Impala. They peeled off just as a large vehicle with flashing patrol lights and screaming sirens rounded the corner. From a distance, it looked like a SWAT van, but as the vehicle barreled closer, The Deacon realized it was only an ice cream truck with police lights mounted on the roof and sound effects coming through the PA system. Detective Brooks sat behind the wheel.

The Deacon and Najee shared a smile, then sprinted across the street to the Chevy Silverado.

"How did you know this would work?" The Deacon probed as he carefully backed the truck out of the driveway.

"If you can't beat 'em, trick 'em! The only thing undocumented Mexicans fear more than death is deportation," Najee replied. "Besides, the Nogales Cartel soldiers are ruthless and reckless. They prefer to rule by force rather than finesse." He checked the side mirror to make sure they were not being followed and continued, "A kamikaze strategy works well when you're playing checkers, but not when you're playing chess."

Nodding his approval, The Deacon eased onto the 110 freeway.

"Boulevard and the Bishop taught you well," he praised with genuine admiration.

Najee thought about Boulevard, The Bishop, his mother, Angel, and all the other loved ones he lost to the game. Saving Angela became even more paramount.

"What's next, mon?" The Deacon's voice tugged Najee out of his pensive thoughts.

Before answering, Najee watched the windshield wipers sway back and forth. They were reminiscent of his life. He pulled out his phone, selected a number provided by Detective Brooks, and expelled a deep sigh.

"It's time to call El Feo."

***

Metro Tires World

Two Hours Later

"¡Pinche pendejos! You have an army and an arsenal at your disposal, yet you let two vatos steal my money?" El Feo fumed. "And you think one of them was a malláte with dreadlocks? Are you fuckin' serious?"

He paced the floor of the tire shop with his fists clinched tightly. His fingernails dug into his palms, and his handsome features were skewed into an evil mask—eyes angry slits, lips curled into a snarl, top teeth grinding against the bottom.

He didn't expect an answer from Casper or Flaco. They were bound by tow truck chains and naked from the waist down with their underwear stuffed in their mouths. Coagulated blood and yellow pus formed a crusty layer where their penises used to be. Earlier, El Feo had poured Tabasco sauce on the open wounds. Muffled groans came from their throats, and tears cascaded down their cheeks. Fear pumped through their arteries.

Their eyes pleaded for mercy, but benevolence was not one of El Feo's stronger attributes. He knew nothing of sympathy, forbearance, or forgiveness.

He laughed at their pitiful pleas with contempt and thought of Angela. He enjoyed giving her the Devil's pedicure, a torture technique where the toenails are savagely ripped from the feet with pliers. She screamed, she cried, but she didn't beg, not even when he gave her the Devil's manicure, a sadistic and painful procedure that involved placing a flathead screwdriver under the fingernail and hitting the handle with a hammer.

Her resilience bruised El Feo's ego. He was looking forward to breaking her spirits tonight by driving a drill bit through her eyeballs, but a more pressing matter now demanded his attention.

"Stand them up!" El Feo ordered.

Four eager to please cartel goons followed the command. Each goon grabbed an elbow and roughly snatched Casper and Flaco to their feet. Domingo, who immediately flew in from Nogales when he heard the news of the robbery, looked the other way. He couldn't stomach what was about to transpire. In contrast, Gustavo, the bodyguard, looked on with peculiar interest.

El Feo ranted and lectured about honor, loyalty, and discipline as he stacked five Goodyear tires over Casper's body. He did the same to Flaco and then removed the lid from a large gas canister.

The tires reached up to the men's torsos and would serve as a reservoir for the gasoline. El Feo held the canister above Casper's head and doused his body with the foul-smelling petrol. He did the same to Flaco and poured the remaining gas directly into the tires. Their feet were soaked in a puddle of flammable fluid.

El Feo struck a match and marveled at the flickering orange and yellow fire. The flame illuminated one side of his face making him look even more sinister. He flicked the match at Flaco, but a breeze blew out the flame.

"Fuck! Somebody give me a light."

Casper and Flaco expelled a collective sigh of relief. They felt the Gods smiling down upon them. Just as El Feo struck another match, his bodyguard rushed forward and shoved his way through the circle of spectators.

Extending a prepaid flip phone towards El Feo, Gustavo excitedly announced, "Jefe, you have a call!"

"Not now, primo. I'm busy."

"It's muy importante! It's about the robbery."

El Feo raised a curious eyebrow and used the burning match to lite a cigar. He snatched the phone from his bodyguard, and said, "You have two minutes of my time starting sixty seconds ago."

Najee got right to it.

"I have your money."

"Who the fuck is this?" El Feo growled.

"My name is Najee," he accepted the blunt from The Deacon, took a drag, and kept speaking, "But the streets call me Sinatra. Perhaps you've heard of me. I made a significant contribution to your organization by killing Benzo Al."

"Ah, yes, Carlos Guzman spoke highly of you to my grandfather, Enrique Estrada. He said you were smart—" He paused to hit the cigar. "So why did you do something stupid like steal-my-fuckin'-money?" His voice rose with each word.

"Correction, I didn't steal your money. I took that shit. There's a big difference."

El Feo adjusted his diamond pinky ring and calmed down, but just a little bit.

"You have enough money to disappear, yet you're calling me. Stop wasting my time and tell me what the fuck this all about?"

"You took something of mine, so I took something of yours."

"What did I take?"

"Angela, and I want her back—alive."

"Why?"

"My reasons are personal."

"Well, this is business."

Najee allowed weed smoke to ooze through both nostrils. "Cool, let's negotiate. Four-point five mill in exchange for Angela."

"Six-point five million and not a penny less. I'll be in touch." El Feo hung up the phone without waiting for a reply. Whether Najee paid the million-dollar tax or not, he was a dead man.

On the way to his office where he had Angela bound and gagged, El Feo lit an entire book of matches, allowed the flames to rise between his fingers, and set Casper on fire. After enjoying Casper's anguish, he flicked his half-smoked cigar at Flaco. His gasoline-soaked body combusted into a ball of flames. The toxic odor of burnt rubber and the foul smell of singed hair and the pungent stench of burnt flesh filtered through the tire shop.

Angela sniffed the air and became nauseous. Killing Pablo Estrada, the former head of the Nogales Cartel, only made room for a younger, more vicious, and deadlier replacement. El Feo wanted his criminal enterprise to be feared like Los Cinco Diablos and the Zetas. Angela's bloody feet and hands were a testament to the lengths he would go to in order to accomplish his objective.

She watched El Feo through the office window. His fists were balled tight, and there was a new sense of urgency in his walk. Angela's heart pounded, she was out of tears, out of prayers, and quickly running out of hope.

"Save me, Najee," she mumbled as El Feo burst through the door and towered over her.

Larry D. Wright

Chapter 8

Never Die Alone

Although El Feo was only 5'8, he made the world around him seem smaller. His giant persona demanded attention when he entered a room. Angela felt his presence even before he twisted the doorknob and rushed into the small office. He towered over her adjusting his pinky ring, a habit he formed when he was nervous or calculating or both.

"How do you know, Najee?"

Silence!

Swack!

El Feo reached back and smacked Angela with an open palm. The blow made her head snap to the side.

"Who is Najee to you?"

Blood trickled from the corner of Angela's lip. She extended her tongue to taste it.

"Fuck you!"

El Feo's anger rose.

"Fuck me?" he asked the rhetorical question while pointing a thumb at himself. "You wanna fuck with me, Julio Armondo Costilla Estrada?" He stormed out of the office and returned brandishing a cordless power drill.

He revved the motor and with the other hand snatched Angela by the hair and brought the long drill bit dangerously close to her left eyeball.

"Najee said he wanted you back alive, but he didn't specify in what condition. I will get a mirror and make you watch while I drill your eyes out, puta. Now, I'm only gonna ask you one more time, who is he to you?"

"You spoke to Najee?" her voice was barely a whisper, but she couldn't hide her surprise, nor could she disguise the passion in her eyes.

El Feo noticed her infatuation.

"Ah, he's your lover!"

"And enemy," Angela added.

"So, why go through all of this trouble to save you?"

"What trouble?"

"He hit one of our stash houses tonight."

Angela laughed.

El Feo yanked her head back and reeved the power tool. The spinning drill bit sliced through her eyelash like a weed whacker. The physical abuse was taking its toll. Angela decided to cooperate but on her own terms. She knew she needed to stall for time.

"Okay, okay!" Angela pleaded. "I'll talk." El Feo lowered the drill, and Angela proceeded, "Najee held Benzo Al responsible for the murders of his family. He hunted us for years and robbed many Los Cinco Diablos stash houses. Your one clavo is only the beginning. He won't stop until he gets what he wants."

"And why does he want you alive all of a sudden when just a few days ago, he and Carlos Guzman wanted you and Benzo Al dead?"

Angela considered Carlos' betrayal and the green light her own organization put on her life. She vowed to never die alone and to make sure Don Julio, Roberto Vargas, and Fernando Rivera paid for their transgressions. In order to do so, however, she needed to survive, not just for her own sake, but for her baby as well. The gears in her brain started churning smoothly. She was sure El Feo didn't have a conscience, but perhaps he still had a soul, Angela surmised.

Her feet were bloody and numb. Her hands were bloody and swollen. The scent of smoldering flesh assured her that El Feo would carry out his threat and drill out her eyeballs. In a world of deceit, sometimes honesty is the only option.

She held her head up, looked El Feo in his eyes, and confessed, "Because I'm pregnant!"

****

"Pregnant? By Najee?" Domingo repeated El Feo's words.

"Shhh, silencio. Someone will hear you." El Feo led Domingo to a quiet corner. "Apparently, he posed as Sinatra in order to infiltrate Los Cinco Diablos but fell for Angela in the process."

"On what? You telling me that Najee and Sinatra are the same vato? El Padrino ain't gonna like this."

"Get off my grandfather's dick and tell me what you heard."

"He's pissed, eh," Domingo reported. "You lost two soldiers and close to six million dollars to the same man on the same night. He wants you to report to Mexico, pronto."

El Feo fiddled with his pinky ring. He was supposed to be heir to the throne, but his grandfather didn't like the vision El Feo had for the future of the organization, so he quietly came out of retirement. They shared the empty leadership seat and had equal authority, yet everyone acted as though Enrique was in charge. This infuriated El Feo. He wanted absolute power and demanded absolute loyalty.

"Fuck him! I'll travel to Mexico ésta lunes. Right now, I need to handle this delicate situation. No one steals from me."

"You mean us!"

"Yeah, us," El Feo responded dryly.

A light clicked on in Domingo's head. "Ay, homes, I know how you can save face and solve this problem before you leave on Monday."

"Shoot, I'm listening!"

"You could kill him," Domingo offered nonchalantly.

El Feo cocked his head to the side and twisted his lips. "That's a stupid idea, ese. Sure, I could kill him, or I could fuck his mother in the ass and stab his children in the eyes. Or I could chop his head off and piss down his throat. Or I could just set his black ass on fire and watch him burn, but that won't get the money back," he emphasized, then added, "Plus, I'm not that type of guy."

He was exactly that type of guy, but Domingo apologized anyhow.

"I'm sorry, jefe. I didn't mean to insult your intelligence, but you can't let this ride."

"We good, primo, and ain't no way I'm gonna let this ride. We're gonna kill Najee and the chica once we get the money back, and I think I know Najee's main weakness." He removed his cell phone and dialed an unlikely ally. "Carlos Guzman always kept an insurance policy. He didn't know if he could trust Najee, so he kept an ace up his sleeve, and like the double-crossing snake he was, he sold it to me."

The call was answered on the fourth ring.

"Reynolds here, who the hell is this?" a gruff and irritated voice grumbled.

He held the phone to his ear with the help of his shoulder as he tightened a rubber tourniquet around his bicep. A burnt spoon and a moist cotton ball and an empty clear baggie sat on the kitchen table next to a syringe loaded with his last jab of heroin. The needle that awaited a bulging vein was the cause of the dark tracks on his forearms and the reason he wore long sleeves in the summer.

"It's me, Julio Estrada."

"Mr. Estrada, how are you?" Special Agent James Reynolds pushed aside the hype kit and took some of the bass out of his voice. "You gotta stop calling me private on those dang burner phones. I'm tryna' avoid the bill collectors and my ex-wife." He chuckled nervously.

"I didn't call to hear about your problems. I called to tell you about mine." El Feo paced back and forth.

"This problem sounds expensive. How can I help?" he offered and picked at a scab. His red hair was disheveled, and his eyes were glassy and unfocused.

"I need you to arrest someone."

"Who is he?"

"It's a she."

Agent Reynolds sat up straight.

"You got my attention, I'm interested. Who is she?"

"A wanted fugitive, the name is Petronella Jackson."

Relocating to his home office, Agent Reynolds logged onto his computer and typed Nella's name into the CODIS database. A mug-shot photo and FBI dossier appeared on the screen.

"She's pretty."

"And deadly," El Feo reminded.

Agent Reynolds put on his reading glasses and clicked on a link.

"She goes by the name Nella and sometimes, Yellow Gurl. The FBI's facial recognition software is linking her to the Giuseppe Murders. Where is she? I can have a criminal apprehension team grab her first thing in the mornin'."

Agent Reynolds listened and scribbled Nella's name, possible location, and connection to Najee on a yellow Post-it-Note. He stuck the note on his computer monitor and briefed El Feo on some new intelligence he had gathered.

"By the way—" He stopped picking at the scab and smelled his fingers. "I have some important info for you."

"I'm listening."

"A credible source reports that an ATF agent has infiltrated your organization. The agent—"

"What?" El Feo cut him off. "Pinche gringo pig, why didn't you tell me this sooner?"

"I'm just finding out myself," the lie tasted bitter.

Truthfully, he and his source, a big-breasted intelligence officer with a serious meth addiction, had been partying for the last week at a low-budget hotel in Hollywood. The booze, the drugs, and twenty-year-old pussy made him have a lapse in judgment.

"Stop wasting my fuckin' time and tell me what you know?" El Feo demanded impatiently.

"My source tells me that an agent posing as a prospect for the Mongols biker gang has a big bust going down soon. Allegedly, he's paying for his next shipment of heroin with cash and five crates of FN MK-16s. Any of this sound familiar?"

It sounded very familiar. The Nogales Cartel was embroiled in wars on all fronts. Linking up with the biker gangs gave them access to guns, lots of them. They exchanged dope for the weapons, giving them the ability to outmatch the firepower of their enemies.

El Feo stopped pacing.

"I need a name!"

Agent Reynolds sniffled, wiped the snot with the back of his hand, and then scratched his forearm. His last fix of boy was in the chamber and his clear baggie with a spider web stamp was empty. The thought of waking up tomorrow morning with the shits and the shakes terrified him.

"Ya' think you could hook me up with some dope, bro?"

"Name!"

"Hey, man, I've been helping you guys out a lot lately. You got boatloads of that shit. All I'm asking for is a little bit to help me get right."

"Name!" El Feo roared.

"His name is Parker—Special Agent Samuel Parker."

Chapter 9

187 On an Undercover Cop

Yesterday's rain brought infernal heat and humidity to the Las Vegas desert. Special Agent Samuel Parker sat in a tricked-out '71 Plymouth Barracuda and cursed the broken air conditioner for the fifth time that afternoon. The blazing hot sun danced on the windshield, and one hundred-and six-degree heat baked the leather seats.

The previous owner of the matte black hotrod was the leader of a white supremacist group, but the vehicle was seized as part of an asset forfeiture order. Parker called dibs on the ride as soon as a flatbed tow truck hauled it into the ATF's Los Angeles impound yard. He had a thing for Harley Davidson motorcycles but felt the 'Cuda could enhance his bad boy image. His assumptions were correct. His outlaw biker buddies loved the display of vintage American muscle, but the ride wasn't suitable for stakeouts. Parker was learning this the hard way.

"Shit, man, it's hot as a motherfucker! Feels like I'm in a sauna with Satan," he complained and dabbed the sweat off his forehead with a black bandana.

Agent Torres, a Tom Cruz look-a-like and ten-year veteran of the Bureau of Alcohol, Tobacco, and Firearms, panned his binoculars in the direction of the Barracuda.

"Just hang in there, buddy. Nine long months of undercover work is coming to an end," he encouraged.

Parker thought about that number—nine long months. It was the same amount of time his wife had been pregnant. She was due any day now. Hell, Tracy might be delivering the baby right now, Parker mused, but unlike regular men who worked regular jobs, his wife couldn't just pick up the phone and call him at work. She couldn't now, and she couldn't when their four-year-old son, Samuel Jr. was struck by a car.

Because Parker was deep undercover attempting to dismantle a heavily armed chapter of the Latin Cobras in Chicago, he didn't find out his son had suffered massive brain trauma and died until two days later. That was three years ago. His wife had forgiven him, but he had never been able to forgive himself.

"The sooner this case is over, the sooner I can turn in my gun and ATF credentials and retire," he mumbled under his breath.

No one heard him. Agent Torres and a backup crew were focused on a white cargo van turning off the main road and headed in Parker's direction.

"Look alive, gentlemen, we have company," Torres warned.

Torres was a stocky-built, ex-Marine in his late thirties. He was a stand-up guy, loyal, cautious, and brave, the type of soldier you want watching your back.

Parker grabbed his club jacket off the passenger seat, stepped out of the car, and slid the black leather vest over his powerful arms and shoulders. As a probationary member of the Mongols, he was allowed to wear the club's colors with the lower rocker reading *CALIFORNIA* but not the official black and white center patch and top rocker that distinguished a full-fledged member.

He leaned against the car, lit a Lucky Strike cigarette, and cautioned his team.

"Gunrunners and drug dealers have two things in common. They're unpredictable," his gruff voice became serious and somber. "We're dealing with both breeds, so everyone keep your heads on a swivel and let's make it out of this alive by any means necessary," he stressed the words, by any means.

Samuel Parker wasn't your typical lawman. He didn't walk, talk, or smell like a cop. He was a big and imposing white boy with shoulder-length, sandy blonde hair, and untrusting ocean blue eyes. His rough looks and *I don't give a fuck* attitude helped him move within criminal circles and infiltrate tight-knit organizations like the Mongols Motorcycle Club.

Today he rocked ripped, grease-stained blue jeans and a black Metallica t-shirt with the sleeves rolled up to show off his chiseled biceps and intimidating skull tattoos. The silver rings on each knuckle, wallet chain, leather vest, and scuffed up biker boots completed his ensemble. The outfit wasn't a disguise, the gear came directly from his own closet. The only thing borrowed was a department-issued belt buckle equipped with a miniature microphone.

Gone were the days of cumbersome black wires and potentially risky microphones taped to an informant's chest. Parker's surveillance device was wireless and transmitted signals to a receiver. In this case, the receiver and recorder were housed in an ankle bracelet. The ankle bracelet fit perfectly with Parker's cover story of being a recent Folsom parolee.

Wired, hot, and impatient, Parker was prepared to cop ten kilos of boy from Arturo Lopez, a major heroin distributor with connections to the Nogales Cartel. The mounting evidence against Arturo was solid, but the case was almost ripped from Parker's hands. Getting a formal introduction from a validated Mongols member who turned snitch, Parker had copped one then three then five bricks of H. That was more than enough weight to bring a CCE indictment against Arturo and his co-conspirators, but since no weapons were involved, Parker's superiors were eager to free up the manpower and hand the case over to the Drug Enforcement Agency.

The DEA was anxious to highjack the investigation. There had been an alarming number of overdoses linked to the Nogales Cartel's Fentanyl laced heroin. When the deaths were isolated to the inner-city, public officials paid no attention to the epidemic. However, once white kids on college campuses and housewives in suburban neighborhoods began to overdose on the highly lethal brand of heroin, it became a high-priority health crisis. Parents wanted immediate answers, and the Department of Justice wanted immediate results.

Parker and his team had done most of the difficult legwork. All the DEA had to do was swoop in, make the arrests, and pose for pictures with the press. It would be a public relations victory for the agency.

Just when the upper ATF brass ordered Parker and his team to shut down Operation Flamingo and brief the DEA on the investigation, the case took a favorable and unexpected turn. Arturo requested guns, high powered tactical weapons. The more the merrier, money wasn't an object, he boasted.

Arturo's sudden request rejuvenated the ATF's interest in the case and kick-started a separate sting that was also leading to a dead end. Before Arturo's request, Parker's investigation into Big Bill's Guns and Ammo had officially stalled. Although there were salacious rumors that the store was fudging Firearm Transaction Records, facilitating straw buyers, and selling firearms to felons, Parker was unable to convince a side hustling store clerk to sell him anything off the books other than a used .22 and a sawed-off 12-gauge shotgun.

These meager purchases didn't amount to the big bust Parker was hoping for before his retirement, and it certainly didn't warrant the man-hours spent at local bars cultivating a relationship with the low-level gun supplier.

However, when Arturo asked for high-powered artillery, Parker took the request to the store clerk who took the request directly to Robert *Big Bill* Berringer, the owner of Big Bill's Guns and Ammo. It was going down, and Parker looked forward to crippling both organizations on his last day of work.

Big Bill climbed out of the van.

Tommy, the side-hustling store clerk, stayed behind the wheel.

"You're late!" Parker accused.

Big Bill was actually a short, balding, German with an infinity for money and guns. He wore black slacks, a crisp, white dress shirt, and gold-rimmed Ray-Ban aviator shades hid his wild eyes.

"If I arrived early, you'd probably think I was an overanxious cop. You're not a cop, are you, Sam?"

Parker was in character and didn't dignify the question with an answer.

"Fuck you! Where are the guns?"

It was the reply Big Bill expected. Anything more or less would have drawn suspicion.

"Follow me."

Big Bill led Parker to the back of the van. Torres cursed under his breath. The men were out of his view. Big Bill opened the double doors. Five green wooden crates and two black metal boxes were in the cargo area. Parker used a pocket knife to pry open the lid of one of the crates. He knew he was out of view and that his team couldn't take pictures of the evidence, so he needed to get Big Bill on audio.

"Nice!" Parker complimented the big, Army-green assault rifles. Ten weapons were packed in each crate. "What models are they?"

Eager to showcase his gun expertise, Big Bill answered, "Swedish made FN MK-16 Special Combat Automatic Rifles. They're standard issue for the U.S. Special Operations Command." He lifted one out of its slot and presented it to Parker. "It has both full and semi-automatic capability."

Parker accepted the gun; it was surprisingly light. Noting that the serial numbers were filed down, he asked, "What about the silencers?"

"You mean noise suppressors?" Big Bill corrected.

He pulled one of the metal boxes toward the edge of the cargo bed and lifted the silver clasps. Twenty-four shiny black cylinders approximately six inches in length and three inches in circumference were neatly stacked inside.

Parker looked up and observed a black GMC Yukon storm up the dirt road leaving a cloud of brown dust in its wake. "Heads up, the guests are starting to arrive." He placed the MK-16 back in the crate and turned to Big Bill. "So, what's the plan?" he asked, knowing the talkative gunrunner would incriminate himself.

"Just like we discussed on the phone. Two gees for each chopper, and the silencers are a stack a piece."

"That's right, I'll pay the remaining three hundred and fifty-two thousand for the ten keys of H and collect my commission on the guns later. We good?"

Big Bill did the math in his head. Arturo was getting a great deal. The guns were not readily available to the public, and even if they were, a drug dealer wouldn't be able to purchase fifty of them equipped with noise suppressors and phony paperwork. Big Bill would make a handsome profit as well, yet he pushed the limits and asked for more.

"Throw in a kilo of that Mexican heroin and we got a deal."

Parker lit another cigarette and blew smoke in Big Bill's face, then gave him the middle finger. Big Bill didn't expect anything less.

The Yukon skirted to a stop kicking up gravel. Arturo and his driver, a gun-toting teenager with a shaved head, stepped out of the SUV. Arturo wore a pink, silk shirt, his favorite color, and the reason the sting was dubbed Operation Flamingo.

There was a nervous edge to Arturo that Parker hadn't seen before. He didn't like it. Movement in the backseat of the SUV caught his attention. The rear door opened, and a Mexican man in an all-white suit emerged. He was tall, twenty-something, and about that life. Pockmarks blemished his bronze face. An angel was tatted on his right fist, and a demon was tattooed on the left.

He was the one in charge, and Parker needed to change that. He dramatically threw his cigarette into the gravel and charged at Arturo, driving his back into the side of the SUV. He shoved a thick forearm into Arturo's neck and pointed an accusing finger in his face.

"I don't like surprises, and I don't like strangers. Who the fuck is he?"

Arturo threw his hands up.

"Chill, man, it's all good. This is my boss, Domingo."

Parker was very familiar with the high-ranking Nogales Cartel capo. If he was here, Parker was either looking at a promotion or a hollow point.

Keeping up the act, Parker raved, "I don't give a fuck if he's Mother Teresa. What the fuck is he doing here?"

Domingo chimed in, "I'm here to do business, eh. Cut the theatrics and let's make it happen," his voice was calm and even.

Parker couldn't believe his good fortune. If he could get a grand jury to indict El Feo's right-hand man for conspiracy to distribute ten bricks of Heroin and possession of illegal firearms, he would be one step closer to dismantling the Nogales Cartel.

He slowly released Arturo, smoothed out his ruffled pink shirt, and dusted a piece of lent off his shoulder.

"Don't take it personal, bro, but I told you from the jump that I get nervous around strangers." Turning to Domingo, he grinned and said, "Let's get it crackin'!"

Keeping an eye on the cartel trio, Parker strolled to the trunk of the Barracuda. This is the position he wanted to be in. His team had an unobstructed view of the meeting. He popped the trunk, removed a hefty duffle bag, and called the men over.

"Yo', come check this out."

Torres focused his binoculars. He finally had eyes on his partner and the targets. Relief swept through him and the other members of Echo Team, which consisted of ATF special assignment agents, Jim Ferguson, and an African American rookie named Zack Carr. The three agents were stationed a quarter of a mile away.

The Nogales Cartel was smart. Due to the strategic location of the clandestine meeting. Torres and his crew couldn't get any closer. It was an open desert space with no businesses in proximity.

Echo Team had to improvise. They positioned themselves on the shoulder of a long stretch of highway and pretended to work on a broke down Buick Sedan. To aid their cover story, the hood was up, and a can of fake smoke oozed from the engine. Torres even poured Gatorade under the car to make it appear as though fluid was leaking from the radiator. It was the best they could do on short notice. If Parker got into trouble, he was fucked.

Parker squatted, unzipped the duffle bag, and held both flaps open so the men could see the thick bundles of cash inside. He stood up, and his tall frame towered over the shorter Mexicans.

"I showed you mine, now show me yours!"

Domingo ignored the request, further demonstrating that he was in charge.

"The guns, let me see the guns."

Parker held his ground.

"Fuck that, let me see the dope!"

Larry D. Wright

The teenager drew his pole.

"You heard the big homie, let us see the guns, gringo!"

Against Parker's disapproving look, Big Bill attempted to be the voice of reason.

"Fellas, fellas, let's not argue. We're all businessmen, right? I'll show you the weapons."

Big Bill led the group to the back of his cargo van, and in the process, he also led them out of view of the surveillance team. Torres cursed under his breath.

Big Bill removed an MK-16 from the crate and handed it to Domingo.

"This bad boy was made in Sweden and can do some damage. It's an FN—"

"MK-16 Special Combat Automatic Rifle," Domingo interrupted. "And it's manufactured in Belgium, not Sweden," he added matter-of-factly. "Can I test fire it?"

Again, against Parker's looks of caution, Big Bill tossed Domingo a fully loaded cartridge.

"Sure, give it a test fire." He also tossed Domingo a silencer.

Parker groaned.

Torres did, too.

Domingo twisted the noise suppressor onto the threaded barrel, jammed the cartridge into the bottom of the chopper, and chambered a round. Flashing a gap-toothed grin, he clicked the switch to full auto and leveled the barrel at Parker.

"There's a rumor going around that you're the policía."

Torres sensed trouble. He wanted to move in, but he hadn't received the prearranged signal from Parker, and jumping the gun could jeopardize the whole operation.

Parker realized he was in a life-or-death situation; a scenario undercover agents feared the most. An agent who goes deep undercover must have guts, intuition, acting skills, and a helluva poker face. Parker possessed all four attributes, and years of working the streets taught him that he must meet aggression with equal force or die right there in the hot-ass desert.

Parker stepped to Domingo.

"You bean eating, piece of shit! Are you calling me a pig?" He was so close he could smell the double mint gum and onions on Domingo's breath. "Get that fuckin' gun outta my face before I take it from you and shove it up your pussy!" He was putting on an Oscar-worthy performance.

Domingo's eyes hardened, and his slim index finger tightened around the trigger. He studied Parker—the chiseled muscles, the skull tattoos, the Mongols biker vest, the determination, and most convincingly, the craziness in his eyes.

"Nah, we got some bad information, ese. You might be a loco gringo, but you for sure ain't no cop," he declared and swiftly swung the assault rifle in Big Bill's direction. "But this vato smells like a rat!"

Big Bill's eyes widened in horror.

"No, please, no! You got it all wrong!" he pleaded as he stumbled back.

Parker opened his mouth to protest, but it was too late. Domingo gritted his teeth and blasted the gun dealer in the chest. For near-silent acoustics, the noise suppressor had steel wool and aerosol foam inside the slender fiberglass tube. The only sounds heard were brass shells hitting the gravel, the sickening thud of slugs penetrating flesh and bone, and Big Bill slamming into the back of the cargo van.

Six circular bloodstains appeared on the front of his crisp, white shirt. Parker watched helplessly as the blood saturated Big Bill's chest and the six small circles became one large, red blob. Because of the high-quality silencer, Torres and the rest of the Echo Team were oblivious to the escalating tension.

The side-hustling gun store clerk cranked the engine and put the van in reverse, but the gun-toting teenager was on him before his New Balance shoes pressed the gas pedal. The young soldier ran up to the driver's side window and let the clerk have it. Bullets shattered the window and struck the clerk in his neck and left temple. He gasped for air before slumping sideways into the passenger seat.

Torres heard the loud report of gunfire.

"Oh, shit, let's move in!" He slammed the Buick's hood and jumped behind the wheel.

Agent Ferguson radioed the Las Vegas PD for backup. He didn't receive good news.

"Vegas has a tactical team on standby!" he shouted over the Buick's loud engine. "But their ETA is five minutes. We're on our own!"

Agent Carr sat in the backseat cradling an M-16. He glanced at his stopwatch, adjusted his body armor, and went over the mental checklist that was instilled into him at the academy.

Domingo aimed the stick at Arturo next.

"You fucked up, homes. You know the price. ¡Manos arriba!" he commanded Arturo to put his hands in the air.

Arturo decided he'd rather die by Domingo's bullets than die by El Feo's sadistic fire. He reached for his strap, pulled it, and aimed, but that's as far as he got. Domingo and the trigger-happy teenager opened fire and blew him down. Arturo's body twisted under the force of hot lead.

Parker considered reaching for his own piece, but intuition and experience cautioned him against it. His cover was still intact, and that's all that mattered.

"The police!" he shouted while pointing at the speeding Buick, then positioned himself on the driver's side of the Barracuda.

Domingo heard the roar of the battered Buick as it turned off the main highway. He slowly and deliberately turned to Parker and tossed him a burner phone.

"From now on, you'll deal directly with me. I'll be in touch, mi amigo."

Domingo snatched up the duffle bag, hopped into the Yukon, and smashed out. The teenager closed the rear doors of the van, dragged the dead clerk out of the driver's seat, and followed the Yukon. Clouds of dust obscured the vehicles as they raced toward the sand dunes and disappeared.

Torres pulled up and slammed on the breaks next to the Barracuda.

"What the hell happened?" he probed as he took in the three dead bodies.

Parker didn't realize he was holding his breath until he tried to speak, "My friggin' cover was almost blown!"

"What! How?"

One name came to mind. "That prick James Reynolds is the what and the how!"

Larry D. Wright

Chapter 10

Cops and Crooks

"What the hell does Agent Reynolds have to do with this, and was that Domingo?" Torres put on his seatbelt and retrieved a box of shotgun shells out of the glove compartment.

"Yeah, that was Domingo. That junkie son of a bitch Reynolds lined me up. I'm gonna kill him!" Parker promised and pounded the steering wheel. He weaved the Barracuda in and out of traffic on Interstate 10 testing the muscle car's big-block engine.

Torres watched the speedometer climb past 90 MPH as he shoved rounds into a street-sweeper, a drum-fed semi-automatic 12-gauge shotgun that's beloved by gangsters and banned by the Feds.

"Hold on, partner, I gotcha back, but I need to know what the fuck is going on."

"Reynolds has been leaking intel to the Nogales Cartel."

"Are you sure?"

"Positive!"

Torres loaded the last round into the street-sweeper. "That's a strong allegation against a twenty-year vet. Got any proof?"

Parker responded with silence. Uncovering Agent Reynolds' dirt also meant exposing his own moral dilemma.

"I just know, okay," he responded half-heartedly and switched lanes.

Torres placed the shotgun on the backseat and looked at Parker. This was not their first rodeo. They had been together through stake-outs with the Crips and shootouts with the Baja Cartel. Their part-nership was forged by bullets and blood, but it was trust that solid-ified their bond.

"Cut the bullshit! If there's something I need to know, spit it out. I'm not running into a burning building without knowing all the facts, feel me?"

Reluctantly, Parker divulged the source of his suspicion.

"Reynolds is banging Ashley Cooper."

"You mean the cute, blonde chick with the big tits who works in intelligence with your wife, Tracy? What about it? Everyone has had a piece of that ass."

Parker took his eyes off the road and gave Torres that look.

"Wait," Torres caught on. "Don't tell me you're screwing her, too!"

Parker's silence confirmed the accusation. Angry with himself, his boot mashed the accelerator. The Hemi engine roared like a silverback gorilla pounding its chest.

"It started a few months ago when we were assigned to that SUV explosion that happened in the Bungalow Projects," Parker divulged, lit a Lucky Strike, hit it, and continued, "We were working late one night, and things just happened."

Torres listened with understanding, but the math wasn't adding up.

"That part is obvious but screwing a big tit, blonde, and getting your cover blown are two different things. What am I missing?"

After thumping the ashes off his cigarette, Parker filled in the gaps, "One night we were talking—"

"You mean pillow talking," Torres interjected.

"Since you put it that way, yeah, we were pillow talking. Apparently, Reynolds was, too. He mentioned that someone was feeding him intel about Los Cinco Diablos. He was also working the Body Snatchers' case."

"Isn't that the crew who were robbing drug dealers and torching the narcotics?" Torres asked.

"That's affirmative, and our cases were semi-related. The leader of the Body Snatchers is allegedly the perpetrator who planted the bomb in the SUV. Reynolds had a better angle on the case, so I was snatched off the investigation and assigned to Operation Flamingo. Ashley used to go on and on about how Reynolds was about to crack the biggest case of his career and receive a Distinguished Service Award."

Patience was not one of Torres' virtues.

"I still don't see how any of this relates to you getting your cover blown."

Parker took a puff off the cancer stick, flicked the left blinker, switched lanes, and revealed the worst part.

"Well, I sorta got jealous and started bragging about Operation Flamingo and how we were gonna bring down the Nogales Cartel. I knew some of the details would get back to Reynolds. In fact, I hoped they did. I just didn't think the rat bastard would sell me out."

Torres threw up his hands in disbelief.

"Com' on, Parker, you know better. You're not some pussy-whipped frat boy. You put all our lives in danger because of your damn ego. Reynolds and Ashley are fuckin' junkies. Remember when you said gun runners and drug dealers are unpredictable? You should've added drug addicts to that list as well."

"I know, I fucked up," Parker conceded.

"Fucked up is an understatement! You compromised the whole mission. We gotta shut down."

"Not necessarily." Parker held up the burner phone given to him by Domingo. "My cover is still good, but we have to get to Reynolds before they do."

"How do you know it was Reynolds and not Ashley?" Torres questioned.

"Motive, incentive, and pattern!"

"You lost me, dog."

"Every criminal activity has a pattern. Recognize the pattern, and you can solve the case," Parker quoted one of his trainers from the ATF academy in Glynco, Georgia. The cigarette bobbed in the corner of his lips as he spoke, "Think about it, the Nogales Cartel and Los Cinco Diablos have been locked in a bloody battle for Southern California for years. What better way to bring down your enemies than to have the police do it for you?"

Torres frowned, confused.

"I still don't get it."

Parker spotted the California Highway Patrol ahead and slowed down before clarifying his theory.

"El Feo is a grimy but smart muthafucker. He doesn't want a truce with Los Cinco Diablos, he wants their drug routes. I believe that while he was openly planning a merger with Benzo Al's brother, Carlos Guzman, he was secretly trying to get as many Diablos soldiers off the streets as possible by feeding Agent Reynolds information about their organization."

Understanding registered in Torres' eyes.

"I bet that's how Reynolds has been making all those cartel arrests. Hell, they're talking about giving this asshole a medal and a promotion. As a Senior Administrator, he'll have access to all the cases his field agents are working."

"That's right. Corruption is a two-way street, and there's not a lot of differences between cops and crooks. If Reynolds is receiving information, I bet my left nut he's giving information as well."

Torres laughed.

"Hold that bet. Your nuts are what got us into this mess in the first place," he joked, and the mood lightened.

The highway patrol officer took the next exit, and Parker picked up speed. The trip to Palm Springs, California, was surprisingly quick. The sun had descended behind the mountains, but the heat lingered.

Parker pulled onto Clearwater Way and parked in front of Reynolds' house, a stylish, two-story palace with floor-to-ceiling windows. It sat at the end of a quiet cul-de-sac. Parker and Torres were thinking the same thing—*how the hell could Reynolds afford such a beautiful home on an ATF salary?*

No lights were on in the home, and the electric blinds were shut tight. Anxious to get it crackin', Parker exited the vehicle gripping the street-sweeper. He had that crazy, determined look in his eyes.

Torres flashed his badge at a nosey neighbor. Parker gave the man the middle finger and pounded on the front door. Receiving no answer, he gave a head nod to Torres. Torres lunged forward and kicked the doorknob. The wood splintered and the door crashed open. Parker stepped through the threshold. His shotgun swept left then right. Torres followed; his Glock 19 panned right then left.

"Spread out," Parker ordered. "Check the bedrooms, I'll check the kitchen."

The trained agents split up and searched the house. Parker found Reynolds first.

"Torres, in here!" he shouted.

Torres rushed into the kitchen and found Parker on his knees leaning over Reynolds' prone body. Reynolds was shirtless, in his underwear, and piss-stained his crotch. His eyes were glass, his lips were purple, and a marshmallow-sized ball of foam protruded from his open mouth.

Parker pressed two fingers against Reynolds' carotid to check for a pulse.

"He's dead!"

Torres noticed the syringe, burnt spoon, and clear baggie on the kitchen table. He picked up the small square baggie and examined the logo. It was a black spider web with 4H printed in the center. He opened the empty bag and rubbed some of the powdery residue between his fingers.

"It's Nogales heroin," he announced and immediately began to feel light-headed. He stumbled back and held the edge of the kitchen table for support. The clear baggie slipped out of his fingers.

Torres crashed onto the tile floor. His body shook violently. Parker noticed the 4H baggie and immediately knew the heroin residue was laced with Fentanyl, a highly toxic drug up to one hundred times stronger than morphine. One does not have to consume the lethal narcotic to be affected. A mere touch or inhalation could be deadly.

In a bold attempt to undermine the Sinaloa Cartel and corner the heroin market, the Nogales organization put a super potent product on the streets. They ordered their distributors to sell it to the consumer 4H, meaning it could be cut at least four times. This was a privilege typically enjoyed by mid-level dealers who copped the heroin raw and stepped on it to increase their profits, but the Nogales Cartel hoped to eliminate the competition by offering a superior product.

In theory, the consumers would receive more bang for their buck and become loyal customers, but in practice, the power move proved to be catastrophic. Users either didn't know they were supposed to cut it before consumption, or they didn't know how to use cutting agents or they foolishly believed their tolerance level for the drug would keep them safe. The results were devastating with rises in heroin overdoses nationwide.

Understanding that time was of the essence, Parker dashed to his car, popped the trunk, retrieved a first aid kit, and sprinted back into the house. He ripped the cap off the Narcan with his teeth, stabbed Torres in his thigh, and pressed the plunger. After a terrifying moment, Torres gasped and desperately sucked in air.

Parker was relieved. He helped Torres into a chair and called the local PD and the paramedics. While waiting, he searched the rest of the premises hoping to find any clues linking Reynolds to the Nogales Cartel. He hit pay dirt in the home office. Parker snatched a yellow Post-it-Note off the computer monitor. It read: *Nella—suspect in the Giuseppe murders, member of the Body Snatchers, may be using the alias, Asia Wright.*

He couldn't believe his good fortune. His thoughts of retirement were replaced with a jolt of adrenaline. It was as if the blood in his veins had been replaced with espresso. The name scribbled in blue ink was very familiar and restored his interest in the failed Body Snatchers investigation. Having the case snatched out of his hands and given to an incompetent colleague had him feeling some type of way. Now he had an opportunity to redeem himself.

On the surface, Agent Parker was a one-man, one-gun cowboy, but deep within, he was simply a dedicated cop who thrived off the next mission. He possessed the determination of a long-distance runner, not to mention he was clever, meticulous, and exceptionally patient. To him, cracking a case wasn't a sprint, it was a marathon, and the race was on!

"I don't know why El Feo wants you arrested, but I know why I do. I'm coming for you, Nella!" Parker declared.

Chapter 11

If I Die Tonight

"Say my name!" Nella demanded while riding Najee's rock, hard dick. On each downstroke, she clenched her pussy muscles and squeezed the base of his pole.

"Oohhh, Nella!" Najee moaned.

"No, say my government name," she insisted as she took him balls deep, squeezed her pussy walls, and rose up so only the head remained in her wet hole. She gently rocked back and forth on the tip of his cock, teasing him, driving him absolutely crazy with passion before sliding down his dick again.

"Petronella Jackson!" Another moan escaped from Najee's lips.

Nella had that flame, and his thick, eight-inch love stick was the perfect size for her snug vagina. On each downward stroke, he stretched her open. When she rose upwards her pussy lips clung to his dick and coated the shaft with streaks of white cream.

"Wrong answer, nigga." She wanted him to give her his last name and was prepared to put that phat monkey on him until he got it right.

Nella squatted over his throbbing dick froggy style. She planted both feet firmly on the bed and rose all the way up so only the fat head lingered in her pink opening, then slammed back down on his thick penis. Her phat booty smacked against his thighs, and his dick head rubbed against her G-spot.

Nella leaned forward so that her soft lips were next to Najee's ear.

"What's my name?" she whispered seductively while bouncing up and down on his long shaft.

This time, Najee got it right.

"Petronella Howard!" he yelled while gripping each of her butt cheeks.

He held them wide open, lifted his hips off the bed, and drove all of his rod into her velvet tunnel. He hit her second G-spot, the one that's deep in her pussy, and her sugar walls spasmed.

"Ay, papi, I feel you all up in me!" she panted with her head thrown back and her mouth opened in ecstasy.

Her body tensed up, her heart thumped faster, her clit stiffened, and her fingernails dug into his chest. Her orgasm started in her pinky toe, flowed through her clitoris, and terminated at her erect and sensitive nipples. Exhausted, she collapsed on his sweaty chest, still rotating her hips in a circular motion and grinding her clit against his tool as she rode out an explosive orgasm. Her sticky, white cream coated his balls, which were the size of hard-boiled eggs and filled with cum.

Najee's climax hit soon after. He rolled Nella onto her right side, got behind her, and lifted one of her legs in the air. In one powerful thrust, he slid his throbbing cock balls deep into her dripping wet cunt. They spooned as he hit her shaved kitty cat with long, slow strokes. Simultaneously, he nibbled on her ear, telling her how much he loved her and how she had some bomb pussy and how he was going to beat her booty up next.

Nella loved when Najee talked nasty and brought the freak out of her. Her asshole tingled at the thought of him eating her out from the back before pushing the huge head into her tight backdoor.

His strokes gradually picked up pace and intensity, sometimes hitting her with short, quick jabs, and switching to deep, strong thrusts all while holding her thick leg in the air and talking dirty in her ear. Nella pushed back on his cock and tightened her coochie muscles attempting to milk the cum out of his testicles.

Unable to hold out any longer, Najee pounded into her guts deeper, harder and faster. He made that pussy talk and get wetter. The bedsprings squeaked, and Nella's big booty wobbled each time it smacked against his thighs. Finally, Najee's body stiffened, and he bit his bottom lip and cum shot out of his dick like a torpedo.

Nella could feel his cock twitch, throb, and squirt jet after jet of warm sperm into her womb.

That was only the first round. Their sex drive was insatiable, their stamina remarkable. They made love like they lived life—fast, wild, passionate, and always on the edge.

Hours later, Nella's anus and pussy were sore. Najee's dick was raw and drained completely dry. The king-sized mattress hung half on its frame, half on the floor, and the black satin sheets had a large, round wet spot. Their bodies glistened with sweat.

After a hot shower together, they cuddled on the couch sharing a bowl of butter pecan ice cream while attempting to watch Hustle and Flow, Nella's favorite hood movie, however, sleep overwhelmed them during the opening credits.

Early the next morning when it was still dark outside and the egg yolk yellow sun hadn't risen above the horizon, and criminals were still sleeping and law enforcement operated with the element of surprise, Najee tapped Nella on the shoulder.

"Wake up, baby!" his voice was urgent. His pupils focused in the dark bedroom.

Nella slept curled in the fetal position. She groaned and brushed his hand away.

"Stop, Bae, you doing too much," she protested sleepily. "No more nookie for you tonight. You tore my kitty up."

Najee grabbed her arm forcibly and jerked her toward him. Nella's eyes widened with alarm. She opened her mouth to voice her disapproval, but Najee held a finger to his lips.

"Shhh!" he urged her to be quiet and held up three fingers. There were three assailants. "Get dressed, now!" He sat a stack of neatly folded clothes on the edge of the bed along with a blue bulletproof vest.

Nella shook off the grogginess and snapped alert. She noticed that Najee had already slipped on a pair of jeans, wheat color Timbs, and body armor. He didn't wear a shirt underneath the bulletproof vest, and his tatted-up biceps looked as black and intimidating as the assault rifle. Nella rushed to get dressed, slipped on a pair of Balenciaga tennis shoes, then she slowly, and quietly retrieved a similar Draco from the closet. The weapon was shorter than an AK, but the curved magazine appeared longer than her forearm.

Najee used a finger to carefully part the blinds of their second-story bedroom window. Nella removed the magazine, checked it for bullets, and jammed it back into the bottom of the rifle as she stood next to him.

"El Feo or Los Cinco Diablos?" she asked.

Najee watched the men maneuver into position. One was black, the other two were white. They moved with smooth synchronicity he hadn't witnessed in El Feo's men or Benzo Al's loyal soldiers.

"Worse, it's the Feds!" he cautioned.

Nella cringed.

"Shit, how did they find you?" her voice was barely a whisper.

Najee shrugged and lined up the black man in his sights. He was young, his ambitious, but inexperienced eyes darted back and forth nervously. Najee swung the barrel to his left and marked another target. He was older, more seasoned, and looked like a popular actor, but Najee couldn't put a name to the familiar face.

He turned to Nella and said, "Look, baby girl, if I die tonight—"

"Stop talking like that," Nella cut in. "The only people dying tonight are these pigs," she assured adamantly and lined up the red-headed white guy.

Najee sensed the end rapidly approaching. He had felt that way for some time now. He felt it in Atlanta when his armored SUV flipped over during a high-speed chase in which Yung Zay was killed. He felt it at Sosa's mansion when Juice and his best friend Rio betrayed him. He felt it during the shootout in the Bungalows when one of his young shooters was gunned down, and he felt it now. There were only so many bullets a gangster could dodge, and there were only so many times an outlaw could elude capture. Some things were inevitable.

Ignoring the nagging feeling, Najee focused on his target. The men moved up the driveway crouched low and in a single file line. Something didn't feel right. They made it too easy. Any perpetrator with a half-decent shot could've easily picked them off like sitting ducks. Nella was a certified murda mami, and she was thinking the same thing.

An unnerving thought occurred to Najee, what if the Feds are not after me? He moved to a different window and panned up and

82

down the serene residential street. A dented Buick and a souped-up Barracuda were the only unfamiliar cars on the block. He scanned past those vehicles looking for unmarked patrol cars. Their absence worried him. He smelled foul play.

"Nella, when you checked into the hospital, what name did you use?" Najee asked.

"Asia Wright."

"What name did you use on the lease for your spot in Pasadena?"

"Asia Wright."

"And what name did you use to rent this townhouse?"

Nella immediately realized she had fucked up. Her look said it all.

"Asia Wright!"

Najee rushed back to the large window.

"It's a setup!"

He and Nella aimed their rockets and lined up their targets, but before they could get off, the haunting sound of metal racking earned their attention. Nella and Najee swiveled around simultaneously. A huge white boy with rippling muscles and crazy eyes pointed a drum-fed shotgun in their direction.

"Freeze!" ATF Special Agent Samuel Parker demanded.

Najee and Nella wisely remained still. Parker had the drop. Nella took in Parker's imposing presence, but Najee focused on his bare feet. He had taken off his boots so he could move stealthily on the hardwood floors and creep up on the suspects. He was clever. He was a professional. He had outwitted both of them, and for that, Najee gave him his props.

The couple kept their weapons waist level and trained at the cop.

"You're a lone ranger," Najee observed. "The black kid is a rookie, the redhead is a bad shot, and Mr. Tom Cruz is moving lethargically as if he's been recently injured. And if you're here, well—" Najee paused for effect. "You already know me, and Nella are about that life."

Parker was impressed with Najee's keen insight but didn't let it show.

"Well—" he also paused for effect. "—if you know anything about a street-sweeper, you know that a single blast of buck shots from this range will kill both of you."

The large, menacing black hole in the barrel could've doubled as a bat cave.

"We'll take our chances."

Nella raised her assault rifle and braced it against her right shoulder.

My girl, Najee thought!

Instead of retreating, Parker took a step forward. The loud and clumsy clunk of boots scuffing the hardwood floors announced the arrival of agents Torres, Ferguson, and Carr.

"It's over! Lay down your weapons," Parker commanded.

Najee noticed that Parker wasn't wearing a wedding band, yet there was a circular indentation on the agent's ring finger. The area was slightly lighter than the rest of his sunbaked skin. He had a weakness. He had a family.

He and Najee were on different sides of the law, but they shared similarities. Nella and their son were the only reason Najee was talking and not shooting. When you have something to live for, dying is that much harder. If he felt that way, then surely Parker must feel the same, Najee surmised. Boulevard had taught him that a bluff is more effective than a bullet. Najee decided to exercise that supreme lesson. He put on his best poker face and tested Parker's resilience.

"Prison ain't an option. We're holding court in the streets, and we're ready to die, but are you?"

Parker knew Najee was trying to draw him into a game of mental chess. He had been around criminals too long not to think like them. He moved his own bishop into position and threatened Najee's queen.

"I actually came for Ms. Jackson but apprehending you in the process is going to be a bonus, and make no mistake about it, I'm going home tonight by any means necessary," he insisted as his finger hooked around the trigger. "But if I wanted you dead, I would've let El Feo's men do the job." He studied Najee's stone face for a reaction. Receiving none, he added, "We intercepted a Nogales Cartel hit team headed this way. How do you know El Feo?"

"How do you know that I know El Feo?"

"Be cool, I'm reaching into my pocket," Parker informed.

"Do it slow," Nella instructed and pointed the chopper in the direction of the bedroom doorway. She lined Torres up in her sights.

Parker held the shotgun in one hand and dug into his front pocket with the other.

"I found this on the coffee table." He pulled out Najee's burner phone and tossed it to him. "I think you better check your text messages."

Najee caught the phone with one hand but kept both eyes on Parker. He worked the icons with his thumb and brought up the latest pics. The gruesome images demanded his full attention. Although he had sucked on Angela's pretty toes on numerous occasions, he barely recognized the swollen and bloody feet in the picture. Her mutilated fingers were in even worse condition. The last image was of a red gas can. The implication was clear. The text message demanded that he report to Nogales, Mexico, within forty-eight hours.

Larry D. Wright

Chapter 12

The Professional

"Coffee?"

"No!"

"Want a smoke?"

"Nah, I'm straight."

Parker sat at the interrogation table with a thick manila file folder, tape recorder, and a Styrofoam cup filled with hot coffee, no sugar no cream. Keeping his stoic glare on Najee, he leaned back, crossed his legs, and fired up a Lucky Strike. After a deliberate moment of silence, he intentionally blew smoke in Najee's face and pressed play on the recorder.

"You said we needed to talk so start talking."

Like many black men, the police made Najee apprehensive. As a child, he wondered why Boulevard would shake like a maple leaf when the police got behind him. He didn't comprehend the tumultuous relationship between the cops and African Americans until his mother gave him *the talk*. From that moment forward, he despised the police and rooted for the villain in movies.

Ignoring Parker's antics, Najee asked a question of his own.

"Where's Nella?"

Parker glanced at his watch.

"By now she's been fingerprinted, photographed, and fed a dry bologna sandwich. Oh, I almost forgot about the cavity search!" he taunted to get a rise out of his suspect.

Najee's jaw muscles tightened.

"When can I see her?" The desperation in his voice was obvious. Hoping Parker didn't notice, he quickly regained his composer, but it was too late.

Parker pulled on the cigarette and took his sweet time answering. He had Najee right where he wanted him, against the ropes.

"You can see her at the arraignment. The two of you are being indicted on a shit load of charges." More thick smoke flowed in Najee's direction.

Najee was shook, but on the exterior, his features remained calm, granite, and unreadable.

"Those charges will never stick," he asserted confidently.

"I find your misguided optimism amusing," Parker remarked between sips of coffee. "What makes you think you can beat these charges?"

Leaning forward, Najee pressed stop on the recorder. His pupils darkened and his voice deepened.

"Because I don't leave witnesses!"

Najee's audaciousness and cavalier attitude irked Parker. He wished these were the old days when you could slap the shit out of a perpetrator and get away with it, but police reforms, camera phones, and angry protestors chanting Black Lives Matter made him hesitant. Besides, he had dealt with wise guys like this before, he reassured himself and suppressed his irritation. Federal judges had handed out over 500 years of prison time to the criminals he had apprehended during his illustrious career. He was looking forward to adding Najee's name to that growing list.

"You're a cocky son of a bitch," Parker accused and turned the recorder back on. "But you're forgetting one thing. You grew a conscience and let those two white girls live when you hit Stix, the Haitian. Remember him?" He opened the thick file folder and slid a gruesome 8x10 crime scene photo across the table.

Stix lay faced down in a pool of dark-red, syrupy fluid. His wrists were restrained behind his back, and his dreads were saturated with blood.

Najee's intestines curled into a pretzel, but he kept his cool and was thankful the air conditioner was on blast. "Control your emotions," he cautioned himself.

Federal agents are trained to detect subtle clues. A look, body posture, or even one's tone of voice could provide an attentive interrogator with vital information.

Najee wondered how much info he had already silently communicated to the observant officer.

If they knew about Stix, they knew too much. Between taking over the infamous Bungalow projects, infiltrating Los Cinco Diablos, and murdering Benzo Al, the move on Stix had become a distant memory. He had kicked in the stash house door wavin' the four-four. After airing out the beefy Haitian bodyguard, he duct-taped Stix and the two skinny white girls who were counting stacks of cash. Najee bagged up over one hundred bands and knocked Stix's noodles loose for not giving up the 411on Benzo Al's location.

Najee should've offed the two white bitches as well, but he went against the grain and let them live. That's the problem with being human. Mortals are bound to their conscience, but bullets have no souls, and the trigger has no heart.

The two white girls posed a potential threat, but he had a few things working in his favor. Witnesses could be bribed or intimidated, and if that didn't work, he had The Deacon and Mufasa. The Deacon was lethal and loyal, and Mufasa ran a squad of Somali hitters from Atlanta who were always eager to murk something.

As if reading Najee's thoughts, Parker flicked the ashes off the end of his cigarette, took a gulp of coffee, and admitted, "Witnesses often disappear or get paid to catch a sudden case of amnesia, but physical evidence is irrefutable."

His statement piqued Najee's curiosity.

"You know something I don't?"

Parker leaned back and grinned.

"I know everything you don't! Puzzle pieces are small, but if you put enough of them together, you begin to see the big picture."

"That sounds like some shit you read in a fortune cookie," Najee shot back.

"Well, how is this for good fortune? I know that you and an accomplice, probably a female, cleaned up Antwan McKinley's Venice Beach penthouse after you murdered him," Parker insinuated. "I have to give it to you. Even way back then you were tenacious and thorough, but you left a puzzle piece."

Najee folded his arms.

"I don't know what you're talking about, officer."

"Sure, you do. You were patient, professional, and proficient, but you made one fuck up." He tapped a dirty fingernail on another photo. "You left your DNA near the murder scene."

Najee unconsciously shifted in his seat. He remembered Twan very well. It was his first lick. He picked up the photo and stared at the Pepsi bottle full of urine. Years had gone by since he'd last seen it. He had cased Twan's spot for weeks waiting on the perfect moment to strike. On the night in question, The Bishop's stepdaughter, Katrina "Katt" Santana, lured Twan from Taboo's Gentlemen's Lounge.

Katt was a thick and sexy Dominican stripper/hairstylist/babysitter/all-around scandalous bitch. The type of woman who made street-savvy hustlers and certified goons turn to mush with a wink from her hazel eyes.

Najee was already posted up in the cut watching, waiting, and wrapping his fingers around the rubber grip of his snub-nose .38. He didn't want to leave his hiding spot for fear he might miss his window of opportunity, so he pissed in the empty Pepsi bottle and carelessly tossed it aside. Amateur's mistake!

Najee pushed the photo back to Parker, and with a straight face, shrugged his shoulders.

"Big deal, you got a bottle of my piss. Y'all gon' have to come way better than that to spook me. Even a public defender could beat that charge. Basically, ain't no telling how long that bottle was there before the murder occurred, and the last time I checked, littering wasn't a federal offense."

Parker was unmoved.

"I figured you'd say something like that, so I saved the best for last."

He removed five more crime scene photos from the evidence file and fanned them out like a lucky gambler presenting a royal flush. He inspected Najee's eyes for a reaction knowing the stone poker face was only a front.

"You may have covered your tracks, but we got Nella dead bang for the Giuseppe Murders."

Najee and Parker locked eyes. Each man silently dared the other to blink first. The Giuseppe Murders had been dominating the airwaves and news feeds for five consecutive days. The case had all the allure of a sensational, high-profile murder mystery. A large amount of cash and five bullet-riddled bodies were found slain in a low-budget hotel in Inglewood, California, but the most salacious detail surrounded the prime suspect, a beautiful, calculating, and deadly woman. The femme fatal rocked a skintight designer bodysuit, camouflage Giuseppe boots, and a matching camouflage bulletproof vest. She was literally dressed to kill.

Najee couldn't resist picking up one of the photos. The image was a still shot from a surveillance camera. The sexy vixen in the 8x10 was undoubtedly Nella. The black bodysuit hugged her voluptuous, 5'6 figure like cellophane. She stood in the hotel's parking lot with a Glock .40 in her hand and an acidic snarl on her lips. Sosa, The Deacon, and The Bishop were close behind, but they wisely wore black Jason hockey masks.

Najee's gaze landed on the other four photos. The bloody scene inside the small hotel room was grotesque and not for the faint of heart. The deceased body of Isaac Ice Miller lay sprawled on the bathroom floor. The barrel of Sosa's AK-47 had been jammed down his throat. The Medical Examiner suspected that Ice was on his knees when he was shot. Blood splatter dripped from the ceiling, and pink chunks of his brains stained the porcelain toilet and sink.

Four more twisted bodies were in the common area. The Bishop had drilled Redbonez in the face, one shot, one kill. Her nose was missing, and the black powder burns on her skin indicated the shot was fired from point-blank range. She got what she deserved, Najee concluded as he made out the Blood gang tattoo on her neck. She had tried to kill him in the Bungalows, worked with Benzo Al to kidnap his son, and murdered The Bishop's stepdaughter, Katt. His only regret was that he didn't pull the trigger himself.

He felt the same way about the dead body belonging to the hotel's housekeeper. The middle-aged hospitality worker was responsible for Nella getting raped by one of Benzo Al's thugs in Amsterdam. Nella made sure the housekeeper paid full restitution with her life. Najee could barely make out the details of her face. The up-close and personal hollow point to the cranium left her unrecognizable.

Two more bloody and mangled corpses were found cuddled up in the bed. Their bodies and the headboard were riddled with gaping bullet holes. It was overkill. Cinnamon and Spice were simply at the wrong place at the wrong time, but that was how The Deacon got down—no mercy, no remorse, no witnesses.

Najee pulled his focus away from the carnage and examined the photo of Nella again. He knew the look on her face was concern for their son, but she had allowed her emotions to get the best of her and failed to mask up.

I taught her much better than that, he thought sadly.

The high-resolution photos were damaging. It would be virtually impossible to convince a jury that she wasn't at the murder scene.

Parker watched Najee closely. He recognized the love in Najee's eyes. He looked at his own wife the same way. He almost felt sorry for him, but he had a job to do. He cleared his throat and hammered the final nail into the coffin.

"Like I was saying, Nella is a cooked goose. There's even video footage of her and the other three suspects entering the room."

Najee didn't realize he was holding his breath until Parker stood up. He went to the mobile TV stand, slid a disc into the Blu-ray player, and pressed play. He sat back down with a condescending grin on his face. A black Lincoln Navigator swerved into the parking lot. Nella jumped out almost before the shiny SUV stopped moving. Three heavily armed masked men followed her lead. In what could've been a scene from the movie Set It Off, Nella smoothly accosted a hotel housekeeper from behind and pressed the cannon against her coconut.

She directed the unsuspecting victim toward door 118, forced her to use the master key to open the door, then roughly shoved her inside. The last masked assailant to enter the room looked directly into the camera and slammed the door. The distinct clap of gunfire narrated what was not caught on tape. Moments later, Sosa and the

Body Snatchers calmly strolled to the SUV and mashed out. The surveillance footage faded to black.

Najee glanced at Parker out of his peripheral. Parker's attention remained glued to the large screen. His grey eyes twinkled with fascination, and if Najee was correct, with admiration as well. All he was missing was a box of buttered popcorn.

"Why did you surrender so easily?" Parker's gruff voice yanked Najee's mind back into the interrogation room.

Najee's shoulders were tense, and the big vein on the side of his neck pulsated.

"Because you had the drop on Nella," he answered a little too quickly.

Chapter 13

Let's Make a Deal

"Actually, I had the drop on both of you."

Najee didn't respond, his gaze landed on Parker's wedding finger. Parker noticed the tan line and awkwardly hid his hand under the table.

"Let me guess," Najee began. "You have a wife, two kids, a minivan, and a modest home somewhere in the San Fernando Valley."

Parker chuckled.

"You're close, but you're wrong about the minivan. I drive a badass 1971 'Cuda. It goes well with my hardcore image when I'm doing undercover work," Parker revealed, and after some thought added, "You're right about the number of kids, though. My wife is pregnant with number two. Our first child was killed in a hit and run accident."

"Sorry to hear that," Najee expressed with genuine empathy. "But why are you telling me this?"

"Because I'm trying to earn your trust."

"Miss me with the reverse psychology shit. I don't trust nobody!"

"You trust Nella!"

Najee looked away and stared at the cream-colored walls. He hated hospitals and police stations, both places sapped his energy and imagination. While in the joint he had learned that law enforcement agencies purposely made their interrogation rooms bland and nondescript to promote sensory deprivation. They wanted persons of interest to be cognizant but not too creative during interviews.

Growing impatient with the cat and mouse games, Najee snapped, "Get to the point, homie! What the fuck do you crackers want?"

"Follow me."

Parker grabbed the mini-recorder and led Najee into the Los Angeles ATF Field Division's operations and command room.

The room was dim, the only light source came from a bank of large LCD screens and a row of flickering computer monitors. Adjacent to the computer monitors, a whiteboard was mounted on the wall. It listed the suspected locations of stash houses, courier routes, and a hierarchical chart of the Nogales Cartel. Black boxes with black lines connected the captains to the lieutenants and the lieutenants to the foot soldiers. The photos of two men shared the number one spot on top of the pyramid.

Najee recognized El Feo, but the older, more rugged-looking gentleman next to him was unfamiliar. The left side of his face was badly burned and looked leathery. A glass eye rested deep in his left eye socket.

Parker pointed a thick finger at El Feo.

"You asked what do we want? Well, we all want him!"

"Who is *we all*?" Najee asked, his gaze remained locked on the mysterious old man with the glass eye. He had the calm poise of an army general and the pedigree of a major boss.

"The Alphabet Boys, that's who! The ATF, FBI, DEA, and ICE and every fuckin' government agency with initials on the back of their windbreakers," Parker ranted. "El Feo's Fentanyl laced smack has caused a twenty-five-point three percent increase in overdoses this year alone. Combine that with his erratic behavior and propensity for violence, and you see why he is public enemy number one. Hell, even other cartels want this monster off the streets."

"So, arrest him!" Najee suggested with a shrug.

"We have a guy who's deep undercover, but it's been weeks since he last checked in. He's probably dead."

Parker patted his pockets searching for his lighter. He found it, sparked up another square, and resumed talking, "And no offense, but this isn't some two-bit, black hustler from the ghetto who we could frame with a bag of dope and a gun charge like usual. We need hard evidence, and El Feo's soldiers are either too loyal or too damned scared to flip on him. In fact, we haven't been able to find any of his drug runners willing to work with us until you came along."

So, these bitches think I'm running boy for El Feo. Good, I can use their assumptions to my advantage and pretend like I'm flippin' on the Mexicans in exchange for Nella's freedom. Yeah, that shit just might work, but I need to make Parker think it's his idea. Najee's thoughts roamed rampant.

"Who says I'm willing to work for you?"

"I do!"

"And what if I say no?"

"You won't!"

"What makes you so sure?"

"Because you're smart, because the whole time you've been sitting here, you've been formulating a plan. Because if you don't, by the time Nella gets out of prison, she'll have cobwebs on her pussy," Parker offered his compelling reasons and gave Najee time to marinate on his proposal.

Najee let the silence linger. It gave him time to arrange the pieces on his chessboard. He couldn't appear too anxious or too eager or too willing to cooperate. After a dramatic pause, he lowered his voice for effect, and said, "If I get you, El Feo, I want full immunity for myself, Nella, and Marcus Fischer."

Parker leaned forward.

"Do you mean Marcus Sosa Fischer, the leader of Block Boy Empire? How are the two of you connected?"

"I owe Sosa. He was out of the game, but I dragged him back in for one last mission. Now he's jammed up on a murder beef."

"Yeah, it's been a bloody week in L.A. All the agencies were briefed on the chop shop shootout that left Alonzo Benzo Al Guzman dead." A light clicked in Parker's head. "Wait a minute, you were there, weren't you?"

Najee pressed stop on the recorder.

"Of course, I was, but it's not what you know, it's what you can prove."

Parker pressed the play button again.

"The coroner said the killing appeared personal. I know about your war with Los Cinco Diablos, and I bet you were the trigger man."

Najee ignored Parker's fishing expedition.

"Miss me with all that. Do we have a deal or not?"

Parker leaned back in his seat and folded his hands across his stomach.

"I dunno', this Sosa twist is out of my jurisdiction. I'm gonna have to run it by my superiors, and Sosa has to be debriefed and new paperwork has to be filed, and of course, the federal prosecutor has to approve—"

Najee stood up, cutting Parker's list of excuses short. As he turned to leave, he said, "You don't have a solid case against me, so I'm finna bounce. Holler at me when you get an answer, but make it quick. As you know, I have to be in Mexico in less than forty-eight hours, and I don't want to be late. El Feo ain't the patient type."

Parker stopped Najee as he reached for the door handle. "Hold up, let's talk!"

"Fuck that, I'm done talking! The deal is simple. Give me Nella and Sosa, and I'll give you El Feo and the whole fuckin' Nogales Cartel." Najee opened the door and stepped into the hallway.

The entire building smelled like the pigs. He moved swiftly down the corridor but not too fast. He wanted to give Parker a chance to catch up. As he passed a row of cubicles, an agent he recognized from earlier that evening looked up from his keyboard. So did a geeky-looking ATF analyst wearing Sony headphones. They appeared startled and suspicious, but Najee thought nothing of it.

As anticipated, Parker was on Najee's back bumper. "Wait!" He grabbed Najee by the shoulder. "How deep are you in with El Feo?"

"Six point five million deep!"

"Whew!" Parker whistled. "That's a lot of debt. That explains what the Nogales blackout team and the photos in your phone is about. Speaking of which, who do those tortured hands and feet belong to?"

The bloody images were permanently engraved in Najee's head. The Nogales hit team who were intercepted outside of Nella's condo were not sent to exterminate him. On the contrary, they were sent to make sure the cartel's paper made it to Mexico and not the Cayman Islands. Najee intentionally withheld that critical piece of information from Parker. He planned to allow the cop to grasp in triple darkness and chase down false leads while he figured out a way to outsmart El Feo and the Feds. He needed to save Angela. He needed to save Nella. He needed to do both at the same time. Deception was the key.

He had used lies, illusion, and misinformation in the past to achieve his objective, but this would be his greatest challenge. Time was running out, so the use of deceit and treachery was necessary now more than ever. The first step was to gain Parker's trust by utilizing law twelve of the 48 Laws of Power, which suggests using selective honesty to disarm your victim.

"The hands and feet belong to Angela Rodriguez. She's my coke plug," Najee revealed half the truth, selectively omitting the real extent of their relationship.

Parker's jaw dropped and his eyes widened.

"Are you talking about the Angela Rodriguez, the Los Cinco Diablos drug runner and sicario?"

Najee nodded his head, confirming Parker's suspicion.

"I have less than two days to deliver the payment for the bricks we were fronted. If I don't make it in time, Angela is dead!"

"This shit just keeps getting better." Parker leaned closer to the shorter Najee. His voice lowered to a raspy whisper. "Do you have the money?"

"Do we have a deal?"

Larry D. Wright

Chapter 14

Fallen Soldiers

Los Angeles ATF Field Division - 2:18 a.m.

"A deal, are you seriously entertaining giving this asshole a deal? You gotta be friggin' kidding me!" Torres ranted as he followed Parker into a small dark office connected to the interrogation room.

The adverse effects of the Fentanyl had worn off, and Torres was back to being tough, stubborn, and devoted to the job. He refilled his coffee mug, turned to Parker, and continued bitching.

"I don't trust that son of a whore as far as I can throw him!"

Parker folded his arms across his wide chest and watched Najee through the interrogation room's two-way mirror.

"I don't trust him either. He's not telling us something, but until we find out what he's hiding, he's our best shot at nabbing El Feo."

Torres dropped two sugar cubes into his cup and stood next to Parker. He watched Najee while blowing cool air on the hot coffee.

"For the record, I'm not feeling this shit. This asshole finagled his way out a murder beef as a juvenile, and from the way he's playing you, it looks like he's improved his game."

Parker let the comment slide and poured himself a cup of Folders.

"We're only shadow boxing. The real fight hasn't started yet," he told Torres while adding almond milk to his Styrofoam cup.

Torres rolled his eyes and sighed deeply.

"Yeah, whatever! Get your head out of your ass, Parker. He's a career criminal. You know damn well that once he leaves this building, he's gonna be in the wind."

"I beg to differ," Parker dissented between sips of coffee. "He's not going anywhere, not without Nella."

"What makes you think he won't abandon her ass and get ghost?"

"One word–loyalty. He's not the type that'll abandon a fallen soldier. Think about it. He has the cartel's money. He could've booked before we showed up, but he's still here and willing to travel to Mexico in order to save Angela Rodriguez."

"That's another thing that doesn't make sense," Torres mentioned as he turned to face Parker. "Here's a guy who has spent his entire life beefin' with Los Cinco Diablos. Now all of a sudden, he's willing to risk his neck for one of their most prominent members. That shit don't add up!"

"You got a point," Parker acknowledged.

He licked his thumb and flipped through the thick file the FBI and the DEA had compiled on Najee. He stopped on a black and white surveillance photo of Najee and The Deacon shaking hands inside of the Bungalow projects.

"Take a look at this, Torres."

Torres examined the photo.

"Well, I'll be damned. You always suspected that Najee was the mysterious drug dealer, Sinatra."

"Now I'm sure of it. Sinatra's sudden arrival on the scene and the subsequent takeover of the projects coincides with the bomb that blew up an SUV just blocks away from the Bungalows."

"I remember that. The type of explosive device used had The Deacon's and The Bishop's signature written all over it. You were working that case, right?"

"Yeah, and it pisses me off every time I think about how it slipped through my fingers." He downed the coffee, crushed the Styrofoam cup, and faced Torres. "There's a lot of shit we don't know, but we're gonna find out. Like I said, the boxing match hasn't started yet, but I'm about to throw the first punch. Get Jeff Bartel in here."

Torres left and returned with Special Agent Jeff Bartel in tow. Fresh-faced, blonde and slender, the talented audio forensic analyst had what it took to succeed in law enforcement. He was efficient, intelligent, diligent, and most importantly, willing to break the rules.

Jeff reached into his shirt pocket for a USB thumb drive and tossed it to Parker.

"You're gonna love this," he promised. The USB stick held doctored audio from Najee's interrogation session.

Parker grinned his approval and patted Jeff on the back. "When a cop says that everything you say can and will be used against you, it's best to take his advice and shut the fuck up!" The three agents laughed.

After laying out his plot, Parker left to round up Nella while Torres reluctantly filed the appropriate paperwork to register Najee as a confidential informant.

Najee sourly considered the unsavory title as Torres fastened a GPS bracelet around his ankle and led him to the elevator.

"Ain't no way I'm about to hoe-up and become a rat. I'ma beat these bitches at their own game!" Najee mumbled to himself.

The elevator doors dinged open, and Torres shoved Najee in the back, pushing him inside. Najee stumbled but quickly turned around with his fist and teeth clenched.

Torres stood on the outside of the elevator and issued a stern warning, with each word, he poked Najee in the chest with his finger.

"I'm gonna be watching your black ass, you fried chicken eating monkey. When you take a piss, I'll be standing at the next urinal. When you take a shit, I'll know if you've been eating corn. Capisce, dick head?"

Najee looked down at the white finger jammed into his chest. His adrenaline surged and his knuckles tightened, but he didn't let the racist agent knock him off his square. After a tense moment, Najee's frown softened into an arrogant smile. He laughed at Torres, chunked up the deuce, and pressed the down button.

As the elevator doors closed, Najee noticed Parker escorting Nella into the interrogation room by the elbow. Tight handcuffs bit into her wrist, and she wore a wrinkled orange jumpsuit with a pair of cheap flip-flops on her feet.

Nella had spotted Najee before he saw her. She couldn't understand why he was in his street clothes laughing with a federal agent while she was dressed in orange and crying on the inside.

When they finally made eye contact, Nella looked away. A teardrop trickled down her right cheek, and her shoulders sagged with doubt and disappointment. Before Najee could assure her that he had everything under control and that she would be out soon, the elevator doors closed and so did another chapter of their relationship.

***

Nella sat in a hard plastic chair and took in her surroundings. The small interrogation room was not dark nor was there a sinister lightbulb swinging from the ceiling like in the movies. Aside from being unusually cold, the room was clean and sterile, yet she somehow knew it held many dirty deeds and filthy secrets.

Parker sat in the seat opposite Nella and sized her up. She had smooth light skin with tiny brown freckles on her slender nose. Her thick, wavy black hair was pulled back into a French bun, and her lips were luscious and ruby red even without lipstick. She was beautiful and sitting there in the wrinkled orange jumpsuit, she looked vulnerable and frail, nothing like the murderer in the skintight, bodysuit, and knee-high Giuseppe boots.

Peeling his eyes away from her beauty, Parker checked his sympathy and reminded himself of the bloody crime scene at the hotel. He was dealing with a validated member of the Body Snatchers. She was a cold and calculating gangster bitch and needed to be treated as such.

Fighting the urge for a cigarette, he opted for a sip of coffee instead and offered Nella a cup.

"Can I get you some coffee?"

"No!"

"Cigarette?"

"Hell no!" Nella declined, irritated.

"Is there anything else I can get you?" Parker asked nicely.

"Yeah, you can get me a phone so I can call my attorney. What's this all about?"

Parker took his time taking another swallow of coffee before leafing through Nella's criminal file.

"Perhaps this might answer your question." He pushed one of the hotel crime scene photos her way.

Nella picked it up and stared at the 8x10 photo in silence. Her hands trembled and her bottom lip quivered. It felt as though she had been kicked in the gut. The still-shot from the hotel's surveillance cameras depicted Nella in the parking lot holding a Glock .40. There was no question it was her. The high-resolution camera even picked up the freckles on her face.

"There's more," Parker stated quietly, but to Nella, it sounded like he was screaming into a megaphone. He slid her several photos showing the utterly shocking and grotesque scene inside of the hotel room. Blood, shell casings, and dead bodies were scattered everywhere. "There's video, too," he added matter-of-factly and took a sip of Folger's.

Nella didn't need to see the other evidence. She knew she let her emotions get the best of her and failed to mask up. She was going to prison for life. Feeling defeated, she put her face in her palms and sobbed, "This has to be a nightmare."

It was as if her worst fear had crept from under the bed and was strangling her in her sleep, but this wasn't a dream. This was real.

"This is Najee's fault!" she screamed in her head. She couldn't believe he let her go down without a gunfight.

Parker watched Nella closely. He had intentionally timed it so she could see Najee in the elevator wearing his street clothes while she was handcuffed and wearing orange. It was part of his strategy to sow mistrust in Nella's heart.

"Look, Ms. Jackson, I'm gonna level with you. Najee was allowed to leave because he cut a deal with us. He threw you and Sosa under the bus and saved himself."

Nella looked up, her eyes were red, and she was on the brink of tears.

"Bullshit, Najee would never flip on anyone, especially me!" Parker's accusations made her suspicious.

As far as she was concerned, Najee was cut from a different cloth and would never talk to the police. He had schooled her to plead the fifth and evoke her right to an attorney if she ever got jammed up by them people. She was positive he did the same thing but was surprised when Parker said he had it all on tape.

Parker held up the thumb drive given to him by Special Agent Jeff Bartel.

"Listen for yourself."

He plugged the thumb drive into the USB port of his tablet, brought up an audio file, and pressed play. Special Agent Bartel did a professional job doctoring Najee's interrogation session. The audio sounded unaltered and authentic.

"Who says I'm willing to work for you?"

"I do!"

"And what if I say no?"

"You won't!"

"What makes you so sure?"

"Because you're smart because the whole time you've been sitting here, you've been formulating a plan."

"Miss me with the reverse psychology shit."

"You trust Nella?"

"I don't trust nobody! If I get you, Nella and Marcus Fischer, I want full immunity for myself."

Parker received the reaction he was looking for and poured more gasoline on the fire.

"He told us about dragging Sosa out of retirement to pull the move at the Los Cinco Diablos chop shop. He also said it was Sosa who killed Benzo Al."

Nella's eyebrows formed an angry V.

"Najee told you guys that?"

"How else would we know that Najee asked Sosa to go on one last mission?"

That's a good point, Nella contemplated. *Only the Body Snatchers knew that Sosa called his boys in to help save her baby from Angela and Benzo Al. Najee had to have told Parker.*

Nella's mind was spinning. She didn't know how to proceed, but she couldn't stand by and let Sosa take the fall for something he didn't do. He had put his life and freedom on the line to help her.

"Sosa didn't kill Benzo Al. He was already dead when we arrived," she assured with passion—a little too much passion.

Parker noticed the fluctuation in Nella's voice and the way she crossed and uncrossed her legs when she mentioned Sosa. Something was there, he just didn't know what. He filed the information in his memory bank and continued the interrogation.

"If Sosa didn't kill Benzo Al, then who did?"

His question was met with silence, so he came from another angle. He pressed fast forward and put jumper cables on her heart.

"It's bad enough that Najee sold Sosa out, but that's not the worst part. He left you to rot in prison while he rushed off to Mexico so he could save Angela Rodriguez. Listen to this." He pressed play again.

"I have less than two days to deliver the payment for the bricks we were fronted. If I don't make it in time, Angela is dead!"

Without thinking, Nella blurted out, "What bricks is he talking about? That bitch Angela is pregnant with his baby. So, when the Nogales Cartel kidnapped her, he hit their main stash house."

As soon as the statement left her lips, she knew she had said too much. She saw it in Parker's eyes. He quickly gathered his paperwork and rushed out of the interrogation room. Nella sat there distraught and confused.

She had lost faith in Najee but not in God.

"Father, forgive me for my sins."

Larry D. Wright

Chapter 15

The Devil's Middle Finger

The smell of frankincense and burnt candle wax drifted through Saint Francis Catholic Church. Sunshine trickled through the colorful stained-glass windows, and dust danced in the light.

Marco Segundo fell to his knees and petitioned God for forgiveness.

"Father, forgive me for my sins," he begged with his head held toward the sky.

The forty-five-year-old Dominican drug lord had been knee-deep in the streets since he was thirteen and had been racking up sins for three decades. Money, murder, and mo' murder was his mantra. Those who knew him would be shocked to see him on his knees at the altar but even when it came to religion, he was a shiesty character. Marco could sense that his time was coming and couldn't think of a better way to cheat death than by aligning himself with God.

A priest wearing a black, satin robe with a hoodie covering his head approached Marco and the baptism tank. He looked more like a Buddhist Monk than a Catholic priest. He made a cross sign by touching his forehead and shoulders, then he blessed Marco with a kiss on each cheek.

Unbeknownst to Marco, his most trusted bodyguard receded into the shadows and disappeared out the back door.

"Are you ready, my son?"

Marco nodded. The priest tilted Marco backward and dunked his torso into a glass tank filled with holy water.

"In nomine Patris, et Fílii, et Spíritus Sancti—in the name of the Father, Son, and Holy Spirit," the hooded priest chanted in Latin.

His heavy hand pinned Marco underwater longer than usual. Marco held his breath and went along with it. He figured that the more sins you had, the longer it took to cleanse your soul, but as his lungs tightened, his eyes widened. He looked up through the clear water and saw the sadistic smile on the priest's lips. Fear and panic seized Marco's soul. He struggled to come up for air, but the priest's grip tightened around his throat. Marco screamed, and bubbles escaped from his mouth and rose to the surface.

The priest found pleasure in other people's pain. He lifted Marco out of the water only to dunk his head again. He was taunting, tormenting, and teasing him with life's most essential element—oxygen. Marco fought for his life, kicking, screaming, and swinging wildly, but the strong priest kept him submerged underwater.

Marco continued to swing, twist, and fight. His fingers clutched at the black, satin robe causing the priest's gold chain and medallion to dangle. The golden image of Jesús Malverde glistened in the candlelight. This was a cartel hit.

The priest pulled Marco up again. Marco took a deep gulp of fresh air and let it out slowly. It was as if he intuitively knew he was breathing his last breath. Many men had suffered the sharp blade of his machete or felt the cold steel of his gun barrel pressed against their warm flesh. He now wondered if they had experienced the same ominous premonition before they died.

After silently praying to Baron Samedi, the God of Death in Dominican voodoo, Marco asked, "Who are you?"

The priest removed his hoodie, placed his lips next to Marco's ear, and whispered, "I'm God's middle finger!"

Marco's body stiffened, and his frantic eyes searched the killer's handsome face. Finally, recognition set in.

"El Feo!" he said the name as if he was chanting Bloody Mary in front of a mirror.

El Feo gripped a fist full of Marco's wet hair and tilted his head back, exposing his throat.

Marco made one last desperate plea, "Wait, dawg! I didn't take the money! It was Domingo, I put that on everything!"

"¡Mentirozo!" El Feo roared in Spanish. "You're a liar! Use the paper you stole from me to buy a tombstone in hell."

Reaching into his robe, he pulled out a knife and viciously swiped the blade across Marco's Adam's apple. The grotesque wound opened, and dark blood gushed from Marco's neck. The holy water turned pink and then became crimson red. The Dominican's dead body floated in the tank.

On the way out of the church, El Feo tossed the real priest a thick wad of blue faces. The real priest was so petrified, his trembling hands almost dropped the roll of hundreds. At the rear exit, El Feo noticed a tall wooden effigy of Jesus Christ hanging in agony. Rusty nails were driven through each of his outstretched palms. It made El Feo think of all the enemies he wanted to crucify.

A black Yukon waited in the parking lot. El Feo's bodyguard, Gustavo, sat behind the wheel. Domingo rode shotgun. El Feo climbed into the backseat.

"¡Vamonos, let's go!" he ordered and fired up a cigar.

Domingo watched El Feo through the rearview mirror. The boss had something heavy on his mind. Domingo assumed it was the move on Marco. El Feo and Marco went way back and made a lot of money and memories together. Domingo offered to do the hit, but El Feo said the green light was personal.

Domingo was cold-hearted, but he couldn't imagine being heartless enough to kill your best friend.

"¿Lo que es bueno? What's good, eh?"

El Feo stared out of the window with a blank expression on his face. Marco's last words bothered him, but he tried not to let it show.

"It's all good, primo. Take me to see the old man."

Domingo sniffed a line of blow and wrapped the remaining powder in aluminum foil. El Feo's silence bothered him. When El Feo says it's all good, it was usually all bad, and Domingo had more troublesome news to deliver.

"Another shipment got caught up at the border. That's two loads this month. What good is paying the government officials if they can't do their jobs?"

El Feo grew more irritated by the news.

"It's the Americans. They've threatened to withhold military and humanitarian aid if the flow of drugs across the border doesn't slow down."

"There's something else you need to know. El Padrino is pissed, homie. He doesn't like the way you're running things. What are you gonna do when Najee makes it to Nogales?"

As Gustavo drove into Mexico, El Feo twiddled his diamond pinky ring and gazed at the long, stretch of steel border wall courtesy of the Trump administration. The drug wars had made Mexico a dangerous place for Americans to travel, and El Feo was counting on that chaos and lawlessness to derail Najee's journey.

Retrieving his satellite phone from the center console, he raised the thick rubber antenna, dialed a corrupt Mexico official, and declared, "I'm not gonna do anything because Velásquez is gonna make sure he doesn't it to Nogales!"

Chapter 16

Slugs and Blood

"Damn, Cuzz!" Najee banged his fist against the steering wheel. "We're never gonna make it to Nogales! We should've did a straight shot through Arizona."

After leaving the Feds building, he cut off his ankle monitor, rented a whip from his Somali connect who owns a body shop, and spent some much-needed quality time with his son. Now he and The Deacon were stuck in traffic on the I-5 South near the San Ysidro border crossing.

The Deacon glanced at the digital clock on the radio. Cars at the U.S./Mexico border stretched back a quarter of a mile, and they were at the end of the line.

"Big up yourself, Soulja, we got this. We had to go this way to shake the Feds. Besides, I'm more worried about the swap out. You already know how dem crazy-ass Mexicans get down. They ain't gonna let us walk up out of there alive."

Najee unconsciously rubbed the Santeria beads he took off Benzo Al's dead body.

"That's kinda what I'm counting on," he professed.

The Deacon looked at Najee sideways.

"You got a funny way of viewing shit, bruh, run it down to me."

Najee inched into the shoulder lane and picked up speed. "It's simple, big homie. Mexicans are beautiful and proud people. They believe in honor, respect, and all that admirable shit," he explained. "I disrespected El Feo, so he has no choice but to defend his honor by killing me."

"Duh!" The Deacon joked. "Getting killed is what we're trying to avoid."

Najee chuckled and worked the low-key rental car through the congested, mid-afternoon traffic. He was glad they didn't bring the Chevy Silverado with the boat hitched. It was too big and conspicuous, they needed to move quick and stealthily.

"Hear me out, my nigga," Najee began to elaborate. "You and The Bishop taught me that revenge is best served cold. You can't go at it with a hot head, remember that? Well, El Feo is a hothead. That's how I'ma burn his bitch ass!"

"I hope you're right, first we gotta get past the border patrol. Tighten up, here they come," The Deacon cautioned.

Close to the border crossing, traffic had come to a dead halt. Three Customs and Border Protection Agents walked the lanes. They selected vehicles at random and questioned the passengers. On occasion, they opened the trunk or hood and performed a quick search.

A fourth border patrol agent walked a K-9 up the lane closest to the guard rail. The German Shepard stopped and sniffed a mid-sized Sedan. The dog wasn't looking for drugs, it was sniffing for money. Large quantities of narcotics are rarely smuggled into Mexico from its Northern perimeter. Illegal currency, however, is a different story.

Thanks to Americans and their insatiable appetite for illicit drugs, the cartels moved billions of dollars in profits back into Mexico each year. The K-9 and his handler were hoping to intercept some of these funds.

Najee watched everything go down. A border patrol agent approached the driver's side window. The Deacon removed a two-shot Derringer from his boot, pulled the hammer back, and placed the small gun under his leg. Najee hoped they didn't get pulled into the Secondary Station where passengers are thoroughly questioned, and their vehicles are meticulously searched. The Federales wouldn't appreciate him smuggling firearms and six-point-five million dollars into their country.

The border patrol agent leaned into the window and eyeballed Najee and The Deacon with scrutiny.

"May I see some identification, please?" the slightly overweight agent asked cordially. His beer belly hung over his belt, and chewing tobacco made his right cheek bulge.

Najee handed over his fake passport and equally bogus California driver's license.

114

"Here you go, sir. How's your day going?"

The border patrol agent ignored the question and asked one of his own.

"Where are the two of you headed?"

Najee had his lines rehearsed. He smiled and replied, "We're headed to Puerto Nuevo to do some fishing."

The agent raised a suspicious eyebrow.

"Where's your fishing gear?" he probed and rested a pudgy hand on his gun holster.

The Deacon slowly eased the ratchet from under his leg and cuffed it in the palm of his hand.

Najee gave him a *be cool* look and continued running game.

"We're not fishing for seafood; we're fishing for women!"

The agent gave Najee a hard look. The Deacon's index finger curled around the trigger. Holding the passport up to the sunlight, the agent inspected the hologram mark on the photo, looked at Najee, then looked back at the photo, and smiled his approval.

"Welcome to Mexico, mi amigos! Have a good time fishing!"

Najee drove forward, and he and The Deacon expelled a collective sigh of relief. They didn't notice that the K-9 handler had removed his sunglasses and was paying close attention to them. He scribbled their license plate number in his notepad, then made a call on his burner phone.

"Dile al Jefe que ya llego el puto que busqua," he told the goon on the other end to inform the boss of Najee's arrival.

On the other side of the border, the DEA and Mexican officials had pulled over two tractor-trailers that were attempting to enter the United States. Drug sniffing dogs had hit on the scent of narcotics. An agent operating a forklift pulled a pallet of teddy bears out of one of the trailers. A kilo of coke was hidden in the belly of each stuffed animal.

The tractor-trailer was a bait vehicle. Amid the commotion, two white chicks who worked as mules for the Tijuana Cartel drove straight through in a nondescript Honda Accord. The Fentanyl pills packed in the door panels had a street value twice as high as the pallet of bricks.

The border was busy. The Deacon watched an agent unload cartons of peanuts from a box truck. A different customs agent directed an Asian couple into Secondary.

"The border is on fire," The Deacon noticed. "Word on the streets is that the U.S. government is forcing Mexico to shut the game down. That Fentanyl is fucking shit up."

"I heard the same thing. That Fentanyl is a muthafucka. Niggas finna' starve in them streets," Najee stated.

He and The Deacon rode in silence until they were well within the Mexican border. Feeling relaxed and optimistic, Najee unfastened his seat belt and pushed the whip up the long stretch of highway.

"We should be in the clear, my nigga! Fire up some of that dondada so I can get right."

The Deacon seemed troubled, he took a quick glance over his shoulder and warned, "Not so fast, mon'. We're being followed! Check your six."

"On what?" Najee looked into the side rearview mirror and groaned. He was so preoccupied with the mission in front of him that he neglected looking behind him.

A black Jeep Wrangler trailed them at a distance. A white, older model Toyota truck wasn't too far behind the jeep.

"How long have they been on our heels?"

"For about a mile. It's a classic two-car team." The Deacon checked the mirror and added, "Looks like they have some tactical training. They'll probably move on us once we make it over this hill."

"Are they El Feo's people?"

"Ain't no telling. There are no secrets in Mexico. If one person knows we're here, a hundred people do," The Deacon preached while pulling a lockbox from under the front seat.

He removed two HK handguns and slapped double-drum clips into the bottom of each. The double drums held thirty-two rounds.

The Deacon jacked a copper demon into each chamber and handed one of the straps to Najee.

"Put yah seatbelt back on and speed up!" he instructed. "Slam on the breaks once we round this corner."

Najee placed the gun on his lap, fastened his seatbelt, and mashed the accelerator. His adrenal glands pumped epinephrine into his blood, preparing him for battle. As anticipated, the passengers in the jeep realized they had been made and picked up speed as well.

"Just tell me when."

"Wait on my signal!"

The jeep was right on their bumper. Najee glanced in the rearview and hit the gas. The jeep and the truck stayed on his tail. The curve came up quickly. They were going too fast to make it. Najee considered slowing down, but he pressed the gas pedal instead. The rental car lurched forward.

As he swooped around the curve, The Deacon shouted, "Now, hit the brakes!"

Najee braced himself for impact and smashed the brakes. The back tires locked up and screeched like a wounded feline. The car swerved leaving black skid marks.

The driver of the jeep was caught off guard. The jeep rammed into the rear end of the rental, and the airbags deployed. The driver and passenger were temporarily disoriented.

Working off reflexes, the driver of the truck slammed on his breaks and swerved to avoid slamming into the jeep. He miscalculated and crashed into the back of the jeep anyhow. The passengers were shaken up some more.

Najee and The Deacon jumped out of the whip, charged forward, and sprayed the jeep. The HK's spit like fully automatics. Bullets ripped through metal, and the windows shattered. The two disoriented goons never came out of their fog or got off a shot. Their bodies jerked from the impact of high-velocity slugs.

The goons in the Toyota truck exited the vehicle shouting in Spanish. They left the doors open for shelter and opened fire with beastie automatics. The Deacon and Najee retreated, taking position by the hood of the bullet-riddled Jeep Wrangler. Thunderous gunfire echoed off the side of the hill.

To deceive a professional, you have to perform like an amateur. The Deacon came up blasting, and the henchman on the passenger side of the truck took the bait. He stepped from the shelter of the metal door, held his assault rifle shoulder level, and squeezed off in the Deacon's direction. Najee caught him slippin' and drilled him three times in the chest and two times in the left thigh. His knees buckled like boiled Ramen noodles.

The driver got back into the truck and slammed it in reverse. The Deacon stood in the middle of the street with his feet shoulder-width apart. He aimed and squeezed off. Six slugs shattered the windshield, striking the driver in the face, neck, and collarbone. The truck careened out of control and slammed into the shoulder bank.

The Deacon ran up to the vehicle, stuck his heat through the window, and put one in the driver's left temple, blood trickled down his sideburns.

After confirming the kill, The Deacon chanted Genesis 14:20.

"And blessed be the most high God, which hath delivered thine, enemy, into thy hand."

Najee met the Deacon in the middle of the road. Najee was turnt up and gave the big homie some dap on the fist.

"That's what it do!" He celebrated.

The Deacon had a somber expression on his face.

"What's the business, cuz? Why you look so worried?"

"I got good news, and bad news," The Deacon reported.

Najee's mood soured.

"Give it to me raw."

"The good news is that these guys are Zetas."

"What's the bad news?"

"Those guys are Zetas too!" He pointed to something behind Najee.

Najee turned around; three armored SUVs barreled their way. A Los Zetas shooter wearing a black ski mask hung out of the moon roof. He brandished a large machine gun with belt-fed rounds. Each bullet was longer than a man's middle finger.

The Zetas are not a group of street thugs wielding guns and machetes. They are highly trained, extremely vicious ex-military commandos and the reason El Chapo is scared of the dark. In the late 1990s, they began working as the enforcement arm for the Gulf Cartel but broke away to form their own criminal organization.

Najee turned back to The Deacon and shook his head. He was mad at himself for getting mixed up with some crazy-ass Mexicans.

"El Feo set us up. They know about the money!"

Larry D. Wright

Chapter 17

A Favor for A Favor

The Zetas pulled up, got out, and got right down to business. The team leader tucked an old Colt .45 Revolver in his waistline and surveyed the damage. Although he was only 5'5, he moved with the swagger of a giant and strolled up to Najee and The Deacon unconcerned about the smoking guns in their hands.

"We know about the money! Where is it?" He was in his late fifties and spoke in a thick, Southern Mexico accent. His salt and pepper beard and well-pressed uniform made him resemble Fidel Castro.

The Deacon wasn't surprised by the silver badge or gold lieutenant bars on the shoulders of his police fatigues. He had worked as a military contractor in many corrupt nations and understood that in Mexico, the policia worked for the drug traffickers or they worked in constant fear.

Najee shifted uneasily and his fingers tightened around the pistol grip. The money was important. It was literally a matter of life and death. If he didn't deliver the loot, Angela and his unborn child were as good as dead. He wanted to lunge forward and rip the lieutenant's heart out of his chest. But then what? The Los Zetas shooter hanging out of the moon roof had a fifty-caliber leveled at his chest.

He and The Deacon were outgunned, but he couldn't see himself getting stuck up for this much paper without putting up some type of resistance. He read the nameplate pinned to the lieutenant's uniform and decided to be polite yet firm and direct. Diplomacy meant everything in Mexico.

"Señor Moreno, no disrespect, but when did Los Zetas start working for El Feo?"

The lieutenant's face twisted into a quizzical frown. He was genuinely confused.

"What ju' talking about? I no work for El Feo," he countered, keeping an eye on Najee and the other on the Jamaican.

Najee pushed the envelope, leveraging the lieutenant's pride and machismo against him.

"You don't have to front. How else could you know about the money, feel me? I'm just surprised that a man of your stature is afraid of El Feo. I'd rather pick fruit for the gringos than do his dirty work."

The lieutenant turned to his goons and laughed.

"Ju' hear this vato, homes?"

The other cartel members joined in on the laughter.

The Deacon and Najee exchanged looks. Diplomacy wasn't going well. Najee nudged his head toward the gunner hanging out of the moon roof. If the shit hit the fan, he wanted The Deacon to blaze him first. He would murk the team leader and anything else moving before they both were gunned down.

The lieutenant suddenly stopped laughing, drew his gun, and jammed it under Najee's chin in one swift motion. His speed and agility caught Najee off guard. The Deacon moved into a shooter's stance with both hands on the pistol grip. He was prepared to empty the double drum into the lieutenant's back. The Zetas aimed their guns at everybody. They were trained to mow down everything in sight and sort the bodies out later.

"Everybody take it easy!" Najee pleaded.

His heart thumped like a Zaytoven beat. This wasn't a hood novel or a Steven Seagal movie. He couldn't pull a karate move, take the gun out of the assailant's hands, and kill ten people with six bullets, he had to play it cool.

"Listen, puto," the lieutenant's voice deepened into a venomous growl. "My veins pump hot sauce not fear. Ju' want me to show you what I think about El Feo?"

The lieutenant snatched Najee up by the collar and pressed the barrel deeper into his throat. Najee smelled tamales and tequila on his breath. The lieutenant was about to finish his rant, but the Santería beads draped around Najee's neck caught his attention.

He studied the unique craftsmen's ship before ripping the necklace off Najee's neck.

"These belong to Alonzo Guzman. Where did ju' get them?" He held up the broken string of beads in his fist.

Najee remained silent, the truth could get him killed, or worse.

Pulling the hammer back with his thumb, the lieutenant issued a sharp threat.

"Don't make me repeat myself!"

Najee sighed and weighed the options in his head. Los Zetas and Los Cinco Diablos were locked in a lethal war over the drug routes through Tijuana and Mexicali. Benzo Al had ordered entire families killed, and the Zetas had retaliated with kidnappings and bloody massacres. One would think killing Benzo Al profited the Zetas, but then again, nothing in the underworld is what it seems. Backroom deals are sealed with handshakes and blood. Hell, Benzo Al and Señor Moreno could even be related, Najee considered.

He took a deep breath. Benzo Al deserved to die. The kingpin was the reason his mother, Boulevard, and Angel were brutally murdered.

Najee held his chin up and divulged the truth, proudly.

"I took them off Alonzo Guzman's dead body."

The Zetas began to chatter amongst themselves in Spanish. Najee caught snippets of their conversation.

The lieutenant lowered his gun and asked Najee for his name, "¿Cómo te llamas?"

"Soy, Najee," he replied quickly, and after noticing the lieutenant's skepticism, assured him that he really was Najee. "Ese es realmente mi nombre."

The lieutenant smiled, revealing a set of crooked brown teeth.

"Ju' got big balls, mi amigo. Ju' smoked Benzo Al!"

"That's what they say," Najee took credit without actually taking credit.

The lieutenant tucked the .45 back into his waist.

"Mexico is no different than America. Everything is about power and politics. El Feo didn't tell me about the money, Domingo did. Now I owe him a favor."

"Domingo is a snake!"

"We're all snakes, homes. Ain't no saints in this game. Domingo is making moves behind El Feo's back. I'm supposed to make ju' disappear to tie up the loose ends, but I owe ju' for killing Benzo Al. Now ju' owe me. That's how it works in Mexico. Un favor por un favor—a favor for a favor."

"¡Gracias!" Najee thanked him.

"Don't thank me, I'm still taking the money, and El Feo is still going to kill ju' and your chica."

Najee shook the lieutenant's hand.

"I'll keep that in mind when I have my gun in his mouth."

One of the Zetas shot the trunk lock, grabbed the large suitcase, and sat it on the hood of the car. He unzipped the luggage, flipped the flap open, and licked his lips at the sight of the shrink-wrapped stacks of money. Beaming with excitement, he held up a thick bundle of loot for the boss to see.

"¡Basta ya! That will do!" the lieutenant affirmed and climbed into the SUV. As the convoy peeled off, he stuck his head out of the passenger side window and shouted, "¡Vaya con dios! Go with God!"

Najee and The Deacon scrambled to the rental car. Najee cranked the engine and laughed.

"Let's get the fuck outta here before they find out we played them with dummy money!"

"Irie!" said The Deacon, which meant *good* in Jamaican slang. He gave Najee a fist pound and checked the passenger-side rearview mirror.

No one followed them. Optimism filled their lungs like a hit of kush from a glass bong. Najee pushed the whip over the hill but slowed down after spotting a roadblock at the bottom. Squinting his eyes in the sunlight, he counted four unmarked government vehicles. He blew past a squad car laying in the cut, and his hopes deflated. The squad car got behind them and hit the lights.

Whoop! Whoop!

"Shit!" They came to a stop in front of a barricade that was set up by the Mexican Agencia Federal de Investigación.

The AFI is Mexico's version of the FBI.

124

Najee didn't recognize the insignia on their uniform. "Damn, cuz, who the fuck are they?"

The Deacon began wiping fingerprints off the burners.

"I have some good news and some bad news!" he answered.

Najee groaned. Armed with AR-15s, the AFI officers snatched Najee and The Deacon out of the car, confiscated their weapons, and had them sit handcuffed on the side of the road.

They watched in silence as the AFI ripped the rental car apart and found bundles of money tucked in all four-door panels, the air conditioner vents, and the spare tire.

After loading the money, the lead AFI officer ordered one of his operatives to uncuff Najee and The Deacon.

"Dejalo los or. Let them go." He gave the two black men the once over and commented, "My name is Velásquez; I work for El Feo. He ordered me to kill both of you, but I owe Angela Rodriguez for saving my life. Tell her we're even and be careful on the rest of your journey. Nothing in Mexico is what it seems. Everyone owes everyone a favor. ¿Entienden?"

The government vehicles rolled out. Najee stood in the middle of the road watching the money and his hopes disappear.

"Fuck!" he yelled and faced The Deacon. "That was obviously the bad news. What's the good news?"

The Deacon put an arm around Najee's shoulders.

"We're still alive!"

Larry D. Wright

Chapter 18

Fist Full of Dollars

"They're still alive!" El Feo told Domingo as he inspected the five crates of Belgium assault rifles his organization had recently purchased from Sammy the crazy gringo biker.

The two men were meeting in a dark, dank warehouse on the outskirts of Nogales, Mexico. Domingo stopped pacing the floor.

"Are you serious, homes? How did he get past Velásquez?" He was really wondering how Najee got past the Zetas. Señor Moreno was supposed to call hours ago.

El Feo removed an FN MK-16 from its slot, screwed on a six-inch noise suppressor, and slapped in a curved fifty-round magazine. Ten inches of firepower protruded from the bottom of the Army-green killing machine.

"My sources tell me that not only did he get past Velásquez he also had a shootout with the Zetas and escaped from Señor Moreno as well. Now tell me how a nigger from the ghetto outsmarted the Zetas without inside help? Better yet, tell me how the Zetas knew about my money?" El Feo swung the barrel in Domingo's direction and lined his chest up through the scope. The double Gs on his Gucci shirt appeared larger than they actually were.

Domingo took a step back and bumped into the table, almost knocking the crates of rifles on the floor.

"Ay, stop playing, primo! You might fuck around and shoot me by accident!" he protested.

El Feo clicked the assault weapon from semi to fully automatic and toyed with the trigger.

Domingo couldn't tell whether he was serious or playing.

"¡Hablo en serio! I'm serious, dog! Stop pointing that pistola at me," he demanded more forcefully.

El Feo lowered the weapon and laughed.

"Stop being a wus, homie. Ain't nobody gon' shoot your scary ass, but check it out, eh."

He led Domingo outside to his Mercedes Benz sprinter van. Gustavo sat behind the wheel with a chrome and black .40 on his lap. He didn't talk much, his look said it all.

Holding the rocket in his left hand, El Feo opened the sliding door with the right. A woman with a black blindfold over her head and two Mexican police officers laid gagged and bound across the back seat. They groaned in agony and showed signs of torture. Both gripped a fist full of bloody dollars, and their eyeballs had been gouged out with a crude and sharp object.

Domingo moved closer to get a better look.

"Oh, shit!"

The two men were Velásquez and Señor Moreno. Instead of tears, blood trickled out of their eye sockets and slowly cascaded down their cheeks. Domingo folded over, grabbed his stomach, and spewed yellow vomit.

"Watch it, homes!" El Feo warned. "These are the new Yeezys."

"What happened to their eyes?" Domingo asked and wiped the corners of his mouth with his shirt sleeve.

El Feo pointed to the DeWalt power drill on the floor mat, blood stained the four-inch drill bit.

"I couldn't let them see where the warehouse is located," he noted with no remorse. "So, I had to get creative."

"I'm saying though, why didn't you just use blindfolds?"

"We ran out, so did Amazon Prime, and I didn't have time to go to Walmart and ask the workers what aisle the cartel blindfolds are on," El Feo answered sarcastically. "Don't go soft on me, homes. This is the world we live in. I had to send a message not to fuck with my money."

"Once again, you mean our money," Domingo corrected.

"You know what I meant. Stop trippin' and line them up against the wall. I would burn them alive, but I want to check out these new pistolas," he ordered.

Domingo cringed and tried to control his weak stomach as he pulled Señor Moreno out of the van. He put his lips next to Señor Moreno's ear and whispered, "Does El Feo know about our deal?"

"No," he stuttered and coughed up blood.

Domingo didn't believe him.

"Tell me the truth, mi amigo. I can save you," he lied and stood Señor Moreno against the warehouse wall.

"Don't let him kill me," he begged desperately. "I swear by my mother, I didn't say anything."

"Good." Domingo sneered, then his eyes darkened.

He twisted Señor Moreno's head and body in opposite directions and snapped his neck. Señor Moreno pissed on himself, and his limp body slumped to the ground.

El Feo heard the body collapse and spun around.

"What the fuck happened to him?"

Domingo shrugged.

"I think he passed out from the pain."

"Fuck it, bring Velásquez and the girl."

Domingo stood Velásquez up against the wall and went back to grab the girl. He shoved her against the wall and removed her blindfold.

"I don't know which one I should put in your mouth first, my gun or my dick?" Domingo taunted.

Angela stared him down, and with no fear in her eyes or trepidation in her heart, she hocked spit in his face.

"Puto!" she yelled. The anger emitted from the pit of her gut. She was not broken.

"Crazy bitch!" Domingo responded with a vicious backhand and put the blindfolded back over her head. "Die in the dark, puta."

El Feo aimed at the targets. Angela held her breath. She tried to be strong, but a single tear slithered down her cheek and rested in the corner of her lips. El Feo braced the FN MK-16 against the crook of his right elbow and placed his left hand on top of the barrel to prevent muzzle-rise. Wrapping his index finger around the trigger, he squeezed off. Polymer-tipped ammo spit from the fully like burnt bread popping out of a toaster. To ensure maximum organ damage, the ammunition was designed to expand after ripping through clothing and penetrating flesh.

Angela screamed! It was the melody El Feo was waiting to hear. He walked to her and snatched off the blindfold. Victory glowed in his pompous eyes. He gently brushed the hair out of Angela's face and wiped her tears with his thumb.

"I knew I could break you," he boasted.

Angela realized she was holding her breath and expelled a deep sigh. She looked down at the bloody and mangled corpse of Velásquez and cringed at the sight. She had no way of knowing she was the cause of his death. She was just glad her body wasn't next to his.

The Nogales Cartel kept her alive for a reason, and she thought she knew why. Najee was coming with the money, and if she was dead, so was the deal. Her heart swelled with hope and also regret. She regretted trying to kill Najee. Even deeper, she regretted cutting off his son's thumb. It wasn't her idea, she was following orders from Benzo Al. How could she explain that to Najee, a proud and stubborn man who is obsessed with revenge? She understood that one day he would make her repent for her transgressions.

El Feo's voice snatched her out of her thoughts. She eavesdropped on his conversation with Domingo.

"I like those guns. Call the crazy white boy and set up a meeting. Tell him we need fifty more."

"I'm on it."

El Feo's sat phone rang. He rarely received incoming calls on his burner line. He and Domingo exchanged looks before he picked up. The individual on the other end commanded respect and did most of the talking. El Feo listened and answered with an occasional yes sir. He hung up in a foul mood.

"Was that El Padrino?" Domingo guessed correctly.

El Feo nodded.

"Yeah, my grandfather is waiting for us at the hacienda. Najee made it to Nogales. I don't know how he did it, but he better have my money."

Chapter 19

Federal Bureau of Prisons

Drako and Bull from East Side Bounty Hunter Bloods mobbed on Sosa while he stood in the chow line.

"Bitch better have my money!" Drako threatened with his face screwed up.

His thick arms and thick neck added to his menacing presence. He was fighting a RICO charge and two homicides but didn't give a fuck about catching another body.

"You gotta pay to stay, Blood!"

"Either that or link up and get on count with the Damu's," an equally big and menacing Watts' native chimed in and purposely bumped Sosa's shoulder.

Sosa ignored the taunts and kept it movin'. The other inmates had been trying to test his gangsta since he arrived six days ago. West Coast federal detention facilities house some of the nation's most ingenious and infamous criminals. After Benzo Al's murder and the bloody shootout between Block Boy Empire and the Feds, Sosa was detained and held in custody at the notorious Metro Detention Center. It had been the worst week of his life, and the media coverage labeling him a wealthy drug kingpin only exasperated the matter.

Sosa grabbed a tray of slop from the window and sat at an empty metal table near the back of the chow hall. As soon as he sat down, the four thugs sitting at the next table moved on him. They surrounded the table and towered over Sosa.

"Ay, nigga, that's my seat!" Stretch from One-Hundred and Eighteenth Street Eucalyptus Gangster Crips instigated. He was tall, tatted-up, and totally treacherous.

Sosa gritted his teeth and tried his best to keep his cool. He had a bond hearing tomorrow and didn't want to do anything that would jeopardize his chances of getting a reasonable bail, so he grabbed his tray and scooted over to the next empty seat.

"That's my spot, too!"

Sosa looked at the empty seats on his left and on his right. "I don't see no names on these seats," he scoffed in his syrupy, dirty South accent.

"What, nigga?" Stretch swiped Sosa's tray off the table. Mashed potatoes and gravy splashed on the floor. Stretch formed a C with his fingers and pounded his chest. "Unless you Crip Nation, I suggest you move the fuck around, cuz!"

Sosa jumped to his feet with his fists balled tight.

"Shit ain't sweet, I ain't no hoe ass nigga!"

Swack!

Stretch took off and slapped the plaque of Sosa's tongue. Sosa stumbled back, caught his balance, and charged forward hitting Stretch with a left and a right uppercut to the chin. Stretch walked through the blows. Street fights, prison riots, and jailhouse workouts had made him a strong and fearless gladiator.

"What that Eleven-Eight EU-Mob like, cuz?" Stretch roared as he countered with a powerful roundhouse to the temple, rocking Sosa and driving him backward.

Stretch advanced and swung. Sosa bobbed and weaved. The crowd cheered for mayhem. The CO hit the panic button. Connecting with a left hook, Stretch followed with a right cross, missed, slipped in the mashed potatoes, and got caught with a knee to the face, blood and snot gushed from his nose.

Rising to his feet, Stretch shook off the pain and squared up. Sosa threw his fist up and danced on the balls of his heels prepared to attack, but he was struck from behind. He fell into Stretch who used the opportunity to knee Sosa in the gut, causing him to fold over.

Reaching into his waistband, Stretch removed a shank. The sharp and lethal icepick had tape and toilet paper wrapped around the handle. Sosa saw a flash of metal, then felt a piercing pain in his abdomen. Stretch moved on him, jabbing him in the stomach quickly and repeatedly.

The CERT team rushed through the door swinging batons, spraying tear gas, and issuing orders.

"Get down! Get down, now!" the commanding officer shouted.

Stretch passed the homemade blade to one of his homies and melted into the sea of inmates. Sosa applied pressure to the puncture wounds, took two steps, and collapsed.

***

Sosa had a hard knock life. His mother was murdered by her pimp, a slick and shiesty hustler named Prince, leaving Sosa all alone in a cold and callous world. The system passed him between different group homes and juvenile detention centers like a two-dollar hoe until Sosa found refuge in the slums. Foster homes raised him, but the streets made him. Having his back against the proverbial wall, he formed Block Boy Empire, and with the help of Benzo Al, he dominated the cocaine trade in Atlanta. His relentless hustle spread like cancer into neighboring counties, border states, and ultimately the entire South.

Members of his Block Boy Empire expanded their own territory, and soon BBE had a presence in every state. They became the inspiration. The trappers hustled to be like them, and the rappers pretended to be them by renting their lavish homes, exotic cars, and shiny jewelry for their music videos.

Sosa was that nigga! He had the sauce, the juice, the key to the streets, and when the Feds turned up the heat, he wisely traded the corner for a corner office. He left the game papered-up with no smut on his name and no debt owed to his plug, but retirement wasn't all gravy.

He tried to do the entrepreneur thing, but his protégé, a disloyal, opportunist named Ice sabotaged his hustle. The cartel wars caused a severe cocaine drought, crippling Ice's finances, so in an attempt to bankrupt Sosa and lure him back into the streets, Ice burned down each of Sosa's soul food restaurants. The plot failed, but the game is a bitch. She doesn't want divorce and alimony; she wants blood and bones. Like a perpetual vacuum, she sucked Sosa back into her embrace.

Sosa contemplated that conundrum as he regained consciousness. He laid in the infirmary with translucent tubes lodged in his nostrils and an IV in his forearm. A clear pouch attached to a metal pole trickled saline into his veins, and handcuffs married his wrists to the bedrail. He opened the hospital gown and examined the large white gauze pad taped to his right side. The five, small puncture wounds just missed his kidneys.

"Dizzam!" he cussed to himself. "I'm in this fucked up predicament because of Najee. If he would've shielded Nella and their son from his drama in the streets, I wouldn't have had to risk my life and freedom to help fight his war. That nigga better come through with the bail money."

Deeply emerged in his thoughts, Sosa didn't notice the two white men standing at the foot of his hospital bed until one of them cleared their throat. They didn't look like cops, but they carried themselves with the arrogant air of law enforcement personnel.

"Uh-hem, good mornin', Mr. Fischer. Or should I call you Sosa?" The tall greasy one who looked more like he belonged in a Heavy Metal band than law enforcement flashed his ATF badge.

His partner swept his leather jacket aside revealing a gold shield clipped to his belt.

"Yeah, I think I'm gonna call you Sosa. I spent all last night reading your file, so it seems like we know each other already." He stuffed his badge in his back pocket and introduced himself. "I'm Special Agent Samuel Parker. That's my partner, Torres."

Sosa's throat went dry, and his underarms began to perspire. He had been sweated by the FBI and the DEA, but this was his first time dealing with the ATF. An old school player once told him that the best way to deal with the pigs is not to deal with them at all. Sosa took that advice to heart and dismissed the two agents.

"My favorite TV show is about to come on. So, whatever y'all got to say, say it, and keep it movin," he stated defiantly.

Parker pulled up a chair and sat in it with his legs crossed. "I don't mince words, so I'll get right to the point. You slipped in monkey shit, my friend. We got cha' dead bang this time. If you're lucky, the judge will show some leniency and give you fifty years. What's eighty-five percent of fifty, Torres?"

Torres unraveled a stick of gum and shrugged his shoulders.

"Shit beats me. Probably somewhere 'round forty-two years. That's a long time with no weed, pussy, fried chicken, or watermelon," he joked.

Sosa gave Torres the middle finger with his free hand. "Fuck you, white trash."

Parker stepped in to cool the tension.

"Listen, buddy, I know—"

"I'm not cha' buddy, and you don't know shit," Sosa admonished.

Parker kept his poise and remained in character as the good cop. He knew from experience you couldn't come at drug dealers head-on. You had to reel them in with reverse psychology.

He sat on the edge of bed and spoke calmly for added effects, "I was about to say that I know you're not scared of us. A guy like you don't give a shit about a fifty-year sentence. You don't care if you're gonna be in your seventies when you get out, right? Who cares if you're wearing a diaper or pushing a walker or didn't get a chance to have any kids because you spent all your best years behind bars? As long as you kept it real, right? Keep it one-hunnit'. Ain't that what you young black guys say?"

Parker let the magnitude of his words marinate. He could see the worry on Sosa's face and gears spinning in his head. Parker cleared his throat and put the clamps on tighter.

"There were dead bodies all over that Los Cinco Diablos chop shop. You shot at law enforcement officers with an AK. Plus, you have a separate conspiracy to manufacture and distribute cocaine indictment hanging over your head."

"You're fucked, dude." Torres blew a big bubble with his gum and let it pop. His antics earned him a *fuck you* look from Sosa.

Parker kept the pressure on, even using Sosa's real name. Being on a first-name basis with a suspect is an old and effective interrogation technique.

"Listen, Marcus, my partner is right, you're screwed, but it doesn't have to be that way. Cooperate with the government, and we can get you a downward departure. You'll be out in a dime. All you gotta do is tell us what you know about Najee and Los Cinco Diablos."

The word cooperate burned Sosa's eardrums. He was a Silverback, not a rat.

"You got jokes, bruh. I ain't nobody's bitch or snitch. So, fuck you, fuck the D.A. and muthafuck the judge, too! It's gonna take a lot more than a few threats to flip a nigga like me," he declared like a true G.

The ATF agents shifted uneasily. If Sosa wanted to play hardball, they would accommodate him. Parker stood up to leave.

"Suit yourself, asshole. We'll see how much of a stand-up guy you are when you're serving a life sentence in Florence, Colorado while Najee is out there living it up. I thought you were smarter than him, but I guess not. He threw Nella and your black ass under the bus without even batting an eyelash."

"Ne–nell–Nella is in custody?" he stammered. His voice dripped with concern.

Parker picked up on the vibes. He felt the same energy when he was interrogating Nella. Sosa's nonverbal clues spoke louder than his words. He loved Nella, she was his Achilles, and Parker planned to exploit his weakness. It was wrong, but in order to be a good lawman, you had to be a great con man.

"Yeah, Nella is in custody. We grabbed her and Najee last night. We got all the evidence we need for the Giuseppe murders. Najee sold her out, and ratted on you for killing Benzo Al."

"That's some straight-up bullshit, on my momma I didn't kill Benzo Al!" Sosa objected and tried to sit up, but the piercing pain in his stomach stopped him.

"That's not what we heard," Parker rebutted. "Listen to this." He nodded to Torres.

Torres reached into his leather jacket for his cell phone, scrolled through his audio files, selected an MP3, and pressed play.

Najee's voice came through the speaker crisp and clear. The doctored version made Najee sound like a snitch:

"If I get you, Nella and Marcus Fischer, I want full immunity for myself."

"Do you mean Marcus Sosa Fischer, the leader of Block Boy Empire? How are the two of you connected?"

"He was out of the game, but I dragged him back in for one last mission."

"This Sosa twist is out of my jurisdiction. I'm gonna have to run it by my superiors."

"Miss me with all that. Do we have a deal or not?"

Torres pressed the stop button, but oddly, he didn't put his phone away.

"Now do you believe us?" he asked, then swiveled toward his partner. "Let's get the hell out of here. If he wants to play the tough thug role and take the fall for Najee, I could give two shits. A conviction is a conviction in my book."

Parker was satisfied with how the meeting was going. He knew from experience that most hardened criminals crack but won't break on the first interrogation session. They still adhered to the code of the streets. However, once the reality of doing football numbers kicked in, loyalty became another seven-letter word. He had witnessed some of the most stomp-down players in the game snitch on their own mama in order to stay on the streets.

Parker flicked a business card on the bed and prepared to leave.

"There are only two types of inmates. Those who snitched and those who wished they did. If you get Najee out the way, you could have Nella all to yourself. Call me when your self-preservation instincts kick in."

Sosa thought back to how wet Nella's pussy got when she held his thick, dick in her small hand. She wanted to buss down and give him some, but her love for Najee stood in the way.

Conflicted with his feelings, Sosa stopped the agents at the door.

"Yo, hold up a second." He felt sick to his stomach for what he was about to do. "What type of deal are y'all talkin' about? I'll do anything to save Nella."

Parker winked at Torres and whispered, "This is going to be easier than I thought."

Torres pulled up a chair, sat next to the hospital bed, and rubbed his hands together.

"Now we're getting somewhere."

Chapter 20

Winner Takes All

"Now we're gettin' somewhere, my nigga!" Najee ended the phone call with Enrique *El Padrino* Estrada and climbed into the passenger side of the beat-up Ford F-150 that he and The Deacon purchased from a Mexican avocado farmer.

The old jalopy had one hundred and seventy-nine miles on the odometer, but was still capable of traversing the country's muddy back roads and rough terrain. Despite the day's events, Najee's 1000-kilowatt smile beamed brightly.

"It's time to turn the fuck up and get Huey P. Newton in this bitch!" The plan to save Nella and Angela was coming together.

The Deacon was amused by Najee's raw energy and enthusiasm. He was once the same way until he learned that soldiers don't run into battle, they march. He cranked the engine, and the tailpipe coughed black exhaust smoke.

"Wah gwaan?" he asked what's going on in his thick Jamaican twang. "Did you make contact with El Feo's grandfather?"

"Fa sho, I'm surprised a cat on his level took my call. Detective Brooks is very resourceful."

"Indeed!" The Deacon agreed.

"I don't trust Parker, so I got Detective Brooks working on getting Nella and Sosa out. I couldn't warn them about my plan, but I'm hoping they stay focused and don't panic."

The Deacon blazed a finger-sized joint and handed it to Najee.

"Here you go, hit this. It's that bag."

Najee accepted the fat joint, took two pulls, and almost coughed up a lung. The bomb weed made his eyes water and his chest contract. "You wasn't jaw jackin'. This that gas fa' real," he approved, took another toke, and passed the bud.

"It's from the islands. The soil is enriched by the blood of the sugarcane slaves."

The Deacon took a hit, let the smoke escape through his nose, and thumped the ashes out of the window. They passed the herb back and forth in silence before The Deacon began kicking science.

"Dig this Soulja Boi, they don't call Enrique Estrada, The Godfather because of his age. They call him that because he's been in the game for a very long time. A lion doesn't survive in the jungle for that long without being cunning and absolutely ruthless. Do yah feel me, mon?"

Najee blew a halo of smoke while gazing at the beautiful countryside. He wondered how such tranquil scenery existed in such a chaotic world.

"Yeah, I feel you, big homie. How should I play it?"

"That's what I'm getting at. This is a cartel boss, not a hood captain. You can't play him. He's from the old world where they combine idealism with extremism. Either he likes you, or he don't. Either he lets us live, or he kills us in the worst way possible."

Najee let the jewels he was handed soak in and formulated his next three chess moves. In his opinion, everyone could be played. You just needed to find out how to turn their strengths into weaknesses.

They took the back roads and hugged the border until they arrived in Nogales, Mexico, right on the outskirts of Arizona. The narrow roads were bustling with cars, pedestrians, and street vendors selling everything from beaded jewelry to blowjobs. Najee and the Deacon bought tacos and two Glock handguns from the same vendor. The hustler across the street sold them a fake Gucci suitcase and a zip of dro.

As instructed, they checked into the Catalina Hotel. A Nogales Cartel operative watched them closely as they entered the small lobby. He didn't bother concealing his actions or the heat in his shoulder holster. His companion lounged in a rocking chair cradling a sawed-off shotgun. Between the mosquitoes, the humidity, and the fear that the hotel door could get kicked in at any moment, Najee and The Deacon didn't sleep well.

Surprisingly, Najee woke up the next morning feeling fresh and rejuvenated. He was working off pure adrenaline. He pushed the old

F-150 South on Highway 15 headed to Cibuta while the Deacon twisted up a blunt. Before they reached Imuris, a Ducati motorcycle swooped up to the driver's side of the truck and ordered them to follow him. The motorcycle turned onto a rough and narrow patch of road, and Najee cautiously followed. A black GMC Yukon waited with the engine idle.

The armored Yukon was covered in dust and the windows were tinted. A beefy Mexican with a serious scowl sat behind the wheel. Najee could make out a shadow in the second row of leather seats. It was a hot day, and the neck and underarms of his Givenchy shirt were soaked with sweat.

The four men exited the vehicles simultaneously. No smiles or handshakes, it was all business. The driver pointed a finger at The Deacon.

"Wait right there!" he commanded, then pointed at Najee. "Put your hands on the hood, ese!"

Najee complied and put his hands on the hood of the Yukon. The hulking driver placed his left hand flat on Najee's back and kicked his legs apart in one fluid motion.

Ex-law enforcement, Najee thought.

The pat-down was quick and efficient. He dropped Najee's cell phone on the ground and stomped on the face, breaking the glass. Next, he confiscated the Glock 19.

Najee protested, "Nah, fuck that, you can keep the bullets, but you ain't taking my strap."

The driver looked to Domingo for confirmation, and Domingo nodded his approval. He took the clip out of the Glock 19, pulled the shaft back to eject the bullet lodged in the chamber, and gave the empty gun back to Najee.

"Happy now?" he mocked.

The Deacon received the same treatment.

The driver inspected the fake Gucci luggage for surveillance and tracking devices. Finding neither, he reported to the cartel goon in the sweaty Givenchy shirt.

"They're clean, ese."

"Gracias, Gustavo," he replied politely and turned his attention to Najee and The Deacon. "My name is Domingo. I will escort you to see Señor Estrada. ¡Vamonos!" He directed them to the Yukon.

Enrique Estrada's hilltop villa was a three-story vine-covered fortress equipped with two Olympic-sized swimming pools, marble pillars, lavish fountains, exquisite statues, and all the toys and gadgets a successful kingpin deserves. Colorful birds, tropical flowers, and tall palm trees swayed in the breeze. The throaty roar of an exotic pet tiger echoed in the distance.

Soldiers with a yellow "*N*" stitched into the sleeves of their black fatigues guarded the compound while holding large machine guns. Najee nudged the Deacon with his elbow and spoke in a hushed tone.

"Damn, my nigga, what kind of choppers are those?"

The Deacon swiped his dreads out of his eyes.

"Those bitches do the nasty! I've only seen them used by the U.N. and paramilitary forces in the Middle East."

"What the fuck have I gotten us into, bruh? This shit is way over my head. Did you hear that roar? We got Pitbulls in the hood, but these muthafuckas got pet tigers and shit. We dead, bruh. We dead!"

"Chill, you got this," The Deacon encouraged. "What's the most powerful type of knowledge?"

"Street knowledge," Najee answered without hesitation.

"That's one-hundred. El Feo knows what it's like to have everything. You know what it's like to have nothing at all. Never forget where you came from or what you're fighting for," The Deacon preached.

Domingo led them to the courtyard. A group of men stood around betting on a cockfight. The roosters had miniature knives strapped to their claws. Only one of them would walk away alive. Cockfights are a parable for humans engaged in business or war. There is no second-place prize, the winner takes all.

El Padrino stood out amongst the crowd. He had the aura of a boss. Curly black hair peeked from under his cowboy hat, and a colorful poncho covered his shoulders. He had the sun-beaten skin of a ranchero and the short but strong body of the mountain-dwelling Sinaloans.

Upon seeing Domingo usher Najee and The Deacon into the courtyard, El Feo frowned and said something in El Padrino's ear. El Padrino ignored Najee and The Deacon then nodded to Domingo. The left side of his face was badly burned. His glass eye never blinked. It was always watching like the eye on the back of a dollar bill.

He approached Najee with an outstretched hand and spoke to him in Spanish. Najee pretended he didn't understand, so El Padrino switched to English.

"So, you're the one who killed Benzo Al? Thank you!" His handshake was firm, his voice even and confident. He was a man used to giving orders.

El Feo was not impressed by Najee. He rolled his eyes and remarked, "I thought you'd be taller."

"And you're exactly what I expected," Najee blasted back.

El Feo didn't know whether to take it as a compliment or an insult.

Sensing the growing tension, El Padrino took charge. "Have a seat, you're my guests." His request seemed more like a command than an invitation.

He snapped his fingers, and the maid filled the five glasses on the table with tomato juice. Another servant brought out freshly sliced papaya, mango, and warm conchas, a sweet Mexican pastry.

The Deacon seemed at ease. As a hired gun for both drug lords and warlords, he had dealt with men of equal or more power, but this was a first for Najee. This was the big leagues. Although Benzo Al was a major boss with colossal influence, El Padrino had survived the game longer and seemed to be in a category of his own. He had a buzz about himself. It was as if you were standing next to an electric fence. He wasn't big and imposing, but when you looked into his glass eye, you could see the devil tap-dancing on a bed of fire.

El Padrino crossed his legs, took a sip of tomato juice, and got right to business.

"Let's be clear, nino. You disrespected my familia. Whether you live or die depends on how you conduct yourself at this table, understood? Now, where's our paper?"

Najee stood up, sat the fake Gucci luggage on the table, and popped the gold locks. El Padrino's bodyguards immediately drew down. The dark barrels of their weapons dared Najee to make another move.

El Padrino calmly raised his hand.

"Tranquilo."

Najee moved slower this time, he flipped the flap open and turned the suitcase toward El Padrino and El Feo who was sitting across from him.

"Here's your paper."

The suitcase was filled with newspapers. The front-page headline read, *Bloody Massacre Near Border*. A photo of the bullet-riddled Jeep Wrangler and the dead Zeta operatives accompanied the caption.

El Padrino picked up one of the newspapers, studied the article, then looked into Najee's eyes. He possessed the type of glare that made you want to avoid eye contact.

"Is this some kind of game? Don't fuck with my intelligence, nino!"

"Señor Estrada," Najee began respectfully. "When I hit your stash house, I had no intention of keeping the money. El Feo took something of mine, so to get his attention, I took something of his," Najee explained. "I was prepared to give back every cent with interest, but me and my associate were robbed by the Zetas. Domingo set us up." He intentionally left out being hijacked by Velásquez. It's not wise to accuse the prince of theft in his own palace.

Domingo jumped to his feet and pulled his iron.

"This vato is a liar, eh. Let me smoke this puto!"

El Feo's lips tightened, and his eyes became angry narrow slits. He had a hunch that Domingo was on some shiesty shit, and the way he was waving his pistol and making threats confirmed El Feo's suspicions.

El Padrino ordered Domingo to sit down.

144

"¡Sientate, pendejo!"

Domingo's trigger finger itched. He didn't know how much Señor Moreno had told Najee or how much Najee was prepared to tell the old man. He contemplated disobeying the order and putting a hot one right between Najee's eyebrows, but The Deacon's deep and malefic voice made him hesitate.

"Yah heard the man. Sit the fuck down!" The Deacon's dreadlocks hung in his face adding to his menacing demeanor, and his no-nonsense tone that told everyone at the table he was about business.

The Deacon didn't speak much, but when he did, people listened. Domingo glared at the tall, dark Rastafarian, but complied and tucked his heat.

El Padrino waited until Domingo took a seat before speaking, "Why should I believe you?" he asked with the calmness of an ax murderer.

"I'm not asking you to believe me. It's the truth. I called El Feo, he didn't call me. Do you think I'm stupid enough to come all this way empty-handed? I had the cheese and could've easily went North instead of coming South," Najee answered persuasively.

That made a lot of sense, but El Padrino wasn't fully convinced. He leaned forward and continued his cross-examination.

"If you knew there was a possibility that I would kill you with or without bringing back my organization's money. Why did you come to Mexico anyway?"

"To save Angela Rodriguez. She's pregnant with my baby," he told half the truth, relying on law number three of the 48 Laws of Power, which suggests concealing your intentions.

"That was foolish of you, nino. As you've seen, Mexico is a very dangerous place, and what if the baby is not even yours?"

"What if it is mine? Isn't that possibility worth the risk?" he pleaded passionately. "You're a man of principles and integrity. What would you have done?" Najee penetrated the old man's head and heart.

El Feo had heard enough. Reaching into his shoulder holsters, he upped two nickel-plated Taurus Millenniums, one pointed at Najee, the other at The Deacon.

"Game over, bitches!"

El Padrino's nostrils flared.

"Sientate, I'm talking to our guests," he chastised.

El Feo glared at his grandfather with scorn and contempt. "I'm tired of you telling me what to do, old man. My uncle left me the keys."

"No, your uncle left you big shoes to fill, and I'll be damned if I let you ruin his legacy."

"Don't mention the word legacy to me. You always talk about how it went down in the old days. Well, in the old days you would've personally chopped this monkey up and scattered his remains all over the ghetto. Am I right or wrong?"

El Padrino took a deliberate long pause before answering, "You're wrong, chico. What he did is valiente—brave. He's willing to die for what he believes in. In our culture that's the highest honor. Am I right or wrong?"

El Feo had to agree that El Padrino was right. It was a silent code they lived by, but he wouldn't admit it out loud. Instead, he spat on the ground to express his disgust.

"You're gonna regret letting him live," he warned and pointed both heats at Najee. "My grandfather saved you but not the chica. You better come up with seven-point-five million or that bitch is dead."

"Aw, hell nawl. The deal was six-point-five mill," Najee objected.

El Feo holstered his weapons and turned to leave.

"The price just went up!"

Chapter 21

City of the Dead

A convoy of three armored vehicles sped away from El Padrino's hilltop villa. For protection, the chief of security positioned El Padrino's Chevy Suburban in the middle. Najee and El Padrino lounged in the back of the bulletproof luxury SUV choppin' it up like two bosses. The Deacon rode upfront with El Padrino's personal bodyguard. The drivers drove with urgency, weaving in and out of traffic, smashing through stop signs, and blatantly disregarding the speed limit.

"When ICE took Joaquín Guzmán into custody, the price of heroin went up," El Padrino recalled El Chapo's capture.

After a brazen prison escape and wild shootout, a joint task force led by the U.S. Customs and Immigration Enforcement agency apprehended the legendary Sinaloa Cartel boss, leaving rival crews scrambling for control of the heroin market.

"We saw an opportunity to transition out of the dying marijuana trade, and we took it," El Padrino continued. "The only problem is that other narco organizations seized the opportunity as well. Now everyone is fighting over the same piece of the pie. It's a fuckin' mess."

Najee could picture the dilemma.

"There's a high demand for product, but there's also too much competition."

"Correct," El Padrino agreed. "One way to get rid of the competition is through war."

"But war is bad for business."

"You're right again, nino. War is bad for business and for the citizens who live on the battlefields. Let me show you something." El Padrino contacted the lead vehicle and instructed the driver to take them to Ciudad Juárez, a city in northern Mexico on the Rio Grande River.

After filling the gas tanks with Pemex Supreme, the entourage of speeding vehicles made the three-hundred-mile trip to Juárez in less than four hours. The golden sunset and the serene mountains overlooking the city made it appear peaceful. However, Juárez is the murder capital of the world. The Zetas, the Sinaloas, the Gulf Cartel, and Los Cinco Diablos made sure of that. Because of its lucrative smuggling routes and proximity to El Paso, Texas, the Nogales Cartel and renegade crews were trying to muscle in on the territory.

Beheadings, shootouts, and machete attacks are common occurrences. Virtually none of the brutal homicides get solved. Shallow graves populate the neighboring desert, and on hot summer days, the stench of rotten flesh overpowers the aroma of the local tortilla factory.

"City of the Dead," El Padrino announced the ghost town as if they had arrived at a vacation resort. "This used to be the city of hope and prosperity. Now, look at it."

Najee took in the boarded-up storefronts and small homes belonging to the poor residents who could not afford to flee. The effects of violence and chaos looked similar to the poverty and despair experienced in Gary, Indiana, and Milwaukee, Wisconsin.

El Padrino ordered the driver to stop. He got out of the Suburban with no bodyguard or bulletproof vest. A group of kids who were playing soccer suspended their game and rushed up to him. El Padrino handed out money and Bibles, further solidifying his reputation as a saint and sinner.

To his enemies and the Feds, he was a criminal and a monster, but to his people, he was a provider and a protector. He turned water into bread, and for that, they were indebted to him. The little kids would one day become his drug mules or loyal soldiers. El Padrino also understood that some may even become his rivals. That was the way of life in the City of the Dead.

Fresh out of American cash, Enrique gave his gold Rolex to a ten-year-old girl and handed his gold-plated Desert Eagle to a fifteen-year-old boy. Hopping back into the SUV, he directed the driver to take him to his mansion on the outskirts of the city. Surrounded by a twelve-foot, black iron gate, the compound was just as impressive as the hilltop villa.

"I like how you roll, especially the way you look out for your people," Najee praised as he and El Padrino strolled through the mansion's garden.

El Padrino accepted the compliment and tossed bread to the pigeons. The birds flocked around him like the kids did in the streets of Juárez.

"Pigeons and people are predictable. Feed them properly, and they'll always come back to you."

"I feel you on that," Najee concurred. He couldn't help taking quick and awkward glances at El Padrino's burnt skin.

El Padrino caught him looking and said, "My face! You want to know what happened to my face."

"I mean, I'm not trying to dip all in your business, but I am kinda curious."

El Padrino's lips parted, his smile was as charming as a hyena's grin.

"I'll make a deal with you, nino. I'll tell you what happened to my face if you tell me what you dreamed about last night."

"Why?" Najee asked with his head cocked to the side. It was the most intriguing question he had ever been asked.

"You can tell a lot about a man by his dreams."

Najee thought carefully before answering, "I dreamed that I killed El Feo."

El Padrino stopped walking, stared at Najee hard, and asked, "How did you do it?"

Najee pulled the empty Glock 19 from the small of his back, and El Padrino's bodyguards immediately reacted. They drew their own weapons and put Najee's dome in their sights.

El Padrino signaled for them to lower their guns.

"Baja las armas, ahora."

The bodyguards slowly and reluctantly lowered their straps but stayed on point. Najee then did something that surprised everyone. He hacked, gagged, and regurgitated the bullet he had swallowed when he was told to put his hands on the hood of the Yukon. Cocking the slide back, he inserted the slug into the chamber and aimed the banger at El Padrino's left pectoral.

El Padrino's bodyguards raised their guns. El Padrino looked down at the loaded Glock pointed at his heart. Again, his lips parted into a smile.

"¡Bravo, well done! You're young, but you've already learned that you don't kill your enemies with bullets. You kill them with ingenuity."

Najee tucked the heat.

"I could've murked El Feo or Domingo or even you at the breakfast table, but I didn't want to get blood all over the cantaloupe. That wouldn't have been polite," he remarked with a smile of his own.

El Padrino's respect for Najee grew. So far, everything his people told him about Najee was on point. He paused at a small pond, put a peso on his thumb, and flicked it into the water. The Chinese goldfish swam around the coins. El Padrino faced Najee and resumed their conversation from earlier.

"Do you remember our conversation about war?"

"Yeah, we both agreed that from an economic standpoint, war is bad for business."

"The other way to beat your competition is by offering a superior product at a lower price." He pulled up his shirt sleeve to reveal a spider web tattoo. It was the same symbol the Nogales Cartel stamped on their bricks of dope and plastic baggies. "We have the best chiva, the lowest prices, and multiple distribution channels, but with all the heat at the border, we no longer have a sustainable and foolproof way of transporting our product into the U.S.," he sounded more like a Wall Street banker than a narcotráficante.

Glancing over his shoulders as if the Feds were watching, El Padrino lowered his voice and resumed talking.

"Your government has an opioid crisis on their hands, but instead of blaming themselves for creating the conditions that drive people to abuse drugs, they blame us and have vowed to dismantle the cartels, starting with the Nogales syndicate. In fact, I believe a mole has already infiltrated our organization. When I find that cockroach—" his words trailed off, and he stomped his foot on the ground as if were crushing a bug.

He looked directly at Najee when he made the threat. Najee's skeleton damn near jumped out of his skin and ran all the way to Compton. Regaining his composure, he glanced at the old and fading tattoo. It looked like it had been done in the 70s.

"Where is this conversation going, Señor Estrada. I know you didn't bring me all the way out here so you could give a few kids some money."

"I like you, nino. You can call me Enrique." He pulled his shirt sleeve back down and adjusted his poncho. "You have big balls and a lot of ambition; I can use you."

"Why me? There are a million muthafuckas with heart and determination. You don't need me."

"Don't get it twisted. I didn't say I need you, I said I can use you. There's a big difference."

"What can I give a man who has everything?"

"Logistics!"

"*Logistics?*" Najee repeated. "Does it look like I have access to any boats or planes or semi-trucks?"

"No, but Angela has access to the tunnels."

Everything started to click. There was a reason he and Angela were not shot and buried in a shallow grave.

"Oh, I get it." Najee stroked the stubble on his chin. "Me and Angela are worth more to you alive than dead."

"This is true. El Feo is shortsighted, but I see the bigger picture."

"Let me see if I got this shit straight. Angela wouldn't talk, but you didn't kill her because she knows where all the Los Cinco Diablos tunnels are hidden, and you didn't kill me because you know I can convince her to tell you where they're at."

El Padrino put another coin on his thumb and flicked it into the pond.

"You catch on fast, nino. If you do this one thing for me, I'll do two things for you."

"Holla at me, I'm listening."

"I won't feed you to my tiger."

"What about the loot I took from the stash house? El Feo is tryna tax me."

"Don't worry, nino. I have eyes and ears everywhere. El Feo got most of the money back, but he has to give you a hard time, or he will lose respect."

"Say less, I understand. What's the other thing you'll do for me?"

"I won't feed Angela to El Feo." The hyena was smiling again.

Najee was almost on the inside of the Nogales Cartel, but he couldn't seem too eager to infiltrate Señor Enrique Estrada's criminal enterprise. As he pretended to weigh the options, he reached into his pocket, found a penny, and made a wish as he tossed it into the pond.

"Sounds like I don't have a choice."

"You don't!" El Padrino assured.

Najee could have sworn he saw flames flickering in El Padrino's glass eye. He was reminded of their earlier deal.

"I told you what I dreamed about last night. Now tell me what happened to your face."

Chapter 22

Rise to Power

"I remember what happened to my face like it was yesterday because I live with it every day," El Padrino reflected while running a hand across his disfigured face.

He led Najee to the swimming pool where he took a seat in a beach chair and nodded for Najee to sit next to him.

Forever a stick-up kid, Najee scoped out the mansion's layout as he sat down. The Deacon was on the same page. He leaned against a palm tree and puffed a wine-flavored Black-N-Mild cigarillo as his eyes monitored everything.

One of El Padrino's bodyguards hovered close by. The butt of a nickel-finished Heckler & Koch 9mm rested against his belly button. The fifty-shot extendo seemed to wrap around his waist like a Gucci belt. Another bodyguard stalked back and forth on the balcony. He rocked a Hawaiian shirt, white linen slacks, and gold-framed Carrera sunglasses. If you looked up Mexican drug trafficker in the dictionary, his picture would appear next to the definition.

Najee got comfortable, eager to hear about El Padrino's rise to power.

"I'm no different than you," El Padrino continued. "And we're both no different than the poor children from the Watts projects or the favelas in Brazil or the slums of Puerto Rico. We detest the bitter taste of poverty and would do almost anything to experience the sweetness of success. My come-up scheme involved simple economics. Get a gun, get some money. Get a bigger gun, get bigger money, but it wasn't so simple after all. I formed a four-man crew with childhood friends from my village, and we all got rich, but money made my life more complicated. How do you say this in English?"

"Mo' money, mo' problems!" Najee sang.

"Yes, nino, more money brings muchos problema. My crew linked up with the Colombians and began importing raw coca from

Cartagena and exporting it to the U.S. via Arizona. Business was good, too good. We paid the policia for protection, but they wanted a bigger cut and proposed an eighty-twenty partnership. They wanted to keep eighty percent of the profits while we did one hundred percent of the work. You see the problem with this unfair arrangement, no?"

"Yeah, I see it. It's extortion. The crooked cops were trying to strongarm you," Najee responded. "What did you do about it?"

El Padrino leaned into Najee. His burnt skin and glass eyeball looked even more sinister up-close.

"I did the only thing you can do to a devil, I burned them alive!"

No cap, he was speaking all facts. Chills crawled down Najee's spine. He could only imagine the excruciating pain he would suffer if his true intentions were discovered. He wanted to ask about Angela but now was not the right time. Desperately trying to avoid eye contact, Najee watched an iguana resting on a log and soaking up the last rays of sun.

El Padrino resumed speaking, "We hunted them down one by one until only their leader was left. He tried to hide, but on Christmas Eve we found out where he lived. My people kept insisting that I do the hit alone. When I think about it now, I should've been suspicious, but back then, adding another body to my long list meant nothing to me.

"Anyhow, I quietly crept into his casa late that night, and that's when I knew something was wrong. It shouldn't have been that easy to break into a police officer's home. Ignoring the red flags, I quickly doused the furniture and the Christmas tree with gasoline. As I was about to leave, someone tugged on the back of my shirt and scared the shit out of me. I turned around, aimed my pistola, and saw a little boy wearing pajamas and holding a teddy bear. He smiled and asked me was I Santa Claus. I'm a man made of concrete and steel, but he turned my heart into mush. There was no way I could kill this kid's father in front of him. I would wait until another day. I told the child to go back to sleep and don't tell anyone he saw Santa Claus."

Najee was anxious to hear the ending.

"I'm assuming you caught up to the leader, bang-bang, took him out, and became the king, but that still doesn't tell me what happened to your face."

"Patience, nino, patience," El Padrino advised and stood up. A Mercedes sprinter van swooped into the tall iron gate. Keeping a faraway look on his face, he finished his story, "I wish it ended that simple, but as I said, money made my life more complicated. As the child ran off, I saw blood on the bottom of his feet. I was curious, so I tiptoed in the dark and cautiously followed the child to his parent's room. That's when I discovered why it was so easy to break in. His mother and father were already dead. The assassin slit their throats while they were still asleep. Blood saturated the pillows, soaked the mattress, and dripped on the floor."

Najee clung to every word of El Padrino's story.

"What did you do next?" he asked.

"I finally realized it was a setup and got the hell out of there. I ran to the front door, opened it, and saw the face of betrayal. My three amigos had guns pointed at me. Reacting quickly, I slammed the door, grabbed the kid, and dove on the floor just as they started shooting. When they stopped to reload, I crawled through the house on my knees looking for another exit, but there was only one way in and one way out. Glass shattered and Molotov cocktails flew through the front and side windows. I had already doused everything with gasoline, so the small casa instantly went up in flames. Me and the kid were trapped."

Najee shook his head recalling how his best friend Rio had betrayed him.

"How did you make it out alive?"

El Padrino started walking toward the luxury sprinter van that had arrived moments earlier.

"I made it out but not alive. Half of me died that day." He lifted his colorful poncho and unbuttoned his shirt to show that it wasn't just his face that was disfigured. He had burns on fifty percent of his body. El Padrino explained how it happened, "Black smoke and six feet tall flames surrounded us. The little kid kept saying, 'puerta-

puerta, and pointing to his bedroom. He was trying to tell me that there was a secret door.

"I scooped the child into my arms, turned sideways to shield him from the flames, and jumped through the fire. Adrenaline numbed the pain. The secret door turned out to be a hidden hatch located on the floor of the closet. We lifted the hatch, climbed in, and crawled on our bellies through a large PVC plumbing pipe that led to the septic tank in the backyard. I didn't realize my clothes were on fire until the neighbor sprayed me down with a water hose."

Fascinated by the story, Najee stood up and walked alongside El Padrino. He watched Gustavo, Domingo, and El Feo emerge from the sprinter van and asked, "What happened to the little boy?"

El Padrino's good eye zeroed in on El Feo.

"My son Julio and his wife Maria couldn't have kids of their own. So, I gave the small child to them. From that day forward, the people in my village called me El Padrino—The Godfather," he revealed.

"Damn, that's deep," Najee remarked. "Does El Feo know you were coming to kill his father?"

Keeping his gaze still on El Feo, Enrique's voice deepened, and he warned, "Nunca hablamos de esa noche con nadia. We never spoke about that night to anyone, and if you know what's good for your health, neither will you."

***

El Feo mobbed through the mansion's side gate and entered the garden area with Domingo and a heavily armed Gustavo close behind. Domingo was on edge. El Feo hadn't said much since breakfast at the villa. When a man isn't talking, he's thinking, and that wasn't good for Domingo.

El Feo was irritated, and seeing Najee choppin' it up with his grandfather like they were old friends made him more heated. He mean-mugged Najee as El Padrino escorted him and The Deacon into the mansion through the patio door. Najee screwed up his grill and returned the glare. A deadly showdown between the two men was inevitable.

"I don't think El Feo likes me," Najee commented to El Padrino.

"He has good reason not to," El Padrino confirmed. "You killed Benzo Al."

His reply shocked Najee.

"I thought that was a good thing! Benzo Al kicked off the beef between Los Cinco Diablos and the Nogales Cartel by killing your son, his father. How many more of your soldiers did he torture or murder in the last decade?" Najee questioned and followed El Padrino down a flight of steps leading into the lower level of the mansion. "Shit, El Feo should be thanking me," he added.

"It's not that simple, nino. My grandson is consumed by pride. You succeeded in killing Benzo Al, which means he failed. Failure is not an easy pill to swallow."

They entered a section of the mansion that could've doubled as a luxurious board room in a Manhattan law firm. Tasteful art and a fully stocked mahogany bar ran along the far wall. A large, round conference table dominated the center of the room. The three items that epitomized the Nogales Cartel rested in the middle of the table on a red satin cloth. Members of their inner circle referred to the human skull, gold dagger, and picture of a bearded Mexican man as the Trinity.

El Padrino explained the significance of each artifact. "The skull represents death. The gold dagger symbolizes life. It's used to slice the palm of the hand across the lifeline. Cutting the lifeline is a reminder that once you're in, there's no getting out. This game is played for life."

The Nogales Cartel initiation ritual intrigued Najee. He picked up the photo of the bearded man and examined it. "Who is ol' boy? I've seen people in your organization rocking gold medallions with his image."

The Deacon had been laying in the cut and hadn't said much since arriving, so all eyes were on him when he provided the answer, "That's Jesús Juarez Mazo, also known as Malverde. He was a bad mufucka. The legend is that he stole from the rich and gave to the poor like Robin Hood. When the lifeline is cut with the dagger, three drops of blood are allowed to drip onto the photo of Malverde. The photo is then burned, and the ashes are used to make Indian ink. All of the Nogales goons are tatted with either an Old English N or a spider web tattoo. They got their shit tight fa' reals."

"Muy bien, amigo. Not only are you a loyal soldier to Najee. You know your Mexican folklore. Jesús Malverde is also known as the narco-saint. He blesses our semi-trucks and boats and planes headed to the U.S."

"If that's the case," Najee countered as he gently sat the photo on the red satin cloth. "Why are the Feds knocking all of your shipments at the border?"

His statement made El Feo and Domingo uncomfortable. El Padrino seemed to be shook as well but recovered quickly. He had a plan that would ease his organization's worries. "That's where you and Angela come in. Vamonos, let me show you the true reason I brought you to Juárez."

Najee and The Deacon made eye contact as they followed El Padrino deeper into the bowels of the mansion. Angela was still alive, that was the news Najee was waiting to hear. A shirtless guard stood in front of a nondescript door. His brown skin, rippling muscles, and Aztec tattoos were just as impressive as the automatic assault rifle slung over his shoulder. A hundred round magazine duct-taped to another hundred magazine protruded from the bottom. He saluted El Padrino, gave a respectful nod to El Feo, gave a fist pound to Domingo, and mad dogged Najee and The Deacon. Najee and The Deacon gave him a *do something, bitch* look and mobbed into the large storage room behind El Padrino.

The storage room was a D-boy's wet dream. Pallets of bricks stacked five feet high were lined up against the wall. There was so much yayo, some of the bricks had fallen off the pallet and remained on the floor like neglected stepchildren. Each brick was approximately the size of a shoebox. Some of the bricks were wrapped in blue plastic, others in red. All had the infamous spider web logo and demeaning stickers of the President of the United States bent over getting kicked in the ass by a donkey. It was the cartel's way of openly mocking the efficiency of the border patrol.

"Perico!" El Padrino exclaimed with a sweep of his hands.

Perico means parakeet in English. It's also drug dealer slang for cocaine, and the reason hustlers call a kilo a bird.

Adjacent to the colorful bricks were more palletized packages, except these were wrapped in plastic. Najee could see the compressed crystalline-white substance within them.

"More cocaine?" he inquired.

This time El Feo answered, "No, dummy, it's meth!"

Najee grabbed his nuts and replied, "I got yo' dummy right here, bitch!"

El Feo rolled his eyes and turned toward his grandfather. "Please let me kill this black motherfucker."

Najee knew he couldn't show any weakness. At every turn, he was being watched, tested, and put through the fire to determine whether he would hold up like gold or melt like plastic. He grilled El Feo with one of those icy, South Central, Los Angeles frowned and said, "The only thing you gon' kill is the off switch on your lips."

El Feo flexed up, but El Padrino stood between the two men.

"Please, grandpa, just let me shoot him once. Nothing lethal, just a hot slug in that big mouth of his."

"¡Silencio! Both of you are driving me crazy," El Padrino chastised and got to the reason they came. "The cocaína, methamphetamine, and marijuana trades pale in comparison to the profit potential of synthetic opioids. Fentanyl is the present and the future. It's cheap, highly potent, and can be manufactured right here in Mexico just as easily as it is produced in Wuhan, China."

El Padrino directed The Deacon and Najee's attention to the thirty-gallon drums lined against the back wall. The plastic, heavy-duty drums were blue with a metal, air-tight, sealed lid. Their street value was higher than the pallets of meth and yayo combined.

One could see why El Padrino has been so successful for so long. He was a gangster who talked like a Harvard Business School graduate.

Larry D. Wright

"The Nogales Cartel is strategically positioned to monopolize the market," he said, sounding more like a slick salesman than a seasoned drug dealer. "We are a vertically integrated organization with manufacturing, wholesale distribution, and a nationwide retail sales force in place. The only component we're missing is—"

"Logistics!" Najee finished the sentence.

El Padrino put an arm around Najee's shoulders and walked him out of the storage room.

"Yes, we're missing transportation. Because of their network of tunnels, Los Cinco Diablos is the only syndicate not worried about the border patrol or the Coast Guards, but you're gonna convince Angela to help solve our problem."

"I'm down to rock with you, but it might be difficult to get Angela on the same page," Najee predicted. "What if she doesn't want to cooperate?"

"That's your problem, nino," El Padrino specified with the calm confidence of a man used to having his orders followed without questions. "We're going to do a test run with the MS-13s. One of those pallets of perico are scheduled to be delivered to the Mara Salvatruchas in two days. You, Angela, and Domingo will make the drop. Got any questions?"

"Yeah, why do you keep calling me nino? That means little boy, right?"

"Yes, but El Niño also refers to a potentially catastrophic storm," El Padrino enlightened. "Go to Angela. I'm sure she'll be happy to see you."

Chapter 23

The Devil's Handshake

Angela snapped out of a bad dream, or was it even a dream? She sat up in bed with the feeling she was not alone in the darkroom. Someone was watching her. She could hear his heavy breathing. She held her own breath and listened. Her fears were confirmed as her eyes became acclimated to the darkness. A shadowy figure sat in the corner. His pistol rested on his thigh. A slim finger coiled around the trigger.

She hoped it wasn't El Feo or Domingo or one of their baby-faced assassins. She had already been held captive for what, two, three, maybe four days now? She wasn't sure. The days were starting to run together. What she did know was that it was only a matter of time before she was raped and murdered or murdered and raped. It could go down either way.

Angela had decided that if she was going out, she was gonna go all the way out. She quickly reached under the pillow for the broken piece of mirror she had hidden when they smuggled her into the Juárez mansion, but it was gone.

"Looking for this?" Najee leaned forward and held up the V-shaped slab of sharp glass.

A sliver of early morning sunlight slipped through the curtains and illuminated the right side of his face. He tossed the broken piece of mirror on the nightstand and blazed a blunt. Yellow flames from the lighter shone on the other half of his face. He watched Angela with mixed emotions.

Love.

Lust.

Hate.

Mostly hate.

Angela's heart thumped faster, harder. Najee reminded her of a lion—beautiful, exotic, dangerous, unpredictable—all the characteristics she desired in a man. Despite the perilous danger she was in, an uncontrollable tingle rushed from her nipples to her pussy. It was like he had his mouth on both places at once. She had to squeeze her legs together and remind herself that he was also the opposition.

She sat on the edge of the bed and said, "Welcome to hell! I knew you were gonna save me. I bet you're still sprung on this hot Latina stash box."

Najee remained silent and responded by blowing halos of THC smoke. It looked like Angels were floating above him. He had to admit that Angela was most definitely a hottie. She had dark, shoulder-length hair that always smelled like sweet shampoo, a beautiful face, perky tits, and a phat ass like J-Lo—the J-Lo from back in the day when Jennifer Lopez was still Jenny from the block.

In addition to her physical attributes, she was running up a check in a major way. Eating swordfish on private jets, politicking with the Arabs in lavish hotel suites in Dubai, leaving the Gucci boutique with three employees helping to carry her bags, and speeding down one-way streets in Lamborghini's with the doors up were stunts she posted to the Gram on a regular. She was ballin' for real, not faking it to make it. She was also dangerous, and Najee didn't let the wrapper fool him into thinking it was candy and not poison on the inside.

"Don't get it twisted, Angela! I didn't come all this way to save you. I came to kill you if yo' triflin' ass ain't pregnant. Go piss on that stick," he ordered and nodded to the pregnancy test sitting on the nightstand.

Angela picked up the box and threw it at him.

"What, you don't trust me?"

Najee calmly picked up the box and tossed it on the bed. "Trust you! Are you fuckin' serious? After what you did to my son?" His anger swelled. "And ain't you the same bitch that tried to get me murked a couple of days ago?"

Angela lowered her head, and her voice softened, "I admit that I've done some dirty shit in this game. I've fucked niggas and then fucked them over, but you know how much I love kids. I fought hard not to involve your son. I put that on everything, and when you find Ice and Redbonez, they will confirm it," she stated sincerely.

"It was Benzo Al's idea. He was gonna kill your son if I didn't cut off his thumb. That's the only reason I did it, I swear!"

Her confession was persuasive. Najee believed her, but he didn't allow her words to soften his heart.

"Ice and that Blood bitch Redbonez is already dead," he revealed. "Now, stop jaw jackin' and go piss on that stick."

Angela pouted like a five-year-old child as she snatched the box and headed to the bathroom. Najee followed her. He leaned against the doorframe and took puffs off the loud.

Angela pulled down her panties and sat on the toilet. "Geez, can a bitch get some privacy?"

Najee twisted his lips.

"Just think of me as your parole officer."

After a twenty-minute wait, the bio strip on the pregnancy test turned blue. Angela was pregnant, but Najee still had reservations.

"How do I know the baby is mine? You were fuckin' me and Benzo Al at the same time," he reminded.

"I know for sure it's not his, so stop trippin'."

"How can you be so sure? And don't try to tell me y'all were still using condoms after all these years."

"I'm sure because I swallowed his cum every time we fucked!" Angela stated bluntly.

Najee's face hardened.

She took pleasure in his reaction. To her, it meant he still cared.

"Geez, Najee, I'm just playing." She giggled. "Benzo Al was sterile—been that way before I even met him, but you got that Navy SEAL sperm, Papi!"

"That's what up. Go get dressed." He took a seat and pointed to the bag of clothing sitting on the dresser.

Angela opened the bag and gazed at the denim jeans, long-sleeved D&G T-shirt, and size six Nike foam running shoes. "I always thought I'd be buried in something more classy."

"We're not going to a funeral. We're going on a mission."

"Where to?"

"The hell if I know. Apparently, you hold all the secrets," Najee remarked and passed Angela the blunt.

She reached for the weed, and Najee stared at the bloodstained gauze wrapped around her hands. One of Enrique's housekeepers had attended to her feet as well. El Padrino made sure she was treated with the utmost respect.

Najee's lips tightened, and anger filled his chest. He could only imagine what type of hell she had been through.

"Did they—"

"No, they didn't rape me," she said, anticipating his question. "Not yet."

They made eye contact. He knew she was dead serious. He lowered his voice just in case the room was bugged, "I got a plan to get us out of here alive," Najee spoke with urgency. "But you have to have faith in me and follow my lead."

"I warned you not to trust them. What did El Feo promise you."

"Not El Feo, I made a deal with the old man."

Angela laughed.

"You mean you made a deal with the devil."

Najee didn't tell her about the other deal he made with the other devil. Instead, he asked, "What chu' mean?"

"They want to know where the Los Cinco Diablos tunnels are located, am I right?"

"Yeah, but fuck that. I ain't risking my life to protect some punk-ass tunnels. I put it all on the line to protect you and my unborn child. Besides, Los Cinco Diablos turned their backs on you, get your revenge by telling El Padrino what he wants to know. I don't see what the big deal is."

"The big deal is this. Drugs don't talk, but people do. It takes a lot of money, a lot of planning, and a lot of skill to drill underground. One big mouth could ruin years of hard work, so in order to keep the location of the tunnels a secret, the engineers and the construction crew are killed once the project is complete. So, best believe that once we show them where the tunnels are located—"

This time Najee completed the sentence.

"They're gonna kill us, too. Fuck, I should've thought of that!" This new revelation put a twist in his plans. He rubbed his goatee and thought of a new plot. After a moment, he snapped his fingers.

164

"I got it!" he said with excitement. "I think I know another way we can come out of this alive. I need to get to a phone. Get dressed."

"Fuck me first."

"What?"

Angela straddled Najee's lap. Her robe slipped open and revealed a pair of perfect tits with brown nipples and a phat pussy.

"Fuck me first, Najee. Bend me over, pull my panties to the side, and beat this pussy up."

"Bitch, you trippin'!" Najee dodged her kisses and grabbed her throat.

"That's the Najee I know. Get mad and take your anger out on this wet-wet," she encouraged him to squeeze tighter.

Asphyxiation makes her cum hard. Whenever she was lonely and alone, she'd tie a silk scarf around the bedpost and choke herself while finger popping her pussy.

Najee stood up, and Angela locked her thick legs around his waist. He drove her into the wall, reached between her legs, and ripped her panties off.

Angela felt something big, black, and hard press against the opening of her vagina, and she moaned into his neck.

"Yes, Papi."

Holding Angela against the wall, Najee shoved the barrel of his Glock into her pussy. Angela's mouth and eyes opened wide. She looked between her legs and saw the deadly dildo stretching her cunt lips.

"Dig this, bitch, if you don't sit yo' little freaky ass down somewhere, I'm gonna blow your ovaries off!" he warned and tossed her on the bed. A lamp fell off the nightstand and shattered on the floor. "Get dressed, we rollin' out in ten minutes."

"I ain't going nowhere," Angela pouted with her arms crossed.

Najee stopped at the door and glared at Angela.

"There's a difference between being brave and being fearless. Fearlessness is a synonym for foolishness and will get you a hot slug in your dome. Now get dressed, we got some coke to move."

***

Margaritas had the best taquitos in Juárez. When Najee told Angela that his plan wouldn't work unless he could get to a phone, she told El Padrino and El Feo she wouldn't talk unless they got her some taquitos with a side of guacamole. Now Najee understood why she was so adamant about only wanting the food from Margaritas. The small but popular Mexican restaurant was busy and noisy.

The large crowd was just the type of cover Najee needed. He placed his order and calmly walked to the back of the restaurant under the pretense that he needed to use the restroom. Once in the back, he made sure Domingo was still preoccupied with the flirtatious waitress. Domingo removed a clear baggie from his pocket, poured a line of coke on a butter knife, and offered it to the waitress. She respectfully declined. Domingo shrugged his shoulders and treated his own nose, vacuuming up the crystals in one swoop.

Great, another strung-out drug dealer! Najee observed as he quickly bypassed the bathroom and dipped in the direction of the payphones.

The international call to Detective Brooks went through without complication. After checking on his son and laying out the elaborate plan to free Nella and Sosa, he made another request.

"Did you torch the fake SWAT utility vehicle after the move on the stash house?"

"No, I got it tucked away. I figured we might need to use it again."

"My man, my brand. Keep that joint on standby because I might need it."

"I'm on it," Detective Brooks confirmed. "Anything else I need to know?"

"Yeah, they're forcing us to escort some weight across the border tonight," Najee talked real fast, and his underarms began to sweat. "The drugs are supposed to be stored at an old horse ranch that Los Cinco Diablos has listed under a shell company named Alvarez Horse Ranch, but I got a magic trick up my sleeve. Look for a beef jerky factory. Both spots are near the U.S.—Mexico border."

"It's going to be hell getting in and out of there," Detective Brooks pointed out.

"I feel you. Angela said Los Cinco Diablos doesn't have a team posted up at the spot, but fuck that, I'm still gonna need guns, big guns, and a fast car."

"Done. What about a burn bag with I.D. and some cash?"

"Good idea, I plan on fuckin' these Migos out of some major paper, and like always, you'll get your proper chop on the back end."

After laying out the plan to Detective Brooks, Najee called Agent Parker. Looking around nervously, he was relieved when Parker picked up the line.

"Yo', listen up because I need to make this quick!" he shouted over the loud mariachi music with the phone held to his left ear and a finger pressed in the other. "Me and Domingo are moving a load of coke across the border tonight," he revealed, but conveniently left out any mention of Angela and The Deacon.

Caught off guard by Najee's sudden and urgent call, Parker knocked over his cup of coffee while reaching for a pen and notepad.

"Exactly when and where?" he grumbled into the receiver.

"The details are sketchy," Najee talked fast while taking quick glances over his shoulder. The Nogales Cartel had eyes everywhere. "The drop will probably take place somewhere in L.A. I think they're testing me," he laid it on thick. "We're delivering one hundred kilos to the MS-13s."

They were actually supposed to deliver one hundred and fifty kilos, but Najee had plans for the other bricks.

"That doesn't tell me much," Parker voiced his disappointment and frantically wiped up the coffee before it leaked onto his files.

"Well, it's all I got for now. Just be ready to move in when this shit goes down. I'll make up an excuse to use one of their cell phones and hit you when I find out more. I gotta go." Najee needed to hurry. Domingo could send someone looking for him at any moment.

"Hold up, you son of a bitch!" Parker tossed his ink pen on the desk.

The information Najee had given him was useless. He had a feeling Najee was holding back just as he did about his true connection to Angela Rodriguez.

"I put my neck on the line for you and the first thing you did was cut off your ankle monitor. How do I know I can trust you?"

"Number one, watch how the fuck you talk about my momma," Najee scolded. "Number two, do you think I'm stupid? That was not an ankle monitor, it was a wireless audio transmitter. If those Migos caught me wearing a wire, they would've sliced my black ass up with a razor blade and poured Tabasco sauce on the wounds. So, the question is can I trust you?"

"Shit!" Parker groaned, partly because he had put Najee in danger, even more, because Najee was smarter than he anticipated. "I didn't know if you were gonna get ghost once you were released from custody, so I needed some insurance."

"Well, your insurance policy almost got me canceled," Najee spoke with force.

"It won't happen again, but remember our deal. If you don't want to visit Nella behind bars, I suggest you get me that damn info about the time and location of the drop," Parker stated, feeling encouraged by the prospect of apprehending Domingo in possession of one hundred kilos. Once he had Domingo in custody, he would make him fold like a lawn chair.

Najee hung up feeling more pressure on his shoulders. He hustled back to the table and slid into the seat next to The Deacon. Domingo and one of his young shooters sat across from them. The shooter had a slim build with peach fuzz above his top lip, probably no more than seventeen but already had three bodies on his conscience.

Domingo eyed Najee suspiciously and took a bite off a carne asada taco. He chewed like a cow grazing grass.

"Ay, homes, who were you talking to on the phone?" he asked in an accusative tone, his drug dealer intuition searching for signs of deceit.

Najee played it off well and answered with a straight face. "I was talking to the police."

Domingo stopped chewing, put down his taco, and glared at Najee to determine whether he was for real or bullshitting. After an intense stare down, he laughed and elbowed his young shooter in the ribs.

"You got good jokes, ese. You had me going for a hot second," he commented with a chuckle and took another big bite of his taco. Food still in his mouth, he turned serious and added, "I did my research. The streets say you keep it one hundred, but I still think you're up to something. The old man may like you, but let's get something straight, ese, I don't. If you ever try to drive a wedge between me and El Feo again, I'll drill you on the spot, comprende?"

Najee noticed the angel tatted on Domingo's right fist and the demon tatted on the left. He ate with his right hand and blasted his gun with the left.

Ambidextrous individuals are skillful, intellectual, and often too faced. Najee kept that in mind as he accepted the challenge.

"Yeah, I comprehend," he affirmed and looked Domingo squarely in the eyes. "And if your research is thorough, you understand that if you ever try to set me up again, I'll drill you first!"

Domingo's shooter, who was actually twenty years old and went by the name Ghost reached for his pole, but before he could up his heat, The Deacon was on the other side of the table choking him out. Najee upped his strap and placed it on the table, the barrel pointing toward Domingo. He only had one shot in the chamber, but one shot is all he needed.

He signaled for the Deacon to fall back. He had made his point, and now was not the time to have a pissing contest and sabotage his plans. The Deacon released his tight grip, and Ghost slumped back into his seat and rubbed his sore neck.

Although Domingo would never admit it out loud, he was impressed by the way Najee and The Deacon handled themselves. They were different than the other blacks he had dealt with in the past. They had their shit together and reminded him of the old school Harlem gangsters he watched on Netflix.

He could've pressed the issue and had them aired out. A slight nod to the cashier who kept a sawed-off Benelli M-4 shotgun hidden under the counter, or a hand gesture toward the cook who was itching to blast the thumper concealed beneath his greasy apron could've ended the situation.

They would lay down their lives to be in the good graces of El Feo and Señor Enrique Estrada. Ironically, their loyalty is what bothered Domingo the most. They weren't ready to ride for him, they were ready to ride because of what he represented—the almighty Nogales Cartel.

Domingo understood this and wanted that type of power and influence for himself. He wanted the game to bow down and kiss his pinky ring, but as long as he worked for El Feo and El Padrino, he would be standing in the shadow of two giants.

He had been planning, plotting, and patiently waiting for his ascension from right-hand man to the main man, and with El Feo and the old man beefing, now was the perfect opportunity to make a power move.

Najee's unexpected arrival was a blessing in disguise, and he needed to keep him alive—at least for now. Domingo almost drooled as he thought about all the paper he could stack if he had access to his own drug-smuggling tunnel.

Yeah, killing Najee could wait, he decided.

"Whatever you say, ese," Domingo dismissed Najee's theatrics like he was swatting a fly and switched the subject to Angela. "What's crackin' with your crazy bitch, eh? Is she gonna be a problem, or what?"

Najee kept one eye on the nervous cashier and the other on the shady cook who had his hand tucked in his greasy apron.

"Don't even trip, I got this!"

Chapter 24

Right Hand 2 God

"Relax, Torres, I got this!" Parker reassured for the umpteenth time.

"Oh, really?"

"Just watch, my guy is gonna come through," Parker tried to sound as convincing as possible, but his partner and the upper brass were busting his balls about his decision to catch and release Najee.

"I like your optimism, but the last time I checked, our suspect went off the radar."

"Well, he just checked in. He's in Mexico."

"Of course, he is. That's where all the fugitives go."

"Asshole!"

ATF Senior Administrator, Douglas Schwartz poked his head into the room.

"Give me an update. What's this I hear about a suspect going to Mexico?" He was a big and beefy commando type who played college football for USC in his prime. Even for a man his size, he moved with the gracefulness of a ballet dancer.

Parker and Torres shared an awkward look between them, but no one spoke. Schwartz invited himself into the office. He wore a gray suit and carried a copy of the novel *To Catch a Thief*.

"I give you guys a lot of rope, don't hang yourselves with it," he sermonized in a deep, authoritative voice. "You cowboys better get your spurs out of your ass and get some traction on this case, or I have no choice but to hand it off to the DEA. We clear?"

Parker protested. "But—"

"Your butt is what you're sitting on. While you guys had your fingers up your asses, the DEA received intel that Enrique The God Damn Godfather Estrada has come out of retirement. Apparently, he's the real mastermind behind the synthetic opioids crossing the border. I want that motherfucker behind bars. Now get out there and get that Fentanyl off the damn streets!" Schwartz did an about-face and floated out of the room.

Torres cracked open a can of Red Bull and sat on the edge of Parker's desk. He had his own reservations about the case, but he didn't like suit wearing bullies pushing him and his partner around. It was times like these that made him want to quit the Agency.

"Do you really think this prick can deliver?" He asked after taking a sip.

"Who else has come this close? Not any of our guys. Agent Ortega has gone off the grid," Parker reminded. "They already trust him enough to deliver a major shipment of coke with Domingo Rojas."

That caught Torres' attention.

"How much we talkin'?"

"One hundred bricks to the El Salvadorians."

"I don't like it."

"What's not to like? We pinch Domingo and work our way up the food chain."

"I get that part. What I don't get is why would the Nogales Cartel put Najee in their business? It doesn't make sense."

It didn't make sense. They were missing a vital piece of the puzzle. Parker realized this as well and was determined to find out what Najee was hiding. He scrolled through the prepaid cell phone Domingo had given him. He was anxiously waiting for Domingo to hit his line and set up another gun buy. After seeing no new messages, he squeezed a rubber therapy ball in his fist.

His psychiatrist—the one his superiors forced him to see after a questionable shooting—claimed it would help relieve stress and curb his urge to smoke. It wasn't working. He needed to hit the streets. He needed to be close to the action. He needed to stop acting like a cop and start thinking like a criminal.

Parker grabbed his leather jacket off the back of the chair, thought about it, and grabbed his pack of cigarettes too.

"Let's roll. It's time we play some games of our own."

"Schwartz is right, ain't it about time we hand this case off to Miller?" Torres was tired of the bullshit. If upper management didn't think they were competent enough to crack the case, then so be it. Less work for him.

"Why? So, the DEA can swoop in and steal the case from us? Been there, done that."

"No, because this has become about drugs, not guns!"

"Trust me, where there's a lot of drugs, there's a whole lot of guns," Parker promised. "Are you with me or what?"

"What cha' got in mind?" Torres asked, shoving his service weapon into his shoulder holster.

"We tighten the clamps on Sosa and Nella. He has a bail hearing this morning at the Ronald Reagan Federal Building, and she has her prelim this afternoon. If we can keep them behind bars, that'll give us leverage just in case Najee gets slick."

***

U.S. District Court

Central District of California

Attorney David Shapiro Esquire looked, walked, talked, and dressed slick. He wore a blue dress shirt with his initials mono-grammed on the cuffs, a black three-buttoned wool gabardine Tom Ford suit, and black oxfords on his size twelve feet. He always made a classy and cinematic entrance into a room, captivating everyone's attention.

He waltzed into the courtroom, set his briefcase on the defense table, and whispered into Sosa's attorney's ear. Turning to Sosa, he extended his palm for a handshake.

Sosa eyeballed the slick lawyer suspiciously. Like most street niggas, he didn't trust white people.

He screwed his face up and asked, "Who da' fuck are you?"

"I'm your best shot at getting out of here," Attorney Shapiro guaranteed and passed Sosa a business card. "Najee sent me."

Sosa examined the fancy business card and ran his thumb across the raised embroidery.

"What does Esq stand for," he wanted to know.

"It means Esquire," Attorney Shapiro stated proudly. "It's a distinguished ranking just below a knight." He seemed to grow taller as he spoke while Sosa's own five hundred dollars an hour lawyer from a prominent black law firm in Atlanta shrunk into the background.

Attorney Shapiro and Najee had known each other for a long time. As a young, up-and-coming lawyer, the Cornell graduate helped Najee get a murder beef reduced to manslaughter. Over the years he had represented many high-profile defendants and earned a reputation of being thorough, expensive, and not afraid to cheat in order to win. He also accepted Bitcoin, which was a major plus for criminals who didn't want to leave a financial paper trail.

The magistrate banged his gavel, and the court reporter read off the docket sheet. The judge looked down on everyone from his wooden throne. His bifocals rested on the bridge of his wide nose, and his lips were tangled in a permanent scowl.

"Counselors, are you ready to proceed?"

Diana Phillips, a hotshot Assistant United States Attorney who was recently transferred from D.C., stood up. She looked like a million bucks with her flowing blonde hair, yellow Yves Saint Laurent blouse, blue pencil skirt, and canary-colored Hermes heels.

"Your Honor," she spoke in a firm, authoritative tone. "The defendant is charged with felony murder, attempted murder, felony possession of a firearm, and racketeering stemming from a drug deal gone bad at Juan's Custom Toys located in the city of Compton—" She paused and flipped through the pile of documents on the table.

The judge frowned at Sosa. He hated blacks and drug dealers. Sosa was a black drug dealer, not a good look.

Mrs. Phillips put on her reading glasses. She looked more like a sexy librarian than a cutthroat federal prosecutor.

"As the indictment reflects, notorious kingpin, Alonzo Benzo Al Guzman, and several other known criminals were gunned down during this bloody melee. The government is prepared to prove that the defendant, Marcus Fischer, did knowingly, willingly, and intentionally fire an AK-47 assault rifle during this bloody altercation.

Furthermore, the government will prove that at least three members of the deceased were affiliated with Mr. Fischer's Block Boy Empire criminal enterprise and acted at his direction."

The magistrate cut in.

"Tell me more about this alleged criminal enterprise."

"Gladly, Block Boy Empire is a criminal gang operating out of Atlanta, Milwaukee, Los Angeles, and elsewhere. Its members routinely engage in acts of violence, including murder, assault, robbery, sex trafficking, and distribution of narcotics."

"I see." The magistrate turned his attention to Sosa and beat him over the head with a frown.

Mrs. Phillips lowered her voice to a dramatic tone and concluded her argument.

"Based on these facts and to protect the public from this vicious career criminal, the government requests that you deny bail. Thank you, Your Honor, the People rest."

The judge scribbled notes on a yellow legal pad and cut his eyes at Sosa.

"Who will speak on behalf of the defense?"

Sosa's Atlanta lawyer attempted to stand up, but Sosa intervened. Something about the stranger's confident swag boosted his hopes.

"Fall back and let the white boy do his thing."

Attorney Shapiro stood up, adjusted the Windsor knot in his necktie, and winked reassuringly at Sosa.

"Your Honor, my colleague did an excellent job laying out the allegations, but they're just that—allegations. The government hasn't submitted a shred of evidence to corroborate that this was even a drug deal. Furthermore, there are no credible witnesses who can place a gun in my client's hands, and the government most certainly can't connect him to these heinous murders."

Mrs. Phillips stood up to protest, "Come on, judge! The defendant was apprehended at the crime scene," she reminded.

The judge banged his gavel.

"Have a seat, counselor!"

Attorney Shapiro waited until she was seated, then resumed, "I'm glad you mentioned the crime scene." He popped the locks on his briefcase and pulled out several invoices. "Your Honor, my client was simply there to pick up his vehicle and got caught in the crossfire. I move to enter the work order and paid invoice into evidence."

Mrs. Phillips jumped to her feet.

"I object!"

"On what grounds?" The judge grumbled.

"The People have not reviewed these documents."

Attorney Shapiro winked at the federal prosecutor before handing her duplicates of the paperwork.

"Thankfully, I made you a copy!" He passed the bailiff the originals and took a seat.

Mrs. Phillips turned beet red as she scanned the documents. She had been blindsided.

The judge analyzed a pink carbon copy work order. It indicated Sosa requested tinted windows, 24" Forgiato rims, and three 15" L7 woofers for his Mercedes Benz a week prior to the shooting. The judge adjusted his bifocals and looked over the receipts. The time and date stamp placed Sosa at the scene of the shooting on official business.

"As both of you know," the judge addressed Attorney Shapiro and Mrs. Phillips. "This is not a trial, and I'm not here to decide innocence or guilt."

Sosa's leg shook nervously, causing the ankle chains to rattle. This was the moment of truth. The judge was about to render his decision.

"With that said," the judge continued. "I conclude that Mr. Fischer's base offense level exposes him to a substantial amount of time, thus, that makes him a flight risk."

Sosa's heart sunk to his balls, and his shoulders sagged. It was all bad.

"However, the defense has submitted convincing evidence that refutes the government's theory. Who knows, he may very well prevail at trial." The judge ripped his glasses off and frowned at Sosa.

"As much as I hate to, I'm going to grant your petition for bail. I'm imposing a five hundred-thousand-dollar cash bond."

Agent Parker and Torres burst into the courtroom armed with doctored audio from Sosa's interrogation, but it was too late. The judge had already made his ruling.

Attorney Shapiro stood up and buttoned his jacket.

"Your Honor, my client is prepared to make bail!

Parker groaned his disappointment.

Larry D. Wright

Chapter 25

Smoke and Mirrors

Nella shuffled into the courtroom like a penguin. Iron leg shackles squeezed her ankles, causing her to take small, awkward steps, and cold steel handcuffs chewed into her wrists, almost cutting off her circulation. The officer had tightened them just to be an asshole. Her hair was a hot mess, she had bags under her eyes, and the stench of jailhouse fear and funk seeped from her armpits.

"Let's go, move it along, Jackson!" A heavyset female bailiff with a short butch haircut gripped Nella's elbow and roughly steered her toward the defendant's table. The lawyer's chair was noticeably empty.

"Damn, this nigga Najee didn't even get me an attorney!" She shook her head sadly and wondered why she at least didn't have a public defender.

Nella had been in courtrooms before. There was the time she put a restraining order on her ex. Then she had to double back and put one on his crazy-ass baby momma, but this was the first time she was the defendant. She was scared, nervous, and alone. Najee had schooled her on what to expect from the dark side of the game, but nothing can fully prepare you for walking barefoot across hot coals.

"Please save me, Najee."

She looked over her shoulder into the gallery hoping, wishing, and praying that her knight in shining armor was front and center, but Najee was nowhere to be found. Her heart broke a little bit more.

Her eyes continued sweeping across unfamiliar faces until her gaze landed on Sosa. Their eyes locked for a hot second but to Nella, it seemed like a million years. His lips parted into a warm smile, and he hit her with a thumbs-up. It was the most encouraging sign she had received all week.

The courtroom's large double doors suddenly swung open, and the gallery came alive with chit chatter. Known for making bold, cinematic entrances, Attorney Shapiro walked—no—he more like floated into the courtroom followed by eight bad bitches from the William Morris Modeling Agency. Tight black Alexander McQueen bodysuits enveloped their curvaceous figures, and knee-high camouflage Giuseppe boots added to their sex appeal. All heads swiveled in their direction.

"What the hell?" Nella couldn't believe what she was seeing.

In addition to the matching designer gear, the models had another thing in common—they all resembled Nella, from the smooth yellow skin down to the cute brown freckles that dotted their faces. Camouflage patterned puffy vests with fur around the hood completed their outfits.

"Order, order in the court!" Magistrate William Duffy demanded and banged his wooden gavel.

The commotion settled, but the spectators kept their gaze fixed on the models as they strutted single file down the middle aisle like they were on a runway during New York Fashion Week. The models quietly commandeered the first row of seats. Some of them even gave Nella a friendly wave.

Attorney Shapiro stopped to shake Sosa's hand. He rejected Sosa's offer to foot the bill, informing him that Najee had compensated his law firm very well.

Judge Duffy, a big and burly Irish guy with silver hair and a heck of a golf swing, was running out of patience.

"Mr. Shapiro, I will not allow you to make a mockery out of my courtroom with your shenanigans."

"My apologies, Your Honor," Attorney Shapiro approached the podium while adjusting his gold cufflinks.

"What's the meaning of all this pageantry?" Judge Duffy scolded.

He was not in a good mood. His hemorrhoids had flared up, and the spicy burrito he ordered from the taco truck gave him heartburn.

"If I may approach, Your Honor. I think you'll find what I have to say interesting."

Assistant United States Attorney Jonathan Dobbs chimed in. The seasoned Princeton graduate had prosecuted many high-profile cases.

"Your Honor, might you remind my fashionably late colleague that this is a courtroom, not a circus!"

The judge gave Mr. Dobbs a stern look. "Might I remind you who's in charge here," he cautioned the veteran prosecutor and hit Attorney Shapiro with an equally harsh glare. "And might I remind you that this is a courtroom, not a circus. I would like to see both of you in my chambers, now!"

Mr. Dobbs mumbled his frustration.

Attorney Shapiro took a moment to talk to Nella. He leaned close to her ear, put a friendly arm around her shoulder, and whispered, "Don't be alarmed, Mrs. Jackson. I have your best interests in mind. All this is part of the plan to get you out of here. Hang tight, I'll be right back." He trotted off.

"Wait, what's going on? Who are you? Better yet, who sent you?" she fired off a rapid volley of questions, but the bailiff was already escorting the mysterious attorney through the side door that led to the judge's chamber.

Irritated and confused, Nella glanced over her shoulder and caught Sosa's attention.

"What the fuck is going on?" she mouthed despite the huge glass partition that separated the spectator's gallery from the courtroom.

Sosa read her lips and shrugged, but he also gave her a reassuring two thumbs-up. He had seen Attorney Shapiro in action and knew he was a beast.

Inside magistrate William Duffy's chambers, Attorney Shapiro and Mr. Dobbs spared with words, "Your Honor, this is a waste of time and government resources," Mr. Dobbs lectured. "And I refuse to partake in this buffoonery."

Judge Duffy chewed two Tums tablets and washed the chalky antacid pills down with a glass of water.

"What do you have to say for yourself, Shapiro? What's with the entourage?"

"They're material witnesses."

Mr. Dobbs scoffed.

"Do you even know how this works? This is a preliminary hearing, not a trial. You don't get to present witnesses."

"Actually, the defense can present expert witnesses, but I'll let you read up on case law in your free time. Besides, I don't plan on putting anyone on the stand today. However, I do plan on cross-examining Detective Herman about the veracity of your video evidence."

Judge Duffy eyeballed the prosecutor.

"You have video evidence to present?"

"Sure do," Mr. Dobbs admitted. "Homicide Detective Steve Herman recovered surveillance video from the hotel. The defendant was accompanied by two male perpetrators who wore masks, but Ms. Jackson can be clearly seen accosting the hotel's housekeeper and forcing her into the room at gunpoint. The housekeeper and four other dead bodies were discovered the next day."

"I see." The judge rubbed his chin.

"Your Honor," Attorney Shapiro offered his rebuttal. "The defense does not contest the contents of the video, only the ill assumption that one of the perpetrators is my client. There are no eyewitnesses, weapons, cell tower records, or DNA evidence that puts Ms. Jackson at the scene."

"The surveillance footage is damaging enough on its own. In addition, the FBI's facial recognition algorithm matched three prominent character features with photos Mrs. Jackson posted on social media posts."

"I strongly disagree. Studies have shown that facial recognition software disproportionately misidentifies African Americans over any other ethnic group," Attorney Shapiro reported the facts. "All eight of the women I marched into court today match the description of the female suspect caught by the surveillance cameras. Are you gonna arrest them, too?"

The Assistant U.S. Attorney turned tomato red.

"This is bullshit!" he roared.

"Enough!" Judge Duffy slammed his palm on the desk. "Just because we play golf on the weekends doesn't mean you can disrespect this court!" He made that clear and popped two more Tums in his mouth. "I'd like to see this video."

The trio watched the video in silence. The judge had to admit that there was a canning resemblance between the suspect in the video and the women in the court's gallery. He could only imagine how a jury would react if they saw eight identical women wearing the same outfit as the killer.

After the footage ended, Attorney Shapiro retrieved a handful of folders from his briefcase. He held them in the air like the Statue of Liberty torch.

"The women you saw today are just the tip of the iceberg. Not only does Ms. Jackson have an airtight alibi, I contacted several other talent agencies with the description of the models and actresses I was looking for, and they all had someone who fits the profile. Take a look for yourself." He tossed the portfolios on the judge's desk.

Judge Duffy picked up a random folder and studied the actresses' headshot photo, but Mr. Dobbs didn't bother.

"This is preposterous, nothing but smoke and mirrors! What is counsel trying to prove?"

Attorney Shapiro opened one of the folders and pointed to the photo of a Nella look-a-like.

"I thought you knew how this works? I'm doing what a good lawyer does. I'm proving that my client is innocent."

"Again, you fail to realize this is not a trial."

Attorney Shapiro made eye contact with the judge.

"I was hoping there wouldn't be a trial!"

Judge Duffy became slightly amused.

"Are you suggesting that I kick the case?"

Attorney Shapiro nodded.

Judge Duffy sat in his leather chair, leaned back, and folded his hands over his round stomach.

"Mr. Dobbs, do you have a rebuttal?"

Mr. Dobbs gritted his teeth.

"Not now, however, I beg you not to dismiss this case. Those families deserve justice."

"So does my client."

"Fuck you, Shapiro!" Mr. Dobbs yelled angrily and focused his attention on the judge. "The People respectfully request an adjournment to investigate this new information."

"And the defense respectfully demands that my client be released on her own recognizance."

***

Nightfall had descended on the city of Los Angeles by the time the U.S. Marshals outfitted Nella with an ankle monitor and released her from custody. She stood on the steps of the 10-story court building, closed her eyes, and inhaled a gulp of the crisp night air. She couldn't wait to soak in a hot bubble bath and scrub the jailhouse funk off her skin, but she needed a ride first. Her cell phone battery was dead, so Uber wasn't an option.

Disappointed that Najee wasn't on deck to scoop her up, she scanned Alameda Street searching for the nearest payphone. Now that cell phones were ubiquitous, finding a phone booth was nearly impossible. As she scanned the block, a matte black Lamborghini SUV gliding on red, 26" Forgis swooped up to the curb. John Legend's soulful voice and booming bass rumbled from the Bang & Olufsen audio system.

Nella dipped into the shadows to make sure the driver wasn't on bullshit. Rockin' with Najee came with a warning label. He killed for that bag and had created a lot of enemies along the way.

Nella watched the driver closely. She didn't know if he was simply a young nigga trying to holler at her or a young assassin trying to spray hollow points at her. The fact that she still didn't know the identity of the mysterious lawyer amplified her paranoia. Organizations were known to get their enemy, or a snitch released from custody only to have that person murdered.

The passenger side window rolled down slowly. Nella braced herself for gunfire, but instead of bullets, someone called her name.

"Nella!"

That don't sound like Najee! she thought.

Nella cautiously approached the Lambo truck and smiled. Sosa smiled back at her.

"What chu' waiting on? Get in, shawty," he invited in his country drawl.

Nella climbed in and drank Sosa's swag with her eyeballs. He had gotten his braids twisted to the back in a zigzag pattern, and his beard was neatly trimmed. Diamonds dripped from his ears and neck like ranch dressing, and his gold Sky Dweller Rolex seemed to glow in the dark. His good looks, intoxicating cologne, and the new car smell turned her on immensely.

Sosa turned down the music.

"That lawyer is a beast, ain't he?"

Before Sosa could say that Najee was the realist nigga in the game, and before he could tell Nella that he believed Agent Parker was feeding them false information about Najee, and before he could reveal that Najee had set up everything with the clever attorney, Nella leaned over and kissed him. Their lips touched and their tongues became entangled.

"Wait, hold up, baby girl." Sosa broke their embrace. "There's something I gotta tell you. Najee set—"

"Shhh!" Nella put her finger against his lips. "I know, Najee set you up, and he abandoned me. Don't say nothin' else. Just drive while I'll show you how much I appreciate you for getting me out of jail while Najee was off playing Captain Save-a-Hoe."

"But—"

"Shhh!" Nella shushed him again, unbuckled his Gucci belt, and unzipped his designer denims.

She pulled his dick from his boxer briefs and his huge slab of meat slapped against his stomach. Nella gasped at its size. It was long and thick with a big vein traveling along its length. Even semi-erect it was the biggest dick she had ever seen. She licked and twirled her soft tongue around the wide head, causing Sosa's throbbing pole to grow thicker and longer and harder.

Nella gripped the base of his cock, stacked one hand on top of the other, and held his Mandingo like it was a baseball bat. When she put her warm mouth around the head and slurped his precum, Sosa said fuck Najee and pulled into traffic. He pushed Najee out of his mind and pushed the back of Nella's head into his lap, forcing more dick down her throat.

"That's right, baby, suck this big monster," he encouraged.

Nella moaned around Sosa's cock and tried to devour all of him, but she couldn't and surrendered at six inches. The luxury SUV hit a pothole, and two more inches slid past her tonsils.

Nella choked on eight inches of dick and had to come up for air.

"Don't stop, baby, you finna make me cum," Sosa moaned and tried his best to maintain control of the vehicle, but her brain game was too cold and he damn near crashed the whip. He pulled onto a side street, killed the engine, and reclined his seat all the way back. "When I buss, I want you to keep sucking and drain this big dick dry."

Nella took him into her mouth again, and when his cockhead hit that secret G-spot in the back of her throat, her pussy walls clenched like a tight fist.

Detective Brooks turned off his headlights and followed the Lamborghini truck onto the dark side street. Najee had purchased a small, cozy house for Nella and their son and had arranged for Detective Brooks to pick her up. Mrs. Brooks had cooked Nella's favorite meal and was taking great care of Lil' Najee. Detective Brooks removed his long lens Nikon camera from its case and snapped pictures of Nella's and Sosa's ultimate betrayal.

His disappointment in Nella grew when he saw Sosa stiffen and throw his head back. He snapped a clear shot of Sosa with his mouth open in ecstasy. Moments later, Nella sat up and wiped her lips with the back of her hand. The Lamborghini's passenger side door opened, the overhead light came on, and Detective Brooks' high-resolution lens picked up a clear shot of Nella leaning over and spitting a mouth full of cum and saliva on the curb.

Detective Brooks didn't know how he was going to tell Najee or if he was even going to tell him at all. It would break Najee's heart, and the burning desire to commit a double murder would consume him.

Parker watched the black BMW follow the black Lamborghini SUV. He gave them some distance, then slowly slid into traffic behind them.

"Someone is following Sosa. Call it in and de-conflict our case with the other agencies."

Torres was already relaying the BMW's license plate number to dispatch. The dispatcher connected him to the new DEA agent assigned to the Sinatra investigation. Torres took a whole page of notes before hanging up.

"The shit just got deeper! The white guy in the 750 is not one of ours. He's an ex-detective turned private investigator," Torres reported, "but that's not the best part."

"You know how much I hate foreplay; stop jerking me off and tell me what you got," Parker chirped while focusing on the red taillights ahead.

"You're gonna love this, not only was he one of the dirty cops who got caught up in that Rampart scandal, his daughter, Dr. Renee Brooks used to write Najee while he was in prison. Wanna take a wild guess who she was married to?"

"That dick head attorney, Shapiro!" Parker guessed correctly.

"And guess who helped Najee beat that murder charge he caught as a juvenile?"

Parker knew the answer, but before he could reply, the cell phone given to him by Domingo lit up. Parker and Torres looked at each other. The game was on.

Chapter 26

Against all Odds

Parker hung up the phone and high-fived Torres.

"Game on, baby!"

The cartel wanted guns, but not just any guns. Domingo specifically requested twenty more of the powerful and deadly FN MK-16 Special Combat Automatic Rifles, and he demanded a lower price this time, take it or leave it. Parker took it.

They planned to swap it out tomorrow night in East Los Angeles. True to an unpredictable drug dealer, Domingo said he would call with the time and location.

"Come alone," Domingo had suggested.

Yeah, right, Parker thought! He would be alone until he signaled for the K9 dogs, tactical squad, and helicopter.

As he and Torres discussed the call, the burner phone lit up again. Parker showed Torres the screen.

"It's Domingo. Why do you think he's calling back?"

"I left my crystal ball at home," Torres joked. "Answer it and find out."

Parker flipped him off and accepted the call.

"This better be good, Domingo. I was just about to get my dick sucked!" He easily morphed into his role as a hardcore biker.

The line went silent.

"Hello, hello!"

"Parker, is that you?" Someone probed in a hushed tone.

Parker recognized the voice. "Najee?" he asked, riddled with confusion. "How did you get this number?"

"I'm the one who should be asking the questions. What's your connection to Domingo?" Najee probed while walking toward the back of the SUV, away from Domingo and Ghost.

Parker ignored him.

"You probably don't have a lot of time, so forget about Domingo and tell me when the shipment is coming in and where I should position my team."

Najee still hadn't gotten in touch with Detective Brooks to confirm whether Nella was still in custody, so he couldn't tell Parker to go fuck himself. He was in too deep and had to play his part all the way to the end. The best deceivers disguise their lies with the truth but never enough truthfulness to foil their master plan.

"We're running the drugs through an old tunnel Los Cinco Diablos abandoned last year," Najee revealed. "It's located about fifteen feet under a vacant T-shirt factory in Tijuana, just West of the Otay Mesa Port of Entry. The tunnel is about a mile long and terminates under a barn five hundred feet on the other side of the border. Look for a place called Alvarez Horse Ranch."

"I'm familiar with that area. What time is the shipment coming in?"

Najee hesitated for a moment. Timing was everything. They were parked on the side of the road in the middle of who-the-fuck-knows-where, and he really didn't know how long the journey through the tunnel would take. If Parker showed up too early, Najee was fucked. If Parker showed up too late, he was even more fucked. Najee needed to give himself some cushion in order to pull his jack move without the scrutiny of the Feds.

He watched a white cargo van and an onyx black Mercedes Benz sprinter van speed in his direction. Their tires kicked up plumes of dust. Najee was sure El Feo occupied one of the vehicles. That wasn't a good sign.

Najee glanced at the face of his Patek. The small hand pointed to the seven.

Thinking fast, he said, "We're rolling out at midnight. Keep your guys out of sight. These guys can smell a pig from a mile away."

"Geez, I didn't know pork smelled that bad! Don't worry, I can read lips from two miles away," Parker responded sarcastically.

This white boy is quick on his toes, Najee laughed to himself and quickly changed the subject.

"I told you the who, what, when, and where. Now tell me what's cracking with you and Domingo."

"That's classified intel."

190

"Man, stop it! You work for the ATF, not NASA. If you want me to continue putting my life on the line, I gotta know what the fuck is going on," Najee stressed. "They already suspect that there is a mole in their organization. Is Domingo the informant?"

"No, he's not," Parker promised. "We lost our guy on the inside."

"You gotta come better than that, Parker! Domingo has a federal agent on speed dial. That means he's either a CI or a suspect."

"Or he could be playing the system like you."

"What's that supposed to mean?"

"It means I know you slipped up and got Angela pregnant. Nella tapped out and told me all about it and a whole lot more." Parker could almost hear Najee's jaw hit the floor. He almost felt bad about fucking with Najee's head, but manipulation was the ugly side of the job. "I gotta give it to you, that little move you pulled with that slick attorney was genius, but I don't think Nella and Sosa fully appreciate you. At least it didn't look that way when I saw them together."

Najee clenched his fists and chewed his bottom lip.

"You know something I don't?"

"Like I told you before, I know everything you don't. Speaking of which, have you met Enrique Estrada?"

"You mean the old guy?"

"So, you have met him? How involved is he in the daily operations of the organization?"

Najee wanted to tell Parker to go fuck himself. He wasn't Alpo, he was built from concrete. Instead, he said, "Nah, dude not in the mix. He just sits around telling old war stories while feeding his pigeons' bread, but back on Sosa and Nella. When did you see them together? Are they out of custody? What chu' tryna' say?" He fired off rapid questions like an NRA cardholder at a shooting range.

"Never mind. Just keep your head in the game and be safe," Parker cautioned. "Now that Benzo Al is dead, rival crews are kidnapping Los Cinco Diablos board members. The Nogales Cartel is not the only gang who wants control of the drug tunnels." Parker hung up and followed the BMW onto the 10 Freeway.

***

The white cargo van and Mercedes sprinter van pulled up and parked behind Domingo's Tahoe truck. The back of the cargo van sagged under the weight of one hundred and fifty kilos. El Feo, Gustavo, and two heavily armed cartel operatives exited the vehicles. Najee recognized one of the gangsters from Enrique's mansion.

El Feo looked cleaner than a brick of cocaine in his all-white Valentino fit. A big silver belt buckle girded his waist, and his white alligator boots matched his cowboy hat. He was the plug. Even his white Richard Milli watch was saucy. It hit for two hundred bands, easy.

He crushed a half-smoked cigar with the pointed toe of his boot and issued orders in Spanish. One of his armed thugs tossed Domingo the keys to the cargo van. Another grabbed Angela. The Deacon moved swiftly and punched him in the throat. The goon stumbled sideways and raised his weapon. The Deacon grabbed the barrel, yanked the goon close to his chest, and headbutted him in the face. The goon dropped the chopper and reached for his broken nose. Circular drops of blood dripped on the pavement.

Domingo crept up and blindsided The Deacon with a stiff right hook to the temple. His fist landed flush with a sickening smack, dropping The Deacon.

Najee rushed Domingo and drove his shoulder into the taller, slimmer man's midsection. Domingo's back slammed into the cargo van. Before he could recover, Najee kneed him in the nuts and blazed him in the jaw with a crippling, UFC-style elbow. Domingo's glazed eyes rolled to the back of his head.

As Najee maneuvered into a fighter's stance and prepared to get off more blows, Gustavo lunged forward and struck him with two shift sidekicks, one to the back of the knees, one to the back of the head. Najee saw white light and crumbled to the gravel next to The Deacon.

"Leave my man alone!" Angela screamed and jumped on Gustavo's back. She held onto his neck and took a Mike Tyson-sized bite out of his right ear.

Gustavo grunted and slung her off his back. Angela stumbled, tripped, fell back, and landed on her ass. "¡Pinche cucarachas!" she called the Nogales Cartel members cockroaches.

El Feo let off half a clip into the air.

"Enough!" he yelled. His voice boomed like the shots from his cannon. "You three are testing my fuckin' patience!"

He was fed up with the disrespect and the antics. He would have smoked Najee, The Deacon, and Angela a long time ago and left them to rot in the desert with the cactus, but he needed Angela alive.

He had the money and resources to excavate his own tunnels, but such endeavors took years to complete, and he needed a way to move product now, today. The plan to take over the organization from his grandfather was already set in motion and having immediate access to a drug tunnel would solidify his position on the throne.

El Feo looked at the pathetic pistolero leaning against the cargo van. The gunman used a black bandana to apply pressure to his bleeding face.

"Carlito, stop acting like a pussy and pull yourself together, homes." Turning to one of his armed henchmen, he said, "Grab the chica. She's coming with me."

Najee stepped between Angela and the henchmen.

"Hold the fuck up, cuz! Touch her and I'ma break yo' fuckin' jaw!" The threat stopped him in his tracks.

El Feo piped up, "You must have me confused with somebody else, homes? This ain't no game. You're about to move over three hundred pounds of coke across the border. Anything can happen. Los Cinco Diablos might be guarding the tunnel. Hell, the tunnel might not even exist. Angela is my insurance policy to make sure you and your Jamaican friend show up with my product."

El Feo had just thrown a monkey wrench in Najee's plans. "I ain't feeling this shit, like fa' real," Najee complained. "I thought Angela was gonna lead me, The Deacon, and Domingo through the tunnel," he scrutinized El Feo's last-minute changes.

"The plan has changed. The chica stays with me," El Feo stated adamantly and shoved Angela into the back of his sprinter van. "You have Angela's map to lead you."

The Deacon caught Najee's eye and silently warned him to chill. El Feo peeped the nonverbal communication and addressed Domingo.

"Shoot them if they try anything stupid."

"My pleasure, eh!" Domingo grinned. His gun was in his left hand, the demon's fist.

"I'll meet you on the other side of the border, and I like your idea about me personally delivering the shipment to the Mara Salvatruchas," El Feo explained to Domingo while fiddling with his pinky ring. "If I show up, they'll understand how important this deal is to both organizations."

"I'm glad you took my advice," Domingo remarked. "If we can establish a distribution pipeline with the El Salvadorians, we're talkin' big paper, primo."

Najee overheard their conversation and pulled El Feo to the side before he got into the sprinter van. Boulevard had taught him that pimpin' wasn't about gunplay, it was about wordplay. If you could pimp a two-dollar ho', you could pimp a million-dollar man.

"Look, bruh," Najee began in a sincere tone while rubbing the knot on the back of his head. "I could give two fucks about how you run your business, but it's way too hot right now for you to be hands-on with that much coke. I think you should fall back and sit this one out."

"How sweet of you to be concerned about my health," El Feo fired back. "But why should I trust you?"

Trust is a word that's used often in the streets, but most of the time it's used in the past tense—*"I trusted that bitch ass nigga!"*

Najee understood the dynamics of the game and used it to sow doubt in El Feo's head.

"It's not me who you shouldn't trust," his words trailed off and his gaze wandered in Domingo's direction.

El Feo followed Najee's eyes.

"Me and Domingo go way back. What are you trying to say?"

"I'm saying he made a strange phone call on the way back from the Mexican restaurant."

"A phone call, seriously? Is that your only evidence? That's what businessmen do, make phone calls, or do you think we communicate with pigeons?"

"Hear me out. This phone call was different. Something didn't feel right, so I asked to use his phone to call my baby momma. Instead of hittin' up wifey, I secretly re-dialed the number. A white guy answered, so I hung up." He deliberately left out the part about his own relationship and conversation with the white guy.

El Feo dismissed Najee's suspicions even though he was beginning to have doubts of his own.

"Ah, that was nothin'. He was probably talking to the crazy gringo who sells guns."

"Or, he could've been talking to the Feds," Najee instigated. "There are no coincidences, only codefendants," he added, knowing that pulling the right thread could make a friendship unravel at the seams.

"What are you suggesting?"

"Like I said, I could give two fucks how you run your organization, but if it was me, I would stick to the script, follow the old man's plans, and let Domingo deal with the MS-13s while you watch from a distance."

El Feo contemplated Najee's proposal.

"I'm gonna take your advice."

"Smart man."

"But my merch better make it to the other side, every gram."

"Angela is a pro at this shit, and she'll do whatever I tell her."

"You still don't understand, homes." A blanket of evil abruptly fell upon El Feo like dense fog. His forehead wrinkled, his lips tightened, and his eyes darkened. He stepped closer to Najee and poked a finger in his chest. "Angela ain't going nowhere until I say so, and if you burn me, I'll burn you, your bitch, and the bastard she's carrying. Are we on the same page?" El Feo ordered one of his men to assist with the shipment. "Check this out, Chili. I need you to roll with Domingo and Ghost. Watch their backs and be my eyes and ears. Okay, Loco?"

They immediately mobilized. Domingo and Ghost jumped in the cargo van. Chili prepared to follow in the Chevy Tahoe.

It took all of Najee's discipline not to grab El Feo by the throat and rip his Adam's apple out. His trigger finger trembled with anger as he did a headcount. Three Nogales Cartel members against him and The Deacon. He liked those odds.

Chapter 27

Against The Grain

Sometimes a gangster must go against all odds. At other times he or she must go against the grain. Najee understood this better than anyone. He was made in the streets and had survived poverty, prison, death, and desperation. He had killed for the drip, taking his hustle cross country and stripping ballers from Hawthorne to Harlem. Now he was smuggling drugs through the deadly Tijuana Cartel territory, his most challenging mission yet.

The Tijuana Cartel, also known as the Arellano-Félix organization, is a powerful and aggressive narco conglomerate. They operate out of the border city of Tijuana, Northern Baja California, and according to the Arellano brothers, wherever the fuck they wanted. Even the sister, Enedina Arellano Félix, is a boss bitch who launders money and orchestrates the export of tons of cocaine.

One of the three original Mexican drug trafficking organizations, the Tijuana Cartel, were formed when el Federacion divided Mexico into plazas. They made national headlines when the group attempted to assassinate El Chapo at the Guadalajara Airport. The shooters missed their target and accidentally murdered Cardinal Posadas Ocampo as he rode through the airport in a vehicle similar to El Chapo's. The organization made the world news again in October 2013 when one of the seven brothers, Francisco Rafael Arellano Félix, was gunned down at a child's birthday party by an assassin disguised as a clown.

Najee kept telling himself that the streets South of the border were no different than the streets of South Central, but not even his own conscience was buying it. He was in a land of greed and lawlessness, a place where the cartel bosses and government officials made no secrets about being equally ruthless and corrupt. His game had to be tight, his intuition had to be on point because one wrong move could mean an unexpected bullet to the back of the head.

Having nothing more than moonlight, an impromptu map, and sheer determination, Najee led The Deacon and the three drug smugglers through the hillsides of Tijuana. They didn't allow him to have a weapon and made him take the lead just in case it was a setup. Keeping him out front would make it easy to put that unexpected bullet in the back of his head.

Najee had gotten them lost twice.

Domingo was beginning to think he was stalling for time. "What's crackin', homes? You got us going in circles," Domingo expressed his frustration.

Najee heard an engine and spotted a pair of headlights. "Get down, there go one-time!" he urgently warned The Deacon, Domingo, Ghost, and Chili.

They crouched low, ducking the Border Patrol agent riding an ATV along a stretch of barbed wire fence. A white GMC Suburban with green Border Patrol decals passed in the opposite direction. From his position with one knee in the dirt, Najee looked to his right and noticed the fence had been cut. The illegal immigrants had left behind empty Campbell's Soup cans, water bottles, charred wood from a campfire, and dozens of shitty diapers. Two stray dogs snarled and fought over the scraps.

Najee used the moonlight to consult Angela's map. They were close. A well-beaten trail hugged the border fence. Najee led the smugglers along the dirt path for a quarter mile until he spotted the dilapidated T-shirt factory.

"There's that joint right there," he announced, pointing a finger. "It's right where Angela said it would be."

The abandoned T-shirt factory had seen better days. Chipped green paint, broken windows, and the tall weeds surrounding the perimeter made the old building look like a dried-up booger. The parking lot was empty, except for a red Dodge Charger sitting on bricks. The whip had been stolen in San Diego, brought across the border, and stripped down for parts.

There were at least one hundred yards of open space between the border fence and the factory. Najee took off running first. The others followed. They were vulnerable and exposed as they made a mad dash and took cover on the driver's side of the Charger. Najee,

The Deacon, Domingo, Ghost, and Chili moved swiftly despite carrying 30 kilos of cocaine in their Army-style backpacks. The extra sixty-six pounds didn't slow them down.

"Shhhh, y'all hear that?" Najee asked. His spider senses began to tingle.

Everyone held their breath and listened. Other than the rustle of leaves blowing in the wind, no obvious threats lurked in the shadows. Once the coast was clear, they sprinted to the front entrance.

Domingo used a pair of bow cutters to cut the heavy chain and padlock that secured the double doors. He pushed them open and stepped inside. A cold breeze swept through the dark, damp factory. White sheets covered what was left of the silk-screening equipment, and vandals had spray-painted graffiti on the walls.

"The spot looks vacant," Domingo remarked and took another step inside, but The Deacon stretched out his arm and stopped him.

"Easy, mon. Looks can be deceiving." The Deacon shined his flashlight toward the ground.

Fresh boot prints were pressed in the thick dust that had accumulated on the floor. The Deacon kneeled down and inspected the footprints. He rubbed some of the dust between his fingers and got a sour feeling in the pit of his gut.

"Somebody beat us here," Najee said what everyone was already thinking.

The Deacon agreed, "Judging from the different sized boot prints, I'd say there's at least four of them." He noticed the direction of the initial footprints and added, "They probably broke in through the loading dock. It looks like they've been dragging equipment in that direction. That would explain the cold breeze."

Just as Domingo, Ghost, and Chili slung their choppers off their shoulders, a black van rolled up and four Mexican men wearing black mechanic overalls and tan stockings to cover their faces jumped out.

"Los Cinco Diablos!" Chili yelled. Those would be his last words.

APC ammo hit him in the chest like a fastball speeding across home plate. The force of the blast knocked him out of his shoes and hurled him back. He landed in the doorway of the building with his toes pointed toward the ceiling. The red circle on his chest was bigger than Flavor Flav's clock.

The men were not Los Cinco Diablos. They were bandidos from the deadly Tijuana Cartel. They had no idea about the potentially lucrative narco-tunnel under the old factory. The group of bandits were stealing machinery and copper out of the building when their lookout spotted five men lugging heavy backpacks. The Tijuana Cartel is notoriously known for patrolling the border looking for smugglers who attempted to use the Mexico/Tijuana corridor without paying the appropriate tax. Their orders were simple—exterminate and confiscate. Tonight, they had hit the jackpot and were more than willing to slug it out.

Everyone fired at once. The skyline lit up with yellow and white muzzle flash. The Deacon grabbed Najee by the backpack and pulled him inside the building. A painful scream followed by a low grunt came from the direction of the van. Ghost had sent one of the Tijuana Cartel members to meet his maker. Fire breathing slugs spit from Ghost's and Domingo's imposing military-style assault weapons. Windows shattered, and air hissed from the van's bullet-riddled tires.

Tech-9s are no match for the bigger, more powerful FN MK-16s, but the remaining three Tijuana Cartel bandits held their ground.

Suddenly, tragically, Ghost's head exploded. His teeth hit the dirt first followed by blood and chunks of his brains. Bullets continued to rip through his prone body.

After seeing his young protege get wet up, Domingo had tears in his eyes and murder in his heart. He charged forward yelling profanities in Spanish and blasting. Slugs zipped through the air penetrating flesh and bone. He kept blazing until bodies dropped and the barrel of his chopper was hot. Realizing his clip was empty, he scrambled and took cover by the front bumper of the Charger. His heart thumped rapidly, which meant he was still alive. Looking to the sky, he kissed his gold medallion, thanked the dope Gods, then ejected the empty clip.

Najee scooped up Chili's FN MK-16, dropped to his stomach, and pressed his right eye against the lens of the scope. He lined the last bandit's dome up with the cross marks and fired at the moving target.

"Fuck!" He miscalculated the recoil from the automatic weapon and hit the last Tijuana Cartel soldier in the shoulder instead.

The blow knocked him off balance, but the Tijuana Cartel soldier didn't retreat, and surrendering went against his oath to do or die. His bloody left arm dangled by his side. He leaned against the van for support, raised the chopper with his right arm, and let off shots in Domingo's direction. Slugs repeatedly smacked the passenger side of the Dodge Charger.

Najee clicked the switch to fully auto, recalibrated his aim, and squeezed. The weapon jerked in his grip as a flurry of merciless lead cut through the lone bandido. His head snapped to the East, his hips twisted to the west, and his condemned soul descended south into hell.

The Deacon snatched up Ghost's weapon and swung the business end in Domingo's direction. The two gangsters made eye contact. The shade was real. Neither of them blinked. Domingo stood up while struggling to shove a fresh, hundred-round magazine into the bottom of the stick. He moved frantically, and his shaking fingers fumbled the clip. Finally, he gave up and stuck his chest out proudly as if to say hit me right here in the third button of my shirt.

The Deacon looked wild and untamed with his sweaty black skin, thick dreadlocks, and savage frown.

Najee stood next to the Deacon.

"If you shoot, I'm blazing my gun, too," he pledged his unwavering loyalty. "But think about Angela and my baby before you do."

The Deacon kept his strap aimed at Domingo with callous indifference, and his eyes hardened like two granite tombstones.

"Watch cha' back!" he advised and applied an ounce of pressure on the trigger.

Three ear-splitting rounds ripped from the killing machine, striking one of the downed Tijuana Cartel bandits in the face as he eased a pistol from his hip holster and aimed it at Domingo's back.

Domingo looked over his shoulder. A dead body in black mechanic overalls lay stretched out on his back next to the front wheel of the black van. His fingers still gripped the butt of his unused pistol as if he could take it with him to the afterlife.

The Deacon could have smoked Domingo, but Angela's life hung in the balance.

"You're welcome!" he remarked through clenched teeth, lowered the smoking gun, and recited a scripture for the soul he snatched.

Domingo took one more look at the dead bandido and walked away. He had too much pride to say thank you and felt too much pain for the loss of Ghost.

"The Tijuana Cartel usually patrols their territory in teams. Grab those other backpacks and let's bounce before they roll back through," he directed as he stepped over Chili's dead body and entered the cold building.

Angela's hand-drawn layout of the building was helpful. They quickly found the hidden entrance to the drug tunnel. It was disguised as a grated drain hole. The Deacon fired up an acetylene torch. The blue flames flickered like the backfire from a SpaceX rocket. He used the hydrocarbon gas-powered flames to slice through ten rusty bolts securing the drain grate in place. Once loose, Najee lifted the heavy metal and sat the grate against the wall.

Domingo flashed his flashlight into the drain. The entrance hole was approximately thirty inches in circumference, just enough room for a grown man to fit through. Inside the drainage hole, a short ladder was bolted into the brick wall. The last rung of the ladder dropped to a metal, porch-like platform. From there, the set-up looked similar to the average house basement. A set of steep steps led down into the dark tunnel.

Najee tossed Ghost's backpack through the hole. It dropped six feet and landed on the porch-like platform with a clunk.

As he attempted to climb down the ladder, Domingo stopped him and said, "Step aside, I'll lead the way from here, homes." If he was going to be the boss, he needed to start acting like one.

"Do you!" Najee replied and took a quick glance at his watch.

"Why you keep lookin' at your watch, eh? You got something more important to do?" Domingo jeered sarcastically before climbing down the rusty ladder and landing on the metal platform.

Najee went next, he chastised himself for being too anxious. Domingo was deep in the game. Players on his level watched and questioned everything, but just as a charlatan can defraud an observant audience, Najee was positive he could deceive Domingo. He just needed to keep his head in the game and continue to root out Domingo's weaknesses without exposing his own. A stomp-down whore from Hollywood once told him that if you can induce the mind, you can seduce the soul. He thought about Candy while climbing down the rusty ladder.

Once on the platform, he immediately noticed an unusual amount of moisture in the air. The Deacon tossed him the other backpack and followed. The trio cautiously made their way down the steps and stopped at the mouth of the tunnel. The pungent odor of sewage water punched Najee in the nose like a heavyweight boxer. The Deacon shined his flashlight into the dark, smelly passageway.

The narco-tunnel was an impressive feat of human ingenuity and proof of the length's criminals will go to in order to get that paper. Hidden 15 feet beneath the T-shirt factory, the tunnel measured 6 feet tall and 2 feet wide. The clandestine tunnel stretched 1,486 yards, a little under a mile. It terminated under a horse ranch located just North of the border in San Diego. The sophisticated passageway was complete with a railway, ventilation ducts, and a plumbing system for underground runoff.

There was only one problem, a major problem. The construction of the tunnel was shoddy. Los Cinco Diablos had killed off all of their skilled contractors, and the horror stories quickly spread throughout the Hispanic engineering community. Simultaneously, the U.S. Customs and Border Protection had started the CBP Tunnel

Task Force, a special operations unit aimed at eradicating transnational drug trafficking outfits. Los Cinco Diablos was quickly losing drug smuggling tunnels and lacked the skilled personnel to construct more. Becoming desperate to keep the dope game in a headlock, they were forced to use inexperienced laborers out of Guatemala to complete the Tijuana project.

Domingo ducked and stepped into the tunnel first. His feet quickly became submerged in a foot of standing sewage water. His shoes and socks were soaking wet, and some of the greasy black sludge splashed into his mouth. Najee and the Deacon snickered while rolling up their pants legs. Domingo was trying too hard to be the head honcho and lead the way.

"What's so funny, eh?" Domingo challenged while wiping the slime off his face. "Laugh now, cry later," he sneered and moved deeper into the passageway, splashing murky water with each clumsy step.

Najee carefully made his way into the mouth of the tunnel. Construction material, hard hats, and dead rats bobbed on the surface of the water. His flashlight bounced off the walls. The network of thick cracks traveling along the ceiling troubled him. As they trekked deeper into the tunnel, it became increasingly apparent why Los Cinco Diablos had abandoned the project. The tunnel was a hazard. The further they traveled, the more dangerous the journey became. The plumbing and ventilation systems were obviously inoperative. Oxygen levels rapidly decreased, causing their lungs to constrict, and the backpacks felt heavier. Domingo paused to catch his breath, and Najee used the opportunity to adjust the extra load of kilos.

The Deacon squeezed past both of them and hit Najee with a dire warning.

"Keep it movin', Soulja Boi. These walls could cave in at any moment and trap us."

Keeping this in mind, Najee slung the extra backpack over his right shoulder and brushed past Domingo.

"Ay, what chu' doing, ese? I told you I got this," Domingo protested and retook the lead.

It was the reaction Najee was hoping for. Ignorance destroyed Troy, and arrogance caused the demise of the Roman Empire.

Eight hundred feet within the condemned tunnel, the water subsided, but the air got thicker, and the integrity of the structure became more questionable with each step.

They came to a fork at the end of the tunnel. The passageway split into separate directions—one outlet going East, the other branching off to the West.

"Ay, yo, which way do we go, homes?" Domingo shined his flashlight in both directions. Standing water flooded the passageway to the West.

Najee passed Domingo the map.

"You tell me, Mr. Big Shot."

Domingo grumbled in Spanish under his breath, snatched the map out of Najee's hands, and shined light on Angela's drawing.

"It says we take a right." Going to the East was cool with him. He hated wading through smelly water. "!Vamonos, let's roll! The Tijuana Cartel probably found their dead men by now."

The passageway to the East stretched the length of two football fields. A concrete wall marked the dead end. Najee aimed his flashlight upward toward the steel hatch built into the ceiling of the tunnel. The steel hatch looked like the wheel on a large bank vault. Domingo reached up and turned the wheel counterclockwise. A waterproof seal released with a hiss. Najee shined his flashlight through the hole, illuminating the large wooden beams that supported the roof of a barn. The distinctive smell of hay and horse manure saturated the air. They were under the stables of Alvarez Horse Ranch.

The opening was smaller than the original manhole they climbed into on the Tijuana side of the border. Domingo sized up the opening and realized it would be impossible to squeeze through with his weapon and the backpack. He had planned on shooting Najee and The Deacon in the back once they arrived at the U.S. exit, but the hatch on the ceiling put a twist in his plot. He needed someone to give him a lift and pass him the cocaine. Reluctantly, he took off the backpack but kept a tight grip on his gun.

Despite the minor setback, a million schemes traversed through his mind, and he could barely contain his excitement. He finally had access to his very own drug tunnel. Now all he had to do was dispose of Najee and his Jamaican goon and give the Mara Salvatruchas the hundred and fifty kilos in exchange for killing El Feo.

El Feo thought he was opening up a new distribution channel with the ruthless El Salvadorians, but Domingo had already set up a deal of his own. He was glad it was dark in the tunnel. The darkness hid his grin.

"I don't see a ladder," Najee pointed out. "How the fuck we gon' get outta this bitch?" He concealed a grin of his own.

"Give me a boost," Domingo requested, strapping his assault rifle over his shoulder. "I'm gonna go up first and check it out."

The Deacon was hesitant. He knew Najee had something clever up his sleeve, but he felt Najee was taking too damn long to execute his plan. They had passed up several opportunities to murk Domingo, take the dope, and blame the hit on the Tijuana Cartel. The Deacon wanted to make a move now, right now—before Domingo realized he was getting played and turned the tables and his gun on them.

Najee could almost hear The Deacon thinking out loud. He knew the big homie was ready to murk something. The nerves in his own trigger finger twitched as well, but he couldn't end it all by throwing a grenade. In order for them to make it out alive and save Angela at the same time, he needed to execute his end game with the precision of a sharpshooter.

Turning to The Deacon, Najee gave the head nod.

"Give him a boost, cuz."

"Fuck him, you give this bum blood clot a boost," The Deacon refused.

Domingo snapped his fingers.

"¡Ràpido, homes! We don't have all day," he barked.

"Awww, hell nawl! Did he just snap his fingers at us?" Najee asked.

"Not us—you," The Deacon corrected with rare laughter in his voice.

Domingo smacked his lips. He didn't like being toyed with.

Najee took one for the team and gave Domingo a lift through the narrow opening. Domingo climbed through, crouched low, and listened. There were eight empty horse stalls in the stable and no other signs of life. Like the T-shirt factory, the ranch had been abandoned.

Domingo couldn't hide his enthusiasm. Angela had come through after all. He kissed his Malverde medallion, stretched out on his stomach, and looked down through the manhole.

"It's all good. Pass me the backpacks."

Najee laughed at him and asked, "Do you know the difference between a pimp and a magician?"

Domingo's face was shrouded by confusion.

"What the fuck, homes, are we playin' twenty-one questions? Hand me the fuckin' backpacks, now!"

"There are no differences. They both deal with tricks, and manipulation is their favorite tool."

The Deacon tried to slam the hatch, but Domingo stuck the barrel of his gun through the hole. Gritting his teeth, Domingo fired off wild rounds into the tunnel.

"Watch out, cuz!" Najee screamed. Slugs ricocheted off the concrete floor.

The Deacon reached up, grabbed the warm shaft of the gun, and yanked it out of Domingo's hands. It crashed on the ground with a clink-clank. Najee moved into position and aimed the heat at Domingo's cranium.

"Fall back or get smoked, bitch!"

Domingo's face sagged with the weight of defeat. He vowed to make Najee suffer.

"This ain't over, mayate," Domingo warned. "We still have your chica, and I'm gonna fuck her in the ass before I slit her throat!"

The Deacon slammed the hatch and turned the wheel clockwise to lock it.

"Big respect, mon'! That move was *irie*." He gave Najee a fist pound. "He's right, though. They still have Angela. What's the next move?"

Najee unzipped Domingo's backpack and quickly split the kilos two ways, giving The Deacon fifteen bricks.

"The next move is to get the fuck outta here and show El Feo why they call us the Body Snatchers."

"What about Domingo? If we take the yayo, the Fed's gotta cut him loose. I don't like leaving loose ends."

"Trust me, bruh, Domingo is dun-dada. I did it this way so that our hands stay clean, and our names don't get muddy. After this fuck up, his own people are gonna take him out."

They filled their backpacks with the dope and sprinted West to the other tunnel. Angela had warned Najee not to make a right turn when they hit the dead end.

"Make sure you go left, not right," Najee recalled Angela's warning. *"The Guatemalans fucked up and started digging in the wrong direction. It took those pendejos a month before they realized their mistake. The true exit is to the left,"* she explained. It was the twist Najee needed.

Najee and The Deacon hiked the length of a city block before the tunnel terminated under a beef jerky plant on Otay Center Drive in San Diego. Detective Brooks had Najee's Dodge Challenger waiting in the parking lot. The door was unlocked. The keys and a cell phone were hidden under the floor mat. They tossed the backpacks in the trunk, and Najee took the wheel. He mashed out of the parking lot, making the 24" Toyo tires burn rubber on the pavement. They hit Interstate 5 just as Parker and his team crashed the front door of the ranch. Within minutes, the spot was crawling with the Feds.

Chapter 28

Profits Over People

Gustavo ran up the hill, hopped in the whip, and passed El Feo a pair of night vision binoculars.

"Let's go, Jefe! The spot is crawling with policía!" he announced out of breath.

They were on the U.S. side of the border parked on Mesa Hill, a narrow dirt road overlooking the horse ranch. Government vehicles swarmed the property like red army ants. ATF agents in unmarked Chevy Malibu sedans, DEA agents in blacked-out SUVs, and ICE personnel in white vans surrounded the ranch.

The DEA pushed to take over and become the agency on record, but the ATF put up a vehement protest. The case was a culmination of months of sacrifice, undercover work, and intense investigation, Senior Administrator, Douglas Schwartz argued. The only thing the ATF brass didn't mention was the press conference that had already been scheduled.

When the desk-dwelling pencil pushers heard about the raid on a mile-long narco-tunnel, they envisioned a long table with a buffet of automatic weapons, stacks of money, bricks of cocaine, and the opportunity to have their faces on the front page of the Sunday newspaper.

When asked why the ATF should lead the troops to execute a transcontinental drug trafficking warrant, Parker and Torres argued that wherever there were cartel narcotics, there were also guns and explosives. The Department of Justice agreed.

An ATF tactical unit wearing Kevlar vests and military helmets received the privilege of crashing the front door. The squadron leader tossed two flashbang grenades into the entranceway. The grenades exploded with deafening noise and bright lights. The tactical unit advanced forward in a close-quarters combat column, which is a single file line meant to reduce casualties in case they took fire. They cautiously worked their way through the main house, moving in unison like synchronized swimmers packing AR-15s. Red beams crisscrossed, searching in the darkness for an armed target like a game of laser tag.

El Feo lounged in the back of his coke-white Rolls Royce Cullinan and watched the raid go down. Cigar smoke overpowered the SUVs' new car smell. He tilted his head back and guzzled Patron straight from the bottle. The tequila went down smooth and warm.

"The mayate was right," he begrudgingly admitted with a slurred voice. The Patron had him tipsy. "I'm glad I didn't meet Domingo at the ranch. That could be me in handcuffs," he commented while looking through the binoculars with bloodshot red eyes.

He watched two agents wearing blue jackets with ATF in big yellow letters escort Domingo out of the horse stables. Domingo held his head down in defeat, and his hands were shackled uncomfortably behind his back. They shoved him into the back of one of the unmarked Chevy Malibu sedans and peeled out.

El Feo waited to see if the Feds brought out any more bodies, but Domingo appeared to be the only suspect arrested. After enough time had lapsed to allow each agency the opportunity to pad the books with overtime, half the fleet of government vehicles dispersed and allowed the CPB Tunnel Task Force in to do their thing. There was nothing more to see. El Feo took a long chug of Patron and gave Gustavo the green light to roll out.

"¿Adónde vamos?" Gustavo asked.

"Take me to mi casa," El Feo requested.

Gustavo cranked the engine and hit I-5 headed to El Feo's downtown Los Angeles penthouse. Even at this late hour, traffic on the freeway was buzzing with partygoers returning from Tijuana and sailors from the nearby Navy base.

Gustavo looked in the rearview mirror and asked, "Our people sent word about Ghost and Chili getting dropped by the Tijuana Cartel, but what do you think happened to Najee and his amigo?"

As El Feo contemplated an answer, his Sat phone rang. Not many people had the number to his private line.

"Who the fuck is this?" He skipped the pleasantries and got right on business.

"Yo, what's up, this is Najee! I got your product. Where do you want to meet?"

El Feo sat up straight and told Gustavo to turn down the music.

"Are you saying you and The Deacon escaped with all the coca?"

"Nah, I'm only sitting on one hundred bricks."

"What happened to the other fifty?" he asked between sips of Tequila, loving the way the liquor warmed his gut.

"Domingo didn't run fast enough and got knocked," he lied without batting an eyelash.

Najee was deep undercover, but he was far from a Jay Reed. He detested snitches and believed in putting his enemies in the grave, not prison. His plan from the get-go was to save Nella by playing the Feds, rescue Angela by running game on El Feo, and hopefully put some spinach in his pockets in the process. So far, so good, but he couldn't forget that he was going up against cunning individuals who were just as ruthless and clever.

"Shit, that means they caught him dirty with a lot of weight!" El Feo punched the back of the headrest, then quickly calmed down. "You were right about the Feds. How did you know they were going to raid the spot?" El Feo asked suspiciously.

"Keep it one-hundred at all times with me, bruh. You can't tell me you haven't felt Domingo's vibe. I've only known him for five minutes, and I can tell that nigga is shiesty. Ol' boy wants to be a boss, and you're standing in his way," Najee preached.

El Feo massaged the back of his neck and analyzed the complications of the game. He despised Domingo's disloyalty, yet he was on the same page. He wanted absolute power, and that desire tugged at him like an addictive drug. He had to have it injected into his veins and planned on doing so by any means necessary, including betrayal.

"Okay, homes, you did good. Muy bien," El Feo praised. "Don't worry about Domingo. I'll have my lawyer check on him in the morning."

Najee twisted his face up.

"Man, fuck Domingo! I ain't worried about him. I'm worried about Angela! Where is she?"

"She's close," El Feo confirmed.

"Look, bruh, cut the bullshit. I'm wet. I'm tired. I've been to Nogales. I've been to Juárez. I've been robbed. I've been shot at. I've done everything you asked me to do. Now it's time to swap it out and go our separate ways."

"I'm afraid it's not that simple, ese."

"Why not? I came through on my end, and Angela gave up the location of a Los Cinco Diablos drug tunnel. The way I look at it, we even."

"The tunnel has been compromised. It's no longer useful to me or my organization."

"That's not my problem."

"I'm afraid it is," El Feo disagreed.

Najee's anger swelled.

"Dig this, El Fake-O, or whatever the fuck yo' name is. I don't give a mad fuck how connected you are. You can pull up and get it! Now, let Angela go, or I'ma —"

"Or you're gonna what?"

The line went silent except for the sound of the two gangsters breathing fire.

"I thought so," El Feo taunted. "You're gonna do exactly as I say, or I'm gonna let my young wolves run a train on your nigger loving bitch. Then I'm gonna make her drink gasoline before I shove a book of matches down her throat, ¿comprende, ese?"

El Feo had once again changed the game in the bottom of the ninth inning.

Najee resented being strong-armed, but he had no choice but to comply.

"So, what's crackin'? What do you want me to do now?"

"I want you to take out Señor Enrique Estrada. I will call you with the details mañana." The words tasted sour leaving his lips. He hung up the phone still not believing it was his own voice putting a green light on his grandfather.

He didn't want to do the hit himself. He feared Enrique too much to look into his eyes and pull the trigger, and he respected him too much to put a bullet in his back. Besides, doing the hit himself would cause divisions within his organization, and using a sicario from another cartel would intensify any current beefs. Wars cost money and lives. El Feo couldn't afford to lose either.

In order to take the throne and gain the support of the board members, he needed an outsider to do the job. Someone efficient. Someone who wasn't plugged with any of the other cartels. Someone easy to frame. Najee was the perfect man for the job. He was El Feo's Lee Harvey Oswald.

El Feo caught Gustavo watching him in the rearview and felt it was necessary to offer an explanation.

"It's my time, primo! May God forgive me, but this is my destiny."

Gustavo remarked, "I could be wrong, but it seems like Najee has been keeping it one-hundred. If he does this last move for you. What's gonna happen to his chica?"

El Feo looked to his left. Angela laid bound and gagged across the leather bench seats in nothing but her bra and panties. She was beautiful, so he hadn't touched her face, but her body was a different story. Purple bruises and red cuts tarnished her beauty. Her perfect imperfections reminded him of a portrait he once saw in a Catholic church. It depicted an angel with burnt wings falling from heaven.

El Feo took a puff off his half-smoked cigar, causing the ashes on the tip to glow fire-orange. Locking eyes with Gustavo in the rearview mirror, his answer came in the form of a demented smile as he dug the hot tip of the cigar into Angela's ass cheek. He could hear her skin sizzle.

"Aaahhhh!" she yelled, but the gag in her mouth muffled her pain. She screamed louder the second time the cigar burned a circle mark into her exposed skin. By the third time, the fire had extinguished, but that didn't deter El Feo.

He pushed in the cigarette lighter, and Angela's eyes widened in terror. Her body trembled in fear when she heard it pop out. El Feo showed her the fire-orange ring, snatched her panties down, and pried her legs open. Angela twisted and fought. El Feo grinned and laughed. Shoving the cigarette lighter between her legs, he pressed the hot end against her clitoris and burned her most intimate body part. This time Angela didn't scream, she had already fainted.

Gustavo's lips tightened, and he gripped the steering wheel tightly. *El Feo is a sick monster,* he thought as he swerved across lanes and picked up speed.

***

Parker rolled into L.A. and kept rolling past the Los Angeles ATF Field Division headquarters. Skyscrapers with glistening glass windows morphed into nondescript office buildings. The office buildings surrendered to small, single-family homes with black bars bolted to the doors and windows.

Domingo didn't like the vibe.

"Ay, where we going, officer? We passed the police station!"

"Shut the fuck up and enjoy the ride!" Parker retorted.

The voice sounded vaguely familiar.

"Sammy from the Mongols motorcycle gang, is that you, homes?"

"Sure is, dog! So much for the disguise." Parker and Torres pulled off the hot ski masks and tossed them into the back seat.

"On what?" Domingo asked in disbelief. "I knew you smelled like a pig."

Torres leaned over and sniffed Parker.

"You smell more like cigarettes and white trash to me!" he joked at Domingo's expense.

"Where the fuck are you rats taking me?"

Torres blew a big bubble with his gum and let it pop.

"The devil has been fluffing your pillow, homeboy. We're taking you to hell."

Parker crossed Slauson Ave and passed Tam's Burger on Figueroa, where early in his career he took down a crew of Five-Nine Hoovers Crips who were plotting to bomb a dope house belonging to their rivals, the Six-Five Menlo Crips.

A quick turn put them on Broadway headed into the heart of the gutter. The maroon-colored Chevy Malibu looked obviously out of place. They drove by trash-littered lawns and wet laundry hanging on clotheslines and lookout boys on the corner packing oversized guns concealed beneath oversized black T-shirts. Crack whores strolled looking for a trick, and heroin addicts staggered looking for a fix. They glared at the Chevy Malibu as if the occupants were the ones doing something illegal and not them.

Parker pulled up to a home surrounded by a chain-link fence and flashed the high beams on and off. A muscular black man in a blue Dickies suit and a shiny bald head mobbed out of the house swinging his left arm and grabbing his nuts with the right. He looked like a cross between Ving Rhames and King Kong. He glanced up and down the block before unlocking the gate and waving the government vehicle through. Parker killed the headlights and pulled all the way to the back.

The muscular black man had neck tatts and a long scar that ran from his left eye, across his nose, and ended on his right cheek. The story of how he received the scar varied. In some variations of the story, he got slashed in a prison riot. In other scenarios, he got cracked with a champagne bottle during a bar brawl. Both versions of the tale were fictitious. Either way, the scar was an asset that helped advance his career. Like Parker and Torres, he was an undercover ATF agent.

"What's up, Tank?" Parker greeted with a pound on the fist.

"What it do?" Tank replied but purposely ignored Torres. He disliked Torres and didn't trust him.

Under the cloak of darkness, they dragged Domingo through the back door and shoved him on the kitchen floor. They were in an ATF crash pad. Most law enforcement teams have one. They are off the books; clandestine stash houses where bad things happen to bad people. Tank sat at the kitchen table, cracked open a bottle of MGD beer, and let Torres and Parker do their thing. He was the cleaner and would thoroughly get rid of any evidence of their crimes, including making Domingo disappear if need be.

Torres grabbed a fist full of Domingo's hair and snatched his head back.

"Domingo Rojas, we got a few questions for you, and we ain't fuckin' around. Comprendo vato loco?" He intentionally sounded like a ridiculous redneck.

Domingo hocked slimy spit in Torres' face.

"Fuck you, puto, I want a lawyer."

Torres lunged forward and kicked Domingo in the rib cage. Domingo fell sideways and winced in pain.

"You want a lawyer?" Torres asked. "Look around, asshole, where do you think you're at?"

As if on cue, a roach crawled across the wall, a pitbull barked, and the ghetto bird rumbled through the sky.

Domingo's hands were restricted behind his back, and the cuffs squeezed his wrists like an angry python. Parker sat him up straight so that his back leaned against the cabinets under the sink.

"Listen, Domingo," he spoke calmly. "We received intel that Enrique Estrada is the real mastermind behind the uncut Fentanyl flowing into the United States. Is this true?"

"I only got one thing to say—lawyer!"

Parker kept applying pressure.

"Is the Fentanyl being processed in Wuhan, China, or does the Nogales Cartel have their own manufacturing facility?"

"Lawyer!" Domingo's voice grew louder.

"You're looking at a lot of time, Mr. Rojas."

"Lawyer!"

"The Federal sentencing guidelines operate off a point system. Your base offense level is already through the roof, and you're also facing a four-level increase for knowingly misrepresenting substances that contain Fentanyl," Parker broke it down. "I suggest you wise up, pal, and consider being a witness versus being a suspect. If you haven't noticed, you're the low man on the totem pole. El Padrino and El Feo don't give a shit about you," Parker picked at Domingo's ego like it was a dry scab. "Why should the man who makes the least money do the most time?"

Domingo resented Parker for diminishing his importance. "You don't have nothing on me. I'm clean, so suck my muthafuckin' dick gringo!"

"Wow, I didn't know you were on the down-low. Thanks, but no thank you, I ain't a homo, I'm happily married."

"That's good to know, ese because your wife is gonna come up missing if you don't let me go!"

Parker's anger boiled over like a pot of hot grits.

"What did you say about my wife, you piece of shit?"

He grabbed Domingo by the shirt collar and slammed him head-first into the oven door. The crown of his head left a deep impression. Parker took off his jacket, rolled up his sleeves, and flicked the garbage disposal switch.

"Game time is over. Uncuff this motherfucker and hold him while I feed his fingers to the sewer."

Tank seemed to enjoy getting tagged in. He snatched Domingo off the floor, spun him around, and kicked his legs apart.

"You can't do this!" Domingo protested as Tank uncuffed his left hand. "I know my rights!"

"Oh, we got us one of them smart wetbacks," Torres instigated and muffed the side of Domingo's face as his phone rang. Irritated by the interruption, he glanced at the caller I.D. The call was from headquarters.

"Tank, watch this asshole. I gotta take this," he instructed and walked into the living room.

Parker got in Domingo's grill.

"You know your rights, huh? What are they?" he asked in a facetious tone. He enjoyed toying with Domingo's head.

"I have the right to remain silent."

"And?" Parker put his right foot on a kitchen chair, raised his pants leg, and pulled a throwaway 9mm from his ankle holster. Every cop who has ever found himself knee-deep in the shit keeps one just in case.

Domingo kept his eyes on the heater.

"I have—I have the right to an attorney," he said, but with less confidence.

"Go on, I'm listening." Parker jerked the slide back and chambered a lead demon. This was one of those *just-in-case* moments.

He pressed the barrel against the nape of the drug dealer's neck. He couldn't tell whether Domingo was shaking from fear or trembling in anger.

"I'm not playing any more games with you," Parker threatened. He had that wild, crazy white boy look in his eyes. "You're going to tell me who's putting Fentanyl on my streets. Then you're gonna tell me about Enrique Estrada. You got that, chico?"

Torres rushed back into the kitchen and whispered in Parker's ear, "We got a problem!"

"You're fuckin' right we got a problem. Overdose deaths have damn near doubled because the drug dealing scum bags are placing profits over people," Parker ranted.

Torres tugged on Parker's shoulder and whispered, "No, bro, we got a problem with the arrest. They didn't find any drugs."

"Are you shittin' me? Did they check everywhere?"

"C'mon, man, you saw how many agents were there. They tossed the place and didn't find a flake of coke, a weed seed, or an aspirin."

"What about guns? We heard gunshots when we pulled up. Did they recover any weapons?"

Torres shook his head.

"I'm afraid not. Just a few expended shells."

"Let me guess, the shells were from an MK-16?"

"You guessed right!" Torres confirmed.

"Well, let's hold him for killing Big Bill, the gun dealer," Parker offered.

"No way, Jose. We don't have any hard proof that he was even in Las Vegas. You're the only one who got a close look at him, so it'll be your word against his. On top of that, Domingo has a valid visa. He's in the country legally, so we can't even put an immigration hold on him," Torres reported and delivered more bad news. "Schwartz is pissed. We're off the case. He wants to see us in his office first thing in the morning. I won't be there, it's time to move on."

"Fuck!" Parker realized that Najee had played him again.

Domingo overheard the conversation and grinned. The shocked look on Parker's face renewed his cockiness.

"Like I told you, I'm clean, ese. You don't have shit on me," he bragged confidently.

"Shut the fuck up!" Parked grumbled, and smacked Domingo across the temple with a throw-away thumper. He needed a cigarette and a stiff shot of whiskey. It was time to get even with Najee, and he knew just how to do it.

Larry D. Wright

Chapter 29

Hell Hath No Fury

Hell hath no fury like a woman scorned. Nella was determined to get even with Najee, even if it meant sleeping with another man. After bossin' Sosa off in his SUV, they drove to his condo overlooking Santa Monica beach. Nella took a hot shower in the marbled, tiled bathroom connected to the spacious master bedroom and called Detective Brook's to check on her son. His wife, Victoria was very cordial and talkative. She said Lil' Najee was a bundle of joy, and she'd have him dressed, burped, and ready to go when Nella picked him up in the morning.

Detective Brooks, however, seemed unusually cold and distant. Nella wondered why he was being so evasive. She even had to coax him into telling her that Najee and The Deacon were on their way back from Mexico. She was happy and relieved to hear that Najee was okay, yet a jolt of jealousy surged through her arteries. She felt he chose Angela over her.

"Alexa, play He Loves Me," Sosa's voice yanked Nella out of her somber thoughts. The sultry vocals of Jill Scott dripped from the speakers. Sosa handed Nella a glass of Merlot and asked, "How do you like my art collection?"

Nella downed the wine in a single swallow. The Merlot knocked the sharp edges off her nerves, still, second thoughts crept into her conscience. She held out her wine glass for a refill and took in the large art canvases. She hadn't noticed them before. Her mind was too preoccupied. The color and symmetry of the paintings were amazing.

"I'm feeling the vibe. You have excellent artistic taste," Nella complemented. "What's the story behind this one?" A manicured fingernail pointed to a piece mounted on the wall above his headboard.

"That comes from the Dominican Republic. It's an abstract portrait of Saint Jude, the patron of lost causes," Sosa answered and blazed a thick blunt. He inhaled, allowed his lungs to become acquainted with the pharmaceutical hybrid weed, and offered Nella a hit.

She declined the bud, sat on the edge of the bed, and slipped on her Balenciaga running shoes.

"Do you consider yourself a lost cause?" she wanted to know.

She had gotten fully dressed, and Sosa saw another opportunity to make love to Nella slipping away. He had to do something or say something quick. He chose to revoke his own player card and sprinkle salt.

"No, I'm not a lost cause, but ya' boy Najee is. He flipped on us and is working with them, peoples." He didn't simply shake the salt shaker, he sprinkled Mrs. Dash, Cajun seasoning, and a pinch of black pepper for good measure.

Nella cringed. If she hadn't heard the audio with her own ears, she would have checked Sosa for slinging mud on Najee's name. She laced up her kicks and stood up.

Sosa hugged her from behind.

"Where you going, shawty?" he asked, pulling her close and kissing her neck.

Nella smelled Sosa's cologne and felt his hard penis pressing against her spine. She couldn't believe that one man was packing all that dick. Her nipples stiffened and the familiar tingle in her panties made her stand bowlegged. It was definitely time to bounce before she did something else that she would regret.

Sosa picked up on the signals and counteracted, "I know you ain't still thinking about ol' boy? How many times are you gonna let him shit on you and get away with it? He doesn't deserve you!" He continued to throw salt.

Nella expelled a deep sigh.

"He's not perfect, but who is?" She defended Najee.

Sosa spun Nella around to face him.

"I'm not perfect either, but I'm the perfect man for you." His smooth lines made Nella blush like a teenager at senior prom. Her smile encouraged Sosa to keep cakin' for the panties. "But it ain't even about me. It's about that nigga. Buddy is a rat, and we both know it."

Nella looked everywhere except into Sosa's eyes. Her gaze landed on the abstract portrait of Saint Jude. Was Najee a lost cause? She wasn't sure, but now that she had time to analyze the situation, she knew in her heart he wasn't a snitch.

"All we know is that the police are some crooked bitches. I jumped to the wrong conclusion earlier. I won't believe anything the Feds say about Najee until he takes the stand on somebody."

"Just pray that somebody ain't you?"

"Najee would never—"

"Shhhh!" He cut her words off with a kiss then another one. "Look around you. He's not here, so let's stop talkin' 'bout him and start talkin' 'bout us."

There's a reason the serpent approached Eve and not Adam. Men think rationally, and women think with their emotions. The nurturer gene in the female species makes them better human beings, however, this flaw in their DNA also makes them easier to deceive. Nella succumbed to Sosa's soft kisses and went with the flow.

Sosa pushed her onto his bed and clumsily undressed her. He got stuck trying to take off her bra and Nella had to help him. Smiling patiently, she reached behind her back and unfastened the three hooks. Her big titties flopped free, and Sosa attacked her left nipple with too much force and too much spit. He neglected her right breasts and awkwardly kissed his way to her stomach and down to her wet stash box. He paused to admire her monkey. It was pretty, shaved, and as phat as a Big Mac. He held her lips open with two fingers, dipped his head between her sexy legs, and literally tried to eat her pussy.

"Ouch! No, boy, don't bite my clit!" Nella rose to her elbows and looked down at Sosa between her open legs. "Stick out your tongue, make it stiff, and lick from side to side real fast but real soft and gentle," she instructed.

Sosa did as instructed but just as he found his rhythm and Nella found her groove, he abandoned his efforts, rolled a Magnum over his dick, and nudged Nella's sexy thighs further apart. He climbed between her legs holding his long cock in both hands. It looked like he was approaching her with a double-barrel shotgun.

Nella said, "Ooohhh, wee, hold up. That shit is too big!" She estimated he was at least eleven inches and thicker than her wrist.

"If you scared go to church," Sosa teased while stroking his dick with both hands. It appeared as though he was cocking a shell into a shotgun.

"Let me get on top so I can control it," Nella suggested.

She straddled Sosa with a knee on each side of his hips, then reached between her legs, held his long dick, and rubbed it against her wet slit, lubricating the wide head with her sweet juices.

She slowly—very slowly lowered herself down on his stiff pole, and her eyes rolled into the back of her head. She sank inch by inch, his thick manhood stretching her tight pussy walls until she rose up again, leaving only the throbbing head in her hot opening. She caught her breath and lowered herself on his dick again, this time taking an additional inch before surrendering and rising up again. She was testing the limits of her vagina, experimenting to see how much meat her velvet tunnel could handle.

Sosa bit his bottom lip and watched Nella do her thing. Her features were twisted into a sexy fuck face, and the brown nipples on her big, bouncing titties looked sweeter than two Hershey Kisses. She slid down another inch and flexed her pussy muscles, enveloping Sosa's stiff erection in some of the hottest, wettest coochie he'd ever had.

Nella felt full and loved the way his girth stretched her pussy to capacity. He was not only long, he was thick. She was only able to take half of his eleven-inch sausage. That was cool with her. She enjoyed riding his dick nice and slow. She felt an intense orgasm building like a wave rolling toward the shore, but Sosa was growing impatient.

He had been waiting on this moment since the first time he saw Nella at Club iCandy. He still remembered how phat her monkey looked in a pair of white leather, booty shorts, and knee-high white Ferragamo boots that made her thick thighs look like two vanilla ice cream cones. From that night forward, every time she was near him, his testicles ached with desire.

Now that he had her in his bed, he was determined to punish that pussy and make it his. Arching his hips off the bed, he lunged up and drove the remaining inches of his huge dick into Nella's snug hole. His thighs smacked against her ass cheeks and his big, swinging balls slapped against her cunt. She moaned and tried to run from the dick, but Sosa pulled her to him so that her breasts were smashed against his chest. He palmed her soft, round booty and pumped in and out of her pussy hard and fast.

"No, no—go slow!" Nella moaned.

Sosa didn't hear her protest, nor did he care. He was too deep in the pussy and too far gone. Keeping a hand gripped on each ass cheek, he pulled Nella down on his dick as he simultaneously shoved his hips up. Thick, white cream accumulated around the base of his dick as he stroked balls deep in and out of her guts repeatedly and relentlessly. The portrait above his headboard shook and threatened to fall off the wall.

Sosa maneuvered Nella onto her back. She was physically present, but her mind had moon walked out of the room. Her thoughts drifted to another place. She felt as though she was lost and trying to find her way through dense fog. She had been Najee's ride or die chick for years, risking her life, jeopardizing her freedom, and blazing her gun all in the name of the streets. She had been kidnapped by Prince, raped by a member of Los Cinco Diablos, and imprisoned all in the name of the game. For better or worse she held it down and remained by Najee's side all in the name of love.

As Sosa put her thick, redbone legs over his shoulders and beat it up like he was performing for an audience, she tried to convince herself that she wasn't doing anything Najee hadn't already done. After all, he had slept with the enemy, even gotten another bitch pregnant.

At least I'm making Sosa wear a condom, she rationalized, but her self-righteous justifications were not enough to appease her conscience. *If I'm not doing anything wrong, why do I feel so dirty and ashamed? It's just sex, right?*

Guilt and regret ate holes in her heart like battery acid as Sosa flipped her over and pounded her out doggy style. All she could think about was betraying Najee. She was about to tell Sosa to stop, she was sorry and had to go, but he suddenly slowed his stroke, and his long dick hit a zone deep in her pussy, a spot she never knew existed. It was a sweet spot no man had ever touched. Her clitoris twitched, and her pussy became juicy.

"Ohhh, yes, stay right there!" She lowered her head on the pillow and arched her back, putting her booty in the air and her pussy at the perfect angle for deep penetration. That elusive orgasm began rolling toward the shore again.

She pushed Najee out of her mind and pushed back on Sosa's iron rod to meet each of his long strokes. This was just sex. She was simply getting even with her nigga for doing her greasy, she convinced herself and began enjoying the moment.

Sosa ruined the mood and started asking dumb ass questions.

"Whose pussy is this?" he demanded and smacked her booty.

"Ouch!" Nella yelled.

Sosa mistook her displeasure for pleasure and quickened his pace. Pinning Nella face-down, ass up, he held her waist and pounded her pussy from the back while spanking her ass.

Swack!

"Who this pussy belong to?"

Swack!

"What's my name?"

Swack!

"Who's your daddy?"

Seriously, do you really want to know who my daddy is? Nella rolled her eyes and didn't answer any of his questions.

Sosa was a sweet man outside of the bedroom, but his sex game was whack and lacked swag, which really surprised her. She thought that with his big dick and all the women hanging on his line, he would be Casanova between the sheets. She failed to realize that he never had a real relationship. All his sexual encounters thus far were void of true intimacy. He was used to one-nightstands with groupies and weekend escapades with gold diggers, and the reason he undressed her so clumsily was because the strippers he was used to fucking were already half-naked.

Asking Nella who her pussy belonged to, made her think of Najee and the way he made love to her. Najee used his dick like a pool stick, hitting her with slow in and out strokes like he was lining up a shot, and then bam, he hits it hard—8 ball in the corner pocket.

"Ohhhh, yes, Najee. Hit it good, big papa!" Nella thought of Najee and her pussy clinched Sosa's dick.

Nella's moans and her tight, pink pussy drove Sosa over the edge. He was so far off the cliff he didn't hear Nella call him another man's name.

Ignoring the wounds he received from getting shanked while at the federal detention center and unable to hold off any longer, he held Nella by the shoulders, thrust balls deep into her swollen cunt one last time, and groaned. Cum shot out of his throbbing penis like a cannonball and filled the Magnum condom. He collapsed on her back sweaty, exhausted, and completely satisfied.

Nella stayed on her stomach and fought back her tears. Sosa's twitching cock still buried in the depths of her vagina was a constant reminder of her betrayal. She had cheated on the man she loved, and the dick wasn't even good.

She wondered how she could ever face Najee again without him discovering her infidelity. Would he be able to hear the disloyalty in her voice? Would he be able to tell by her walk that she had given another man what belonged to him? Would her pussy feel different? Her mind was a confused mass of intertwined thoughts, and her heart was twisted like two pretzels entangled in a kamasutra position.

She didn't realize Sosa had left the room until she heard his voice coming from the shower.

"You straight, shawty?"

Nella scooped up her clothes. She had to get out of there. "Yeah, I'm good!" she answered, pulling her shirt over her head. She looked everywhere in the room for her panties, even under the bed.

"Come get in the shower with me, baby," Sosa invited.

Nella couldn't find her underwear, so she quickly slid on her jeans without them.

"Give me a minute, I'll be right there," she lied, grabbed her shoes, snatched her cell phone off the charger, and tiptoed barefoot out the front door.

Sosa heard the front door slam.

"What the fuck?" He stepped out of the shower and lifted the porcelain top on the toilet. He kept a small caliber firearm duct-taped inside the tank above the water line.

He cocked the nickel-plated .32 and crept out of the bathroom to discover that Nella had ghosted him. He stood in his living room dripping water on the hardwood floor as he hit her line.

Nella picked up on the first ring and apologized, "I'm sorry, Sosa, but I made a mistake?"

"Made a mistake about what?" Najee asked.

Nella heard Najee's voice, and her heart damn near jumped out of her left titty.

"Oh, my gosh! Where are you, baby?"

"I got a better question. Where are you?" Najee cross-examined.

Nella knew better than to lie, but she couldn't exactly tell the truth either. She took a deep breath and blurted, "The U.S. Marshall released me about an hour ago, and I took the Blue Line from downtown to Santa Monica. I'm about to get a room at the Ocean Inn." Nella's arteries stopped pumping blood while she waited for Najee's response. She hoped her voice didn't betray her.

After a long pause, Najee replied, "Nah, scratch that idea. Get rid of your ankle bracelet. The Feds are starting to put listening devices in their GPS monitors. I'll slide through and pick you up at the old Alive 365 headquarters. Remember where it's at?"

How could she forget? The old seafood plant was where the Body Snatchers met up to split the loot after they hit a lick. "Yeah, I remember," Nella answered softly. "I'm not too far away."

"That's what's up. I'll be there in a hot one. One other thing—"

Nella held her breath.

228

"I'm listening, bae."

"Welcome home, my queen! I know it's been a rough couple of days, but I had it all under control. My man's David Shapiro has been on the payroll since I was a shorty."

"Wait, you're the one who hired the lawyer?"

"Come on, Lil' mama, you know your king wasn't gonna let you go out backward! I hired him to represent Sosa, too. Speaking of Sosa, what were you apologizing about?"

Nella felt stupid, she had played herself.

"I—we—see what happened was—I gave him some directions, then I realized I had made a mistake. I thought you were him calling back to say he was lost."

"Damn, that's fucked up. Anyway, Lil' mama, good lookin' for being so understanding and loyal. We've been through a lot together, and I wouldn't be the man I am without a woman like you," Najee expressed with sincerity. "I've never loved anyone as much as I love you, real talk!"

His words pierced her heart like Cupid's arrows. They hung up with Nella torturing herself with questions. As she was putting the phone in her back pocket, it lit up again. This time she looked at the caller ID carefully before answering.

"Look, Sosa, what we did was a big mistake. I'm in love with Najee."

"A mistake, you callin' me a mistake?" he asked. "A mistake is what you make when you trace outside the lines or mark the wrong answer on a test. A mistake ain't letting a nigga nut in yo' mouth, and then ridin' his dick," he expressed with hurt in his voice.

His words stung. What she did was wrong, and the way Sosa described their encounter made her feel like a random thot.

On reflex, she looked over her shoulder. The same car she saw parked on Ocean Boulevard slowly rolled down the street. Nella put her head down and picked up the pace. The suspicious vehicle stayed on her trail. She dipped into the lobby of a posh, ocean-front hotel and strained her eyes to get a good look at the driver. The driver of the BMW made a quick U-turn rather than pass by the glass lobby doors and blow his cover.

Nella hustled toward the rear exit with her phone pressed to her ear.

"Like I said, Sosa, I'm very sorry for leading you on, but it's just not meant to be. I hope we can remain friends."

"Yeah, whatever!"

"And Sosa—"

"What?" he asked sourly.

"Please don't tell Najee," she begged.

Sosa walked into his room and gazed at his alarm clock. A pin-sized hole housed a hidden camera lens. He pulled Nella's missing panties out of his pants pocket and sniffed them. His grin broadened. He wasn't going to tell Najee that he fucked Nella, he was going to show him!

Chapter 30

The Game Is Dirty

Parker stormed out of ATF Senior Administrator Schwartz's office determined to show Najee this wasn't a game.

Schwartz followed Parker into the hallway.

"You got twenty-four hours, Agent Parker, then I'm pulling the plug!" he issued a stern warning. "And where the hell is Torres?"

"That's a good question," Parker said to himself.

Torres wasn't picking up his phone. Parker didn't look back and kept marching. His boss had chewed a new hole in his ass for the tunnel debacle and promised to make his life a living hell. The failed drug bust was an embarrassment and a scarlet stain on the U.S. Bureau of Alcohol, Tobacco, Firearms, and Explosives' reputation. The overhyped raid even made the front page of the Metro section, and to add insult to injury, a reporter compared the ATF's investigation to a limp pickle.

The pencil pushers in Washington D.C. demanded answers. Parker didn't have any, but fortunately, although Schwartz was a hard-nosed boss, he had faith in his unit. Parker was one of his best undercover agents, and his success at catching bad guys was exemplary. Once a Special Assignments guy himself, Schwartz understood that sometimes you get shit on the bottom of your boots when you're in the field, so he pulled a few strings and bought Parker some time, but not a lot of it.

Tik Toc!

The clock was ticking.

Parker hurried into his office to prepare to hit the streets and hunt down Najee, but there was no need to. Najee was already in the building. He reclined in Parker's chair with his Versace Chain Reaction sneakers propped up on the desk.

Najee looked over the top of the critically acclaimed masterpiece, *To Catch a Thief*, and said, "Excellent book, I hear it's based on a true story."

Parker swiped Najee's shoes off his desk.

"What the hell are you doing here?"

Najee tossed the book on the cluttered desk and picked up a framed picture of Parker's wife.

"I was about to ask you the same thing. Shouldn't you be out looking for me?"

"Real cute, asshole." Parker snatched the picture frame out of Najee's hand and carefully put it back in place. "You embarrassed the Bureau and made me look like a fool. I thought we had a deal?"

"We did. I fulfilled my end of the bargain. I delivered Domingo and helped uncover an elaborate drug tunnel in the process. Now it's your turn to back off Nella and Sosa."

"Back off Nella and Sosa, huh?" Parker scoffed. "I admire you, Najee—Sinatra or whoever the hell you are. You're willing to go to hell and back for your criminal friends. Do you think they would do the same for you?"

"There you go again tryin' to mind fuck me. If you know something I need to know, then pull my coat."

Parker sat at Torres' empty desk.

"I know—"

Najee interrupted and finished the sentence, "—everything I don't know, I got it. Tell me something new."

Parker leaned back and crossed his legs.

"What I don't know is what happened to the hundred keys of coke?"

"There never was any dope," Najee lied with a straight face.

"Why not?"

"Because I told them it was a setup."

This revelation aggravated Parker.

"Why the hell did you do that?"

"To get closer to El Feo," Najee admitted. "Do you really think the Nogales Cartel would trust us with that much weight? It was a test."

"You said *us*. Who were you with?"

Najee wanted to cringe. The more you talk, the more susceptible you are to say something incriminating. Playing it off cool, he replied, "I was with the trinity—me, my gun, and God!"

Parker noticed how Najee looked up and to the right, a body language sign of deceit. It was time to pull his own shrewd move and leverage Najee's loyalty against him.

"The government's objective has changed," Parker divulged. "We no longer want Domingo or El Feo. We have a new target."

Najee's eyebrows crinkled.

"Who is he?"

"Enrique 'El Padrino' Estrada, The Godfather! He's the mastermind behind the highly toxic and inexpensive opioids flooding the streets, and I'm gonna be the one who takes him down."

"Why you telling me? Do yo' thing, cowboy."

"I'm telling you because we don't know where he's at, but you do, and you're gonna lead us to him."

"That's news to me. You got me all the way fucked up, like fa' real!" Najee stood up to leave. "The deal was to get you a high-ranking Nogales Cartel member, and I did."

"We didn't have anything to charge Domingo with, so we had to cut him loose, but you planned it that way, didn't you?"

Najee confirmed the accusation.

"Dig this, white boy, I'm not one of your CIs trying to work off a case. I came here today out of courtesy. I said I would lead you to him. I didn't say he would be dirty, nor did I promise a conviction. I'm out this bitch!"

"Not so fast! You're not as smart as you think," Parker countered. "Once the Feds got you, we got you for life, so sit your black ass down, now!" he commanded.

Najee remained standing. The two men glared at each other. It was a battle of wills, two big egos arm wrestling.

Parker delivered a devastating mental blow.

"Look in that top drawer. There's something you need to see," he insisted.

Najee pulled on the top file drawer and removed a thick manila folder. He opened the flap, looked at the surveillance photo paperclipped to the front page, then frowned at Parker. "You dirty muthafucka!"

"Angela Rodriguez, a.k.a Ms. Loca from Barrio Boyle Heights," Parker sang. "A modern-day Griselda and a high-ranking member of Los Cinco Diablos—that is until they tried to assassinate her last week," he elaborated. "Your baby mama is wanted for moving a lot of coke, Najee. Oh, and I can't forget about the nasty way she kills her enemies with her Spanish Guillotine. I would hate to run across this hot tamale when she's on the rag."

"You'll never find her!"

"Sure, we will. El Feo was pushing for a merger in order to gain access to the Los Cinco Diablos narco-tunnels, but El Padrino wanted a war. A war that would not only give him control over Los Cinco Diablos drug routes but also show the other cartels that the Nogales organization is back on top. The only problem is that Los Cinco Diablos have too many loyal soldiers, and wars are expensive. To solve that problem, the Nogales Cartel has been feeding Los Cinco Diablos soldiers to one of our Intelligence Officers, a strung-out tweaker named Agent James Reynolds. What better way to fight a war than to let the Feds take out your enemies for you? When you murdered Benzo Al—"

"Allegedly murdered Benzo Al!" Najee corrected.

"Either way, the death of Benzo Al accelerated El Padrino's plans, and he ordered El Feo to kidnap Angela."

Najee shifted uneasily on the balls of his feet. The beef between El Feo and his grandfather started to make sense. El Padrino really was the mastermind.

The Nogales Cartel was sitting on a shit load of product but had no way to move it. Frustrated with the Border Patrol and the way El Feo was handling the situation, El Padrino came out of retirement and started dealing the cards. Angela's knowledge of the tunnels made her the queen of spades in a game of stakes poker.

Najee was growing impatient with playing verbal tug of war with Parker. He wanted to hit the streets and drag his knuckles like a silverback gorilla.

While flipping through Angela's criminal dossier, he bluntly stated, "Spit it out, white boy. I don't roll with either cartel. So, what are you getting at?"

Parker cut to the chase and made his Machiavellian intentions clear, "Agent Reynolds died from a Fentanyl overdose on Saturday, so El Feo is going to be looking for another dirty cop to do business with. He might not give up his grandfather or anyone from his own organization, but how quick do you think he'll give me Angela if I give him a get out of jail free card in exchange?"

"Y'all pigs are dirty!" Najee hissed through tight lips.

"It's a dirty game, homeboy. Either you deliver El Padrino, or your child will be born behind bars and have to visit his mother in prison for the rest of her life."

"Fuck you!" Najee roared, flung the manila folder at the wall, and stomped out of the office.

Parker stayed on his heels and in his ear all the way to the elevator.

"While you're thinking about it, think about this. Drug exportation accounts for a significant portion of Mexico's annual GDP. We're talking double-digit billions with a capital B. Without the cartels and American recreational drug use, their economy would collapse within a few months. With so much at stake, it's no surprise that the Mexican government allowed the cartels to operate with impunity. I want to put a stop to that."

Najee pushed the down button on the elevator.

"Save the John Wayne speech. The white man has his hands in the pot, too. The ghetto is flooded with dope," Najee reminded. "But I don't know one person from the hood who owns a boat or an airplane. Y'all didn't give a fuck about drugs flooding the inner city until white people started OD'ing."

"You may be right but look at it this way. African Americans have been hit especially hard by the opioid crisis, both in terms of overdose deaths and incarceration," Parker laid out the cold, hard facts. "Sure, a few college kids and suburban housewives may get caught up, but their families are gonna put them through rehab, and if they catch a case, they'll most likely get a slap on the wrist and probation. You and I both know the outcome ain't the same for black people trapped in the same predicament."

The elevator doors opened. Najee stepped in without speaking and pressed the lobby button. First El Feo flipped the script, now Parker. El Feo wanted El Padrino to die in the streets. Parker wanted him to die in prison. Najee was trying to keep his hands clean, but both men wanted him to do their dirty work. He was in a catch twenty-two. Either decision placed his life and the safety of his family in imminent danger.

Parker continued making his point, "El Padrino is destroying your community by putting a product on the streets that is four times more potent than his competitors. Inexperienced users and full-blown addicts who think they're buying heroin or real pharmaceutically manufactured pills are dropping like flies. If black lives really do matter to you, you'll step up and do something about it," he finished laying on the guilt trip.

As the elevator doors closed, Najee grabbed his nuts with one hand and gave Parker the middle finger with the other. Once outside, he checked his phone. He had a text message from El Feo.

He got The Deacon on the line and stated, "Strap up, it's going down tonight!"

Chapter 31

Natural Born Killers

Hustlenomics 101: *Get there before the other guy.*

Najee whipped his Dodge Challenger Demon through the cold and unforgiving back streets of Los Angeles. Gang graffiti marked the territory of each hood, with a tap of the gas, the aftermarket supercharged engine roared like a lion riding a Harley Davidson. He parked down the street from Metro Tire World, one of the Nogales Cartel's strongholds. The tags on the walls let it be known that they were trespassing on Primera Flats turf.

El Feo told Najee to meet him there at 9:00 p.m. to drop off the hundred bricks, pick up Angela, and get instructions regarding the move on El Padrino. Najee and The Deacon arrived an hour early and posted up in the cut. The Dodge Challenger's black paint and black Forgiato rims blended well with the night sky.

The Deacon thumped gray ashes off the end of a thick blunt and passed it to Najee.

"Wah gwaan, Soulja Boi, how are things with you and Nella?"

Najee hit the loud, and after holding it in his chest for too long, he coughed up smoke.

"On life, my nigga, you be having that Mardi Gras!" Najee praised. "But on the reals tho', look in the glove compartment."

The Deacon opened the glove and spotted a small, black, velvet box. He lifted the top and saw a flawless gem inside. His lips creased and revealed two rows of yellow teeth.

"Irie, mon! When is the big day?" he asked while examining the big, sparkling, diamond engagement ring.

Najee gazed up the block into darkness.

"I don't know, cuz. I haven't popped the question yet."

"What cha' waiting for? Every Pharaoh needs a Nefertiti. How long do you expect her to wait while you make up your mind?"

Najee hit the blunt again and passed it.

"That's what I've been asking myself. We spent the afternoon together, cashed out at the Gucci store, took my son to the park, and did some grown-up thangs when Lil' Najee went to sleep. The sex was fire, but something didn't feel right."

"Sounds like you found what every street nigga is looking for—a family. What didn't feel right?"

"The pussy felt different! It was good, but I mean—"

"You trippin', my nigga."

"Not only that. Her phone kept blowin' up, but she wouldn't answer it."

"Yup, you most definitely trippin'. She probably doesn't want to talk to any of her old friends after La La betrayed her. Just give it some time and keep in mind that the sista has been through a lot lately. On top of that, you've been off doing your thing and got another baby on the way. That's some heavy shit for a woman to process."

The Deacon kicked real live game, but Najee still had an ill feeling in the pit of his gut.

"I hear you, big homie. Maybe I am trippin'. Parker finger fucked my mind this morning and got me ready to spazz out."

The Deacon spotted action up the block. A white Rolls Royce SUV followed by a black Chevy Tahoe swooped into the tire shop's parking lot. A group of menacing men got out of the vehicles. Their heads swiveled from left to right like a convenience store surveillance camera. One of the men held the car door open for El Feo. He got out, shoved a pearl handle 357 in his belt, and looked up and down the block, his penetrating eyes searching the shadows for danger.

The Deacon clocked his moves through a pair of Swarovski night vision binoculars.

"Don't let that Yankee bleach ya' dome. We can chop it up later," he promised and pointed at the tire shop. "Right now, we got movement up the street. It's game time!"

"Let's get it!" Najee pulled twin Glocks from under the driver's seat. "How many soldiers is El Feo rolling with?"

He checked one of the clips, slapped the magazine back into the bottom, and cocked the slide back. The chic-chic sound of a Teflon demon sliding into the chamber was sweeter than a note from a Bee-thoven symphony. Najee gave his other Glock the same treatment.

"He has four soldiers with him, but I doubt Domingo is packing, especially if El Feo put a green light on him." The Deacon went silent before delivering the worst part, "Check it out though, bruh. They got Angela with them, and she don't look too good."

The Deacon passed Najee the binoculars, then tucked a Draco into the sling sewed into the lining of his black leather trench coat. He shoved a Desert Eagle into his shoulder holster to balance the weight of the assault weapon.

Najee glared into the binoculars. What he saw made his heart pound with murder. Angela was bare feet, and El Feo had her dressed in a short black miniskirt. The skimpy outfit barely concealed her coochie or the butterfly tatted on her ass cheeks. She looked drunk or drugged or both. Staggering on wobbly legs, she tried to pull her skirt down but lost her balance. She stumbled and fell into El Feo, causing one of her dress straps to fall off her shoulder. Her left breast slipped out, exposing an erect brown nipple. All of the men, except for Domingo, burst into laughter. Domingo appeared nervous and apprehensive.

El Feo shoved Angela off him into the arms of Lowdown and another Nogales Cartel shooter named Solo. They each held an elbow and dragged her into the tire shop.

Operating off adrenaline and emotion, Najee was ready to turn up.

"Let's mash on 'em right now while they slippin'." He reached for the door handle, but The Deacon grabbed him by the arm.

"Hold up! We can't run up and start blasting."

"Fuck that, cuz! Fuck the scheming. Fuck the scamming. Fuck the planning. We ain't in Mexico no more. We in my city and I'm ready to murk something!"

"I feel you but recognize game. I do this guerilla warfare shit. Dem blood clots are strapped up and have the numbers. If we attack them in the open, they can spread out and flank us. I suggest we wait and see if El Feo comes correct and release Angela when we return the kilos. If he tries to pull it, then we can get into some gang-ster shit and move on 'em in close quarters where their numbers become a liability." The Deacon's proposal made a lot of sense.

Najee gave him a fist pound.

"Cool, we'll do this your way, but if dude gets on some bull-shit, I'm blazing my gun, like fa' real," he promised and made a move to exit the vehicle.

The Deacon stopped him again.

"Slow ya' roll, Soulja Boi. We got a late arrival to the party," The Deacon announced while looking through the binoculars.

A maroon-colored Chevy Malibu circled the block, came back around, and parked in front of the tire shop's garage door. From their angle, they couldn't get a good look at the driver.

"Think it's them, peoples?" Najee questioned as he fingered both triggers of his Glocks.

"Nah, I doubt it. He's alone, plus he's not trying to hide. He practically drove into the spot," The Deacon explained. "Hit El Feo on the hip and tell him we about to pull up."

"I got a better idea." Najee pulled his blue Balmain puffy jacket over his bulletproof vest. "Let's just go through the front door!" He liked the thought of keeping the element of surprise on their side.

El Feo paced back and forth on the greasy garage floor. He wore black Louis Vuitton slacks, a black silk shirt, and black cowboy boots with silver caps on the toe tips. His diamond pinky ring shim-mered like ice, his gold Malverde medallion glistened like fire, and his red Richard Milli hit for a respectable 400k—twice the amount of his white one. Gustavo, Lowdown, and Solo lingered in the shad-ows. Like El Feo, they were armed and on edge.

Domingo was literally in the hot seat. He sat in the middle of the garage in an uncomfortable chair. An equally uncomfortable look clung to his face like a Halloween mask. He had witnessed other men in his position sitting in the same chair with El Feo's scrutinizing eyes dissecting their stories. It never ended well for them.

El Feo stopped pacing and faced Domingo.

"So, run that shit by me again, homes."

Domingo broke it down, "When we got to the end of the tunnel, Najee and the other vato robbed me."

"They robbed you, huh?" El Feo asked with his hands on his hips, not even attempting to disguise his skepticism.

Domingo swallowed to wet his dry throat before speaking again, "Yes, primo, they took the yayo!"

"And you just sat there while they ganked my shit?"

"What could I do, dog? They had pistolas."

The sound of the front door opening and closing interrupted El Feo's interrogation. Heavy footsteps swept across the customer waiting area.

"Watch it, ese!" El Feo whispered and upped his piece.

Gustavo, Lowdown, and Solo quickly mobilized, put their backs against the wall, and aimed the barrels of their deadly MK-16s toward the lobby.

Najee walked into the tire change area dragging a large, Army green duffle bag. He smiled and said, "This is a tough neighborhood. Y'all should think about locking the front door."

The Deacon followed Najee into the garage area, tossed his heavy, Army duffle bag at El Feo's feet, and posted up with one hand tucked inside his trench coat.

El Feo looked down at the large duffle bags, then hit Domingo with a contemptuous scowl. The lines in his forehead deepened, and his eyes hardened. Kneeling on one knee, he unzipped one of the duffle bags, removed a compressed brick of cocaine, and examined the spider web logo.

"Give me a cuchillo," he requested a knife.

Solo produced a switchblade, opened it, and handed it to El Feo.

El Feo punctured the kilo and scooped a large mound of coke onto the blade. He vacuumed the powder into each nostril, loving the way the drug exploded in his head like colorful fireworks. It was straight drop, no cut, authentic cocaína from the mountainous region of Western Mexico where the altitude, soil acidity, and rainfall created the perfect atmosphere for coca leaf cultivation.

While El Feo stuck the knife into another bird, Najee quickly surveyed the layout of the tire shop and made note of the exits. He and The Deacon were strategically positioned so their backs faced the front entrance. Two garage doors were off to the left. Further to the back of the tire shop, an exit sign hung over the rear door. He didn't see Angela and determined she was being held in the back office.

El Feo licked his thumb and wiped the white residue off the bridge of his nose.

"This is some good shit. Want to try some, homie?" He held the knife out to Najee. A jab of cocaine rested on the tip of the blade.

"I'm good, do you," Najee declined and got on business. "That's one hundred white girls, fifty in each duffle bag," he reassured. "Now, where's Angela?"

"Not so fast, amigo! I still need to know what happened to the rest of the perico."

"Talk to ya' mans over there," Najee nodded his head in Domingo's direction. "After Ghost and Chili got slimed, we split the keys three ways and kept it moving. When them peoples showed up, we got in the wind, but like I told you on the phone, your mans, Domingo didn't run fast enough."

"Fuckin' mentirozo!" Domingo jumped out of the chair, calling Najee a liar.

El Feo sniffed the coke off the blade and rolled up one of his sleeves.

"Entertain me some more, Domingo. What happened next?" The high-quality nose candy made his dick hard and his skin tingle.

"After those two pinche putos robbed me, the Federales showed up out of nowhere and raided the spot. It was that crazy gringo from the biker gang!"

"You mean the same crazy gringo you were supposed to kill in Las Vegas? It's not looking good for you, Domingo!" El Feo rolled up his other sleeve.

Domingo's bowels loosened. He clenched his ass cheeks to keep from shitting on himself.

"I fucked up, homes," he admitted and looked down at his shoes.

"You damn right you fucked up! What kind of deal did you cut with the gringo?"

"That's what I'm trying to tell you, eh. I didn't have to cut a deal. They don't got shit on me."

"So, the Feds just let you go?"

"They had to."

"I don't believe you." El Feo turned to Lowdown. "Take this piece of shit out back and shoot him!"

Domingo turned iPod white, and his kneecaps shook with fear.

"No, wait! I'm tellin' you the truth! Najee took the yayo, so when the pigs hit the spot, they didn't find nothin', man. I put that on everything!"

"You know what? I changed my mind, don't shoot him."

A sigh of relief escaped from Domingo's chest. For a moment he felt safe, but his hopes were quickly extinguished.

"I have a better idea. I'm gonna burn this lying motherfucker while he's still breathing!"

Domingo fell to his knees and hugged one of El Feo's legs. "Please, jefe, please! Don't kill your own primo. I would never cross you!" He broke the sacred oath and begged for his life. A disappointing groan came from Lowdown and Solo.

El Feo laughed, the hunting sound reverberated off the tire shop's grungy walls. Power is a potent aphrodisiac. The thrill of being feared matched the euphoria produced by cocaine.

"Calm down, homes. I was just fucking with you! Get off your knees and get it together. You're making a fool of yourself and the organization," he commented and dialed a number on his cell phone. After speaking with the party on the other end, he added, "I actually believe you."

Najee and The Deacon shifted uneasily. If El Feo believed Domingo, that meant he didn't believe Najee. Lowdown eye-fucked Najee from a distance. The Deacon gripped the Draco. The tension in the air thickened.

The garage door lifted up a few feet. A tall figure ducked underneath and entered the tire shop. He had the calm and confident strut of a cop. Najee immediately recognized the Tom Cruz look-a-like and quietly relayed the info to The Deacon.

The Deacon took a quick look over his shoulder. The front exit was still clear. This brought more worry than comfort. The Spartans created illusions on the battlefield and were able to thoroughly crush their adversaries by pretending to be weak and vulnerable.

Exiting the front door is what the Nogales Cartel wanted, The Deacon concluded.

A strategically placed team of shooters waiting in the cut, or a skilled sniper positioned on a nearby roof would be detrimental to Najee's and The Deacon's health.

El Feo put an arm over the man's shoulders like they were old pals and introduced him.

"Gentlemen, meet the newest member of our familia—Special Agent Torres!"

Torres had left the garage door open on purpose. Anything could pop off, and he had enough experience to know that you never walked into a room without having a way to run out.

Gustavo inched closer to Najee. His face was pale and sweat bubbled on his top lip.

"No, no, no, this ain't good!" he told Najee. His voice was strained with urgency.

Najee didn't like the way Gustavo pushed up on him, putting his left hand in his coat pocket, he gripped the butt of his heat and remarked, "Everybody in this room is a criminal, including Agent Torres. So, why are you so spooked? You know something I don't?"

"I know everything you don't!"

The familiar phrase stopped Najee in his tracks. His eyes widened, and his chin hit his chest. He recalled the way Gustavo was always watching but rarely talking or participating. His mannerisms were professional, his pat search thorough, his fighting skills proficient. He was the police.

"Oh, snap! You're the missing ATF agent?"

"Shhhh, not so loud!" Gustavo shushed Najee. "I'm not missing. I'm still on assignment just deeper in the mud," he talked faster than a meth head speed balling.

"What's the deal with Agent Reynolds? Why didn't he rat you out?" Najee probed.

"Agent Reynolds' clearance wasn't high enough to get information about my assignment, but it was only a matter of time before he discovered my identity, so I went off the grid. At the same time, I knew the Nogales Cartel had a rogue agent on the payroll, but only a chosen few knew his true identity. I didn't find out it was Agent Reynolds until they gave him a hotshot and killed him."

His reply raised more unanswered questions.

"You've been on El Feo's security detail long enough to see a lot of shit go down. If you're still undercover, why haven't you had him extradited to the U.S. for prosecution?"

"Bureaucratic red tape, government impotence, corruption— take your pick. El Feo is smart, and he has money and a lot of connections. That's a dangerous combination. I've built an airtight case against him, but he has the Agencia Federal de Investigación in his back pocket. They convinced our government that Enrique Estrada is the real threat, and the DOJ suddenly changed my mission."

"Whoa, this shit is bigger than Nino Brown and way out of my league. I'm just trying to save Angela and move on to the next. All that other shit don't have nothin' to do with me."

"That's where you're wrong. These guys are natural-born killers. They don't leave loose ends or witnesses."

Najee's jaw muscles tightened. He knew better than to get caught up with the Migos. He watched Agent Torres, El Feo, and the other Nogales Cartel goons. They were on edge. Something was about to pop off. Najee turned back to Gustavo.

"Why are you telling me all this? You know fa' sho' I'm knee-deep in the mud, too. Aren't you afraid that I might blow your cover?"

"It's too late, my cover was blown the second me and Torres made eye contact. Torres blew your cover last night. El Feo knows about the side deal you cut with Parker," Gustavo spoke out of the corner of his mouth trying his best to be inconspicuous. "I overheard the conversation, but I had no idea El Feo was talking to Torres until now."

"Put me up on game. What did you hear?"

"They were planning a murder."

"That's old news. I already know about the murder plot against Señor Enrique Estrada. El Feo wants me to do his dirty work, but I have too much respect for the old man to back door him."

Gustavo watched Torres whispering to El Feo. El Feo's entire body stiffened. Gustavo began to drift away from Najee.

"They were not talking about killing El Padrino," he revealed while raising his heat.

"Then who were they talking about killing?"

"You!"

Chapter 32

No Love, No Mercy, No Regret

Gustavo has one rule—shoot first. He raised his FN MK-16 waist level, braced the stalk against his stomach, and swung the business end in El Feo's direction.

"Watch out!" El Feo and Torres split up, moving in opposite directions while drawing their weapons.

Gustavo felt the cold trigger against his index finger and pulled it. The FN swept to the left, spitting fire and live ammo at El Feo as he dashed to the back office.

El Feo dropped to the ground, rolled onto his side, and let his pearl-handled pistol bark. The 357 jerked violently in his palm.

"Die, you fuckin' rat!" he yelled with venom in his vocal cords.

Gustavo ducked out of the path of danger. The bullets missed him and slammed into Najee's chest. The Kevlar absorbed the brunt of the unexpected blast, but still knocked the wind out of his lungs. Najee was thrown against a rack of Michelin tires. He groaned in agony. The room seemed to spin counterclockwise, and his legs betrayed him. He collapsed on the greasy floor with his hand still concealed in his coat pocket.

"Najeeeee!" The Deacon screamed with salty tears in his eyes and bitter vengeance in his heart.

He went for his tool, but Lowdown and Solo unleashed a lethal torrent of gunfire in his direction. The Deacon leaped over the counter, took cover, and reached for his Draco, but the fifty-shot banana clip got entangled in his jacket sling.

Lowdown and Solo stood side by side blazing. Holding their FNs at hip level, they swept the menacing barrels in a back-and-forth motion. Bullets knocked huge holes through the wooden counter. The Deacon yanked his Desert Eagle from his shoulder holster, stuck the long, chrome barrel through one of the huge holes, and let off four rounds. Three of them struck Lowdown in the torso, puncturing his kidney and bladder.

Hot slugs in your belly had a way of making you reevaluate some of your decisions. Lowdown realized two things—one, he wasn't about that life, and two, he was not ready to die. He dropped his gun, abandoned his crew, and staggered toward the open garage door. The Deacon showed no love, no mercy, or no regret. He lined up Lowdown's melon and double-tapped the trigger. The back of Lowdown's skull split open, and his memories splattered on the wall.

The Deacon didn't have time to say a prayer for Lowdown's condemned soul. Angry bullets whistled over his head and ricocheted off metal. Paper, wood chips, and glass rained around him. He needed to move, but Solo had him pinned down under automatic gunfire.

Gustavo caught Solo slippin'. As agents were trained to do when engaged in close quarter gun battles, Gustavo maneuvered into a modified Weaver stance, turned his torso sideways, and stood with his size twelve feet shoulder-width apart in an attempt to make his body a more narrow target. His heart raced, thumping against his ribcage like 808 kick drums, but his gun hand remained steady. He was a soldier. He aimed his chopper at Solo and fired. The green-tipped polymer ammo viciously ripped through Solo's flesh.

El Feo quickly scrambled to his feet, squeezed off wild rounds for cover fire, and sprinted to the back office. He untied Angela, grabbed a fist full of her hair, and snatched her out of the chair. Angela struggled, but she was too weak, and El Feo was too determined. He grabbed her by the neck and pressed the iron against her right temple.

Torres had been in many shootouts and also learned about close quarter combat at the ATF National Academy. He gripped his .40 cal in both hands, stood with his left foot slightly forward to make his body appear slimmer, and dumped the whole clip into Gustavo.

Gustavo didn't see it coming. His body crumpled under the barrage of gunfire. Blood leaked from the bullet holes and quickly saturated his shirt.

Out of ammo, Torres dropped the .40 cal, pulled his P380, and hid behind a large, red, tool cabinet on wheels. He used the tool cabinet for cover and rolled it toward the open garage door.

The Deacon rushed to Najee's aid. Domingo sprinted to Low-down's dead body and scooped up his chopper. As The Deacon grabbed Najee by the jacket and attempted to drag him to safety, Domingo opened fire.

"Ahhh, shit!" The Deacon felt fire in his leg.

A round penetrated through his thigh, causing blood to skeet from the femoral artery. The Deacon returned fire, but his hand-eye coordination was off, and his erratic bullets missed their mark. Warm fluid rushed into his boot and made his sock soggy. He became dizzy, but still raised his arm in preparation to shoot again, but he saw double visions. There were two Domingos. His military training kicked in. Preserve your ammo, seek cover, and above all, don't panic. He squeezed off two rounds, one at each shadow, and retreated into the customer lobby.

Najee laid curled up in the fetal position. Domingo slowly and cautiously inches forward with the FN extended in front of him. After the loud gunshots, the tire shop became eerily calm and quiet. Domingo looked around and saw nothing but death and destruction. He watched Najee's chest for signs of breathing, seeing none, and debated whether he should drill a slug into Najee's head just for the fuck of it. His trigger finger was indecisive.

Najee made the decision for him. Holding his breath and playing dead, Najee fired three rounds with his hand still hidden in the pocket of his Balmain jacket. Two slugs bang Domingo in the face, one in his chin and one just above his right eyebrow. Black blood gushed from his mouth. His body fell sideways and landed in a puddle of engine grease. He died with his eyes wide open. They stared at Najee in utter shock and disbelief.

Najee rose to his feet and upped the Glocks, with the left hand he aimed downward and shot Domingo in the back of the head. Domingo's brains turned into oatmeal. Using the right-hand Najee sent slugs at Torres as Torres ducked under the garage door. Najee chased after the crooked cop. He continued blasting with a Glock in each hand, but Angela's screams diverted his attention, and Torres escaped.

Najee turned on his pivot foot and pointed both guns in the direction of Angela's voice. El Feo had Angela in a rear chokehold. His 357 was pressed tightly against her cheek. He used her body as a human shield and made his way to the rear exit.

Najee kept both Glocks trained on El Feo and tracked his movements, but he couldn't get off a clean shot.

"Let Angela go, coward! This shit is about me and you!"

El Feo gripped Angela's throat tighter and continued to move backward. "That's where you're wrong, ese. This shit is bigger than both of us. This shit is about power, and I want it more than you!"

El Feo sent flames in Najee's direction. Najee swiftly took cover behind the bullet-riddled counter. He raised up, extended both guns over the countertop, felt the sudden and invigorating rush of electricity flow through both trigger fingers, but thought twice about shooting. He made eye contact with Angela.

Her eyes said don't do it.

Najee didn't do it.

"Fuck, fuck, fuck!" he roared out of frustration.

He lowered his guns and watched helplessly as El Feo gripped Angela's throat and escaped through the back door.

Najee heard The Deacon groan, so he sprinted into the lobby area. The Deacon laid on his side in a puddle of blood. His blue jeans were stained red. He was in bad shape.

Najee squatted next to his friend, mentor, and brother from the same struggle.

"Where you hit, my nigga?"

"In the leg, I think the bullet hit an artery."

Najee opened the rip in The Deacon's jeans and examined the gunshot wound. The prognosis was grim.

"Don't even trip, big homie, it's just a scratch," he lied for The Deacon's sake.

The FN left a deep laceration in The Deacon's leg, and he was bleeding profusely.

"Let's get you out of here," Najee suggested. Police sirens screamed in the distance.

"Forget about me and go save Angela. At first, I wasn't feeling this mission but now I see how important family is to you. I'll meet you at the church later." The Deacon refused help, tried to get up on his own, but collapsed.

Najee knew it was The Deacon's pride talking and not his common sense.

"You're my fam, too. It's you and me, baby boy from the womb to the tomb." He put The Deacon's arm over his shoulder and helped him onto his feet. "You lost a lot of blood, but you're gonna make it. Detective Brooks' daughter, Renee, has a small medical practice. She'll fix you up like new."

"Bless up, you're a true soldier," The Deacon complimented.

Najee took possession of the Draco and headed straight for the front door, but The Deacon stopped him.

"Nah, let's fade out the back way."

"Good idea," Najee agreed and switched directions.

The Deacon grimaced in pain and stopped walking. He balanced on his good leg but leaned most of his weight on Najee.

Najee held the Deacon up and warned, "We gotta groove up out of here, cuz. The spot is finna' be crawling with the twelve."

"Just give me a second, this is important." The Deacon gasped out of breath. "Do you remember what I told you about the differences between a shotgun and a sniper's rifle?"

"Of course, I do. You said snipers are trained to be patient, persistent, and precise. I said I still prefer shotguns because they do the nasty."

"That's exactly the mentality I want you to have," The Deacon professed as he held onto Najee and hobbled on one leg headed out the back exit. "It's time to get nasty. Forget everything I said and don't hold back nothin'. Embrace your hate, utilize your pain, unleash your rage, and send those motherfuckers to hell!"

Chapter 33

Ear 2 the Streets

Najee drove like a bat out of hell. After dropping The Deacon off at Renee's medical practice, his adrenaline dissipated and reality set in. He was back at square one and no closer to rescuing Angela than he was on the day she was abducted. Only now the situation had grown more urgent. There was no reason for El Feo to keep her alive. Najee estimated that Angela and his unborn child would be dead by sunrise.

Desperate times called for desperate measures. It was a risky move, but instead of going home, Najee banked a U-turn and headed to talk to the only person who could provide El Feo's location. He eased onto the freeway and mashed the gas pedal. The horsepower surged through his foot, traveled up his leg, and made the seats vibrate. American muscle, the phrase isn't limited to cars, it's also a synonym for the people's grit and determination. Najee had both of those attributes along with motivation and a whole lot of ammunition.

He pulled into Palermo's parking lot and blessed the young valet with a crisp Blueface.

"I'm going to be in and out," Najee told the valet. "Park near the exit."

Well-dressed dinner clientele spilled out of the Italian restaurant as Najee mobbed inside rocking blue jeans and bullet holes in his jacket. The bartender spotted Najee and reached for the trusty Louisville Slugger he kept hidden under the counter.

"What the hell are you doing here?" he barked.

Najee lifted the hem of his shirt and revealed the butt of his blicky.

"I'm here to see Carmine. You got a problem with that?" He didn't wait for a reply.

He adjusted the Gucci backpack slung over his right shoulder and kept groovin' to the rear of the restaurant. Once in the storage area, he was confronted by Fat Tony, Carmine's large and intimidating bodyguard.

Fat Tony wore an expensive black pinstripe suit with a red silk tie. His wide shoulders made his shaved head look small. Not taking any chances this time, Fat Tony upped his piece on Najee.

"You either got big balls or a small brain. Didn't we tell you not to come back without going through the proper channels?"

"Move out of my way," Najee calmly ordered. "Me and the old man got business."

"What kind of business?"

"That's none of your business," Najee fired back aggressively, but then decided to change tactics.

Never agitate a lion when you're trespassing in the lion's den. Najee slung the backpack off his shoulder, unbuckled the flap, and showed Fat Tony five kilos.

"Tell Carmine I got a gift for him."

Fat Tony stuck his nose inside the bag and his attitude changed.

"The boss loves gifts wrapped in duct tape. Follow me."

He led Najee to Carmine's office and knocked twice before entering. Carmine sat at the poker table devouring a plate of spaghetti with large garlic meatballs. His son, Niko, was going over the books, tallying up who paid their debts and who needed their kneecaps broken. Fat Tony leaned over and whispered in Carmine's ear, "It's the black guy again. He has a backpack full of nose candy."

Looking up from his plate of food, Carmine frowned at Najee.

"What do you think this is, some kinda social club?"

Niko jumped to his feet and reached inside his blazer. "You want me to put a friggin' slug in this moulie's watermelon?"

Carmine rolled pasta onto his fork as he gave Najee a thorough once over. He was impressed by Najee's calm confidence and gangsterism. Most importantly, he noticed the dedication and desperation in Najee's eyes.

He waved his son off, and with a mouth full of pasta, said, "Fugget about it. He's a friend of the family, one of Detective Brooks' connects. What's your name again, kid?"

"The streets call me Sinatra, but I prefer to be called Najee."

Carmine dabbed marinara sauce from the corners of his mouth.

"Sure, I've heard of you. You did the job on that fat fuck, Benzo Al. Nice work, but you better have a damn good reason for barging into my establishment without an appointment!"

Hustlenomics 102: *Know who the fuck you're fucking with before you fuck with them.*

Carmine's ruthless reputation preceded him. Najee knew he was a Made-Man and a mob boss with a seat at the round table in New York, but he still had a price. Everyone does. El Padrino had taught him that humans are just like pigeons. Feed them well, and they will always return.

Najee thought of this maxim as he sprinkled breadcrumbs and respectfully apologized, "Forgive me for the intrusion, Don Carmine, but I've hit a dead-end, and I need your help." He unbuckled the backpack and dumped the five kilos onto the poker table.

Carmine picked up one of the tightly wrapped packages, felt its weight of 2.2 pounds, and examined the spider web logo. The Nogales Cartel stamp spoke for itself. They guaranteed a high-quality product.

"You got my attention," Carmine affirmed and passed the brick to Niko for inspection.

Niko smelled the wrapper. It smelled like mustard and motor oil. Some organizations use mustard and other ingredients to conceal the odor and confuse the drug-sniffing K-9s. Niko nodded his approval.

Carmine was pleased.

"How can I be of assistance?"

"I need to know where I can find El Feo."

Carmine waved his fork in the air.

"More information, huh? Gezus friggin' Christ. Do I look like Google maps?"

"No, you look like a man who keeps his ear to the streets."

Carmine looked at the bricks of cocaine, then looked back at Najee. The coke was worth at least eighty racks wholesale, double that amount if they were whipped and re-compressed and triple that on the streets. The general consensus in the underworld was that El

Feo was bad for business and needed to be dealt with, but most crime families gave him a wide berth to operate, and those who did oppose him were locked in bloody turf wars.

Carmine would've given up the 411 on El Feo for free and paid for a front-row seat to watch the niggers and the wetbacks kill each other, but the consequence would come in the form of bullets if word got out the Salerno Borgata was involved, and for that risk, Carmine needed to get paid.

He put the kilos back into the leather bag, passed the backpack to Niko, and stated, "The Nogales organización has crossed the line. Their heat has made the whole game hot, but if I'm gonna get my hands filthy, it's gonna cost you more than five birds."

"Understandable, there's more where those came from," Najee reassured.

"I heard you had fifty."

"Where did you hear that?"

"The streets, of course!"

The two men stared at each other. Carmine's gentle grey eyes and raspy voice concealed tales of murder and racketeering. As odd as it sounds, Najee liked the Mafioso's dark vibe. He was looking forward to doing more business with him in the future.

Turning to leave, Najee looked over his shoulder.

"I'll double my offer. Just get me that info—tonight!"

***

It was well past midnight when a call came through, but it wasn't the one Najee expected. Nella's phone vibrated in her Birkin bag. It was the fifth time it rang in the last fifteen minutes. Nella cursed herself for forgetting to turn it off after she deleted all of Sosa's threatening text messages.

Najee strolled into the kitchen in his boxer briefs with no shirt on and stood behind Nella. Ella Mai bumped in the background. Fresh out of the shower, Nella wore nothing but black, lace Dior lingerie and Shea butter skin cream. Najee's erection rested in the crease of her ass cheeks, and she could feel his warm, minty breath on the back of her neck.

"What up, Lil' mama? For the last couple days, somebody been blowin' yo' line up like a Taliban suicide bomber. You gon' answer that joint, or what?" Najee quizzed while wrapping his strong arms around Nella's sexy waist.

His soft lips left a trail of delicate kisses on the nape of her neck and down the middle of her back. When he got to her bra, he used his teeth to expertly unfasten the hooks, and Nella's breasts bounced free like coconuts falling from a tree. He cupped them in his palms and gently twirled each stiff nipple between his fingers.

Nella moaned and reached back to rub Najee's smooth bald head.

"Just ignore it and keep doing what you're doing. I'm changing my number tomorrow anyway."

Najee stiffened and his spider senses tingled.

"Who you tryna' duck?" He spun Nella around so he could look into her eyes when she answered.

Nella's heart pounded and her palms became sweaty. Her phone vibrated again. She looked at her purse sitting on the kitchen table. The distraction gave her a reason not to look into his eyes. Najee could read a bitch like a Lock Down Publications novel.

Using his index finger, Najee lifted Nella's chin and recalibrated her focus.

"Look at me. Who you tryna' duck?" he asked this time more firmly.

"Nobody!" Nella answered quickly and awkwardly.

"Then answer it and tell nobody they fuckin' up my vibe, or do you want me to tell 'em?"

Nella couldn't hold eye contact, so in order to avoid suspicion, she did the next best thing. She turned the tables. Stomping to her purse with a black girl attitude, she grabbed her iPhone.

"Here you go." She extended her arm and offered Najee the phone. "If you don't trust me, answer it yourself and see who it is." She bluffed and held her breath.

Najee snatched the phone out of her hand.

"Shit, you ain't said nothing but a word."

Nella didn't expect that reaction and panicked. Thinking on her toes, she added, "I don't have nothing to hide. Go through my phone all you want, but best believe when you're done, I'm gonna have a thousand and one questions about the little Mexican bitch you got pregnant!"

That did it. Najee stopped in his tracks. The last thing a man wants to do is have a long conversation with a black woman about the other woman. It never ends well. Najee gave the phone back and pulled her into his arms.

"Handle yo' business and come to bed so we can finish what we started before Lil' Najee wakes up," he insisted and gave her a playful smack on the ass.

Nella waited until she heard Najee moving around in the bedroom, then she checked her phone. She had several missed calls and one new image. All of them were from Sosa's new line. She had blocked his old number, which infuriated him, and that's when the threats started. He had gone from a perfect gentleman to thirsty to straight-up stalker.

She brought up his latest message and froze. It was a pic of her missing panties.

The caption read: *You left these at my condo. Answer yo' phone or I'ma tell Najee.*

Najee suddenly appeared behind Nella with his own phone in his hand. His abrupt and unexpected presence startled her. Nella's spooked soul damn near squirted out her asshole and trickled down her leg.

"Boy, don't be sneaking up on a bitch like that!" Nella joked, hiding her iPhone in her Birkin bag. She turned and saw that Najee was not in a joking mood. His lips were bent down, and his eyes were angry black marbles.

"Wha—what's wrong?" Nella stuttered.

Najee put his finger to his lips to quiet her.

"Somebody just sent me a text message that got me ready to turn up."

Nella's heart sank into her socks. She didn't want Najee to find out about her and Sosa this way. She wanted to be a woman and tell him herself.

"Baby, we need to talk." She reached out for Najee's hand.

He pushed her away.

"Not now!" Najee put on a pair of black Dickies, laced up his blue Chucks, strapped on his bulletproof vest, and pulled a black hoodie over his head.

Nella followed him into the spare bedroom.

"You're scaring me, baby. What's going on."

Najee remained silent and moved with urgency. He placed a SIG Sauer, an HK MP5 tactical weapon, and four flashbang grenades on the mattress. Nella watched him load the magazines and screw a noise suppressor onto the barrel of the SIG.

"Come here!" Najee commanded.

Nella didn't know whether she should run or get on her knees and beg for her life. She reluctantly approached Najee, and surprisingly, he pulled her into his arms.

"I just got a text message from the Italians. They know where El Feo is holding Angela," Najee revealed. "I gotta move on him before it's too late."

Nella squeezed Najee tight and placed her head against his chest. She could hear his heart beating. It was strong just like his will. He was a warrior. She knew she couldn't talk him out of his mission. It was not her place to decide his fate or destiny. It was her duty to support him.

She kissed his lips softly and asked, "What do I always say before you go on a move?"

"Hurry back so I can hit that kitty." Najee laughed.

Nella playfully punched Najee in the arm.

"Boy, I'm serious." Standing on her tippy toes, she slipped her tongue in his mouth.

Najee cupped her booty and pulled her close to his chest. Nella loved when he did that. His hands were so strong yet so gentle at the same time.

"I'm just fuckin' with you, baby," Najee said after breaking their passionate kiss. "A woman has a wise dome. That's why you're my wisdom. I listen to everything you tell me, and best believe I'm gonna follow my heart and use my mind!"

Chapter 34

Set It Off

"Are you out of your mind?" Detective Brooks paced across the Persian rug in his home office. His hair and pajamas were disheveled, and his LAPD mug contained strong black coffee and a stiff shot of Jack Daniels.

Najee smashed through the ghetto banging King Von and working the stick shift. The asphalt jungle was his home. He felt alive and invincible in its rough and unforgiving streets.

"No, I'm not out of my mind, but I'm fully confident we can pull this off," Najee stated with firm conviction. "I just got off the phone with Carmine's son, Niko. He gave me the rundown on El Feo's location."

"Carmine must like you a lot."

"What makes you say that?"

"You're alive!" Detective Brooks stated bluntly. "Where is El Feo hiding out?"

Najee kept one hand on the steering wheel and sent a text message with the address of a downtown Los Angeles high-rise.

"The element of surprise is still on our side. El Feo won't expect us to set it off at his penthouse, feel me?"

Detective Brooks pinched the corner of his eyes and shook his head. He had been retired from the LAPD for a number of years, and his private investigation firm was thriving, but to a soldier, nothing compared to being deep in the trenches slugging it out with the bad guys. The unparalleled thrill was like an injection of Viagra directly into the dick vein. After completing a mission with Najee, he would go home with flowers and a stiff penis and chase his wife around the house naked.

Like a moth drawn to flames, the game was pulling him in.

"What did Niko say about security?" he inquired.

Detective Brooks' curiosity brightened Najee's mood. He had been rocking with Detective Brooks for a hot minute, and his loyalty was unquestionable.

Najee checked his rearview mirror, pressed the clutch, shifted gears, and switched lanes before saying, "Niko said El Feo is shook, but out of pride and arrogance, he hasn't beefed up security, at least not yet. For now, he's still rolling with a three-man crew, two armored SUVs, and heavy artillery."

"And that doesn't scare you? I'm practically shittin' in my pajamas listening to you describe what we're up against."

"Keeping it one hundred, I'm a little spooked, too, but there's no courage without fear."

"That'll go great on your tombstone!" Detective Brooks replied dryly.

"I understand if you wanna sit this one out—" Najee paused and chose his words carefully, "I can't sugar coat it, though. We're going in vertical, but there's a chance we may leave up out that bitch horizontal. Ain't no guarantees."

Detective Brooks knew the price.

"There never is!" he admitted.

"Listen, man, you investigated my mother's murder and helped me track down the muthafuckas responsible. You also helped me become a wealthy man in the process. I trust you, and you can trust me," Najee expressed sincerely. "We're not taking on the entire Nogales Cartel. That's stupid and suicidal. All we're doing is creeping up on El Feo and a couple of undertrained goons while they're slippin', feel me?"

Detective Brooks put the coffee mug down, picked up the Jack Daniels, and took a long swallow straight from the bottle. "I don't know why I let you talk me in to doing some of the shit we do," he said with a smile forming at the corners of his lips. "But I'm in! What's the plan?"

"We get in, we get Angela, and we get out alive! The only hold-up is acquiring the floor plans. Do you think your connect down at the Urban Development Commission can get us the blueprints this late at night?"

Detective Brooks sat at his desk and logged onto Zillow.com.

"He's on vacation at Club Fed for a fraud indictment. Besides, we don't need him. Everything is online nowadays. I just logged onto a real estate portal. The property managers advertise heavily on this site."

Detective Brooks typed the address into the search bar and images of the posh high-rise came up. It was a sleek, fifteen-story glass oasis and home to the beautiful and elite.

"Here it is right here, Manulife Tower. These bastards want an arm and a left nut just to lease a studio apartment. I wonder what they charge for a condo with a view?" Detective Brooks complained.

"Stay focused," Najee instructed. "Click on the penthouse and tell me if they offer video or a three-sixty virtual tour of the layout."

"Already on it, I'm sending interior images of the penthouse to your phone now."

Najee received the images and slowed his speed. The last thing he wanted to do was crash and kill himself while texting and driving.

"The penthouse is two stories with the bedrooms on the upper level," Najee observed. "That works in our favor. El Feo is probably hiding Angela up there. If we have to slug it out, she won't get caught in the crossfire."

"If—you mean when we slug it out," Detective Brooks corrected. "We got another problem, too. I see why El Feo feels so comfortable in this building. The place is a fortress. There's a bank, a Starbucks, and a jewelry store on the first floor along with armed guards. You need a key card to enter the premises after business hours."

"What about security cameras?"

"The exterior and lobby got electronic eyes everywhere, but surprisingly, there are not a lot of cameras on the floors occupied by the residents. The property managers placed an emphasis on anonymity. It's crazy how rich folks covet their privacy over security."

"Wealth and privilege can be a gift and a curse. The last thing a successful businessman or politician wants is to get caught on camera escorting some blonde bimbo to his honeycomb hideout," Najee offered his hypothesis, then asked, "What about elevators?"

"There's two of them, but it looks like only one goes to the penthouse, and it requires a key card, too."

"I figured the building would be locked down tight. The freight elevators are usually a weak point though. Delivery people come and go every day. There should also be an interior staircase. Either one should put us on the penthouse floor."

"I'm pulling that up now." Detective Brooks clicked on the link. "The plan shows a flight of steps on the Westside of the building. They run from the underground carport to the roof. Staircases are a security guy's nightmare because they're required by code."

"Precisely, that gives us two escape routes."

"That explains how we're getting out, but you still haven't explained how we're gonna get in the building and get up to the penthouse without being noticed by security or one of the residents or one of El Feo's soldiers. We're talking dozens of potential witnesses and collateral casualties if this thing goes sideways."

Najee seemed undeterred by the possibility of citizens or the security detail derailing the operation.

"You ever hear of organized chaos?" he asked.

Detective Brooks stood up and started pacing again.

"You are out of your mind, aren't you? You're gonna call in a bomb threat to get the building evacuated?"

"Is that a question or a statement?"

"It's both, there's no way El Feo is going to evacuate the building. Besides, if you call in a bomb threat, security will alert the bomb squad."

"That's exactly what I'm hoping for. When security calls the SWAT team, we'll be the first responders and walk straight through the front door. They won't even look twice at our weapons or vests. You know the lingo, so you do all the talking," Najee laid out the plot and added, "You still got any of that old LAPD riot gear?"

"Sure do," Detective Brooks confirmed. "You know what, Najee? Your plan is just crazy enough to work! I'll meet you on Fifth and Figueroa so we can change into tactical uniforms and go over the plan one more time before we execute."

Fifteen minutes later, Detective Brooks was strapped up and ready to ride out. He placed the SWAT team gear, two Kevlar helmets, two illegally modified AR-15 assault rifles, and extra ammo inside the ice cream truck he and Najee used to pull off the move on the Nogales Cartel stash house. The truck had chunky, all-terrain tires, law enforcement decals, and a paint job that mimicked a SWAT utility vehicle.

He paused for a moment to think of how he was going to tell Najee about Nella and Sosa. After meditating over it, Detective Brooks whispered a short prayer, backed out of his garage, and smashed off without realizing he was under surveillance.

ATF Agents Parker and Tank spotted Detective Brooks pulling out of the driveway of his suburban home.

"We got movement!" Tank warned, and the men ducked low in their seats.

Tank waited for Detective Brooks to bend the corner before cranking the engine and slowly pulling away from the curb.

"What I tell you, Tank? Criminals are creatures of habit," Parker insisted. "I knew if we sat on Brooks long enough, we'd catch him up to no good."

Tank gave Parker a fist pound and stated, "He's packing some heavy heat and impersonating a Special Weapons and Tactics officer. Where do you think he's headed?"

"Who knows, this is a big city with a lot to get into," Parker replied, then a light clicked on in his head. "Holy shit, I should've seen this coming! Najee is going after El Feo! They're about to set it off!" He couldn't contain his excitement. That familiar rush of adrenaline pumped through his body, making his eyes wide and his heartbeat faster.

"Follow Brooks and don't let him get away," Parker instructed and called Torres for the umpteenth time.

Once again, Torres's cell phone went straight to voicemail. Parker gazed out of the windshield with an absent look plastered on his face. Something wasn't right!

***

Larry D. Wright

Manulife Tower

"Something ain't right!" El Feo repeated for the sixth time since security called and gave him a heads up about the bomb threat. He paced back and forth in his plush living room before stopping to snort a line of coke off the glass coffee table.

The booger sugar made him more paranoid. El Feo rushed to the bank of security monitors and checked the six screens. Everything looked kosher, but he was still on edge. He liked being on edge. Over the years his intuition had kept him out of prison, and more importantly, it kept him alive.

"Yo, Chino, go check it out, homes," El Feo ordered, and after some thought, sent another soldier with him. "Shadow, I want you to roll with Chino. You vatos keep your eyes open until we find out if this bomb threat is legit."

"I wouldn't worry about it too much," Torres tossed in his two cents. "Some smart ass probably made a prank call. Happens all the time. It's more of a nuisance than anything. The bomb squad will come, run a K-9 through each level, and that'll be that."

El Feo was pleased to have a knowledgeable cop on the payroll. The bribe money was well worth it.

"Will we have to evacuate the building?" he asked.

"Not unless they find an actual bomb. I doubt the Chief will issue an order to evacuate these families in the middle of the night on a humbug. Like I said, I wouldn't worry too much." Torres sank into the soft leather sofa, kicked his boots up on the coffee table, popped a handful of almonds in his mouth, and cracked open a bottle of Modelo beer.

He was enjoying his new career as an outlaw. The Agency didn't seem to appreciate the years of sacrifice he had put in, so like a free agent, he sold his talents to the highest bidder. Money talks, bullshit runs a marathon!

El Feo nodded his approval. What the crooked cop was saying made sense. Convinced the bomb threat was a prank, he walked out onto the terrace of his swanky crib. The terrace wrapped around

266

two-thirds of the penthouse and offered breathtaking views of the Los Angeles skyline.

Gazing at the dazzling lights below his feet usually made El Feo feel as though he was standing on top of the world, but tonight his spirits were at an all-time low. Domingo was dead. He still couldn't believe it. He still couldn't accept it. He knew his right-hand man was an ambitious snake who wanted to be in his shoes, but everyone wanted the number one slot. It's the nature of the game, and Domingo was still sangre—blood—familia. A life must be taken in exchange for his life. No, fuck that, everyone in Najee's family must die, even the dog.

El Feo's mind was comforted by the images of revenge. He leaned over the rail of the terrace, looked down, and was surprised to see a big tactical vehicle with police lights and the number twelve on the roof.

"Damn, the bomb squad got here quick!" he said out loud.

Chapter 35

Come and Get Me

Najee's plan to get inside the building worked brilliantly. He called the building's security desk, disguised his voice as a disgruntled Arab, and made the bomb threat. As anticipated, the night security crew called the police. The dispatcher said she'd deploy a team, but it was the fourth false alarm of her shift, and she didn't seem too enthusiastic.

"We only got a few minutes to execute the plan before the real bomb squad arrives on the scene," Detective Brooks said as he pulled a thick, green, bulletproof vest over his head and strapped on a Kevlar riot helmet.

Najee swallowed hard, felt the steel trauma plate protecting his chest, and said, "Let's rock and roll, baby!"

Detective Brooks pulled up to the high-rise and deliberately parked in front of the double glass doors. Security buzzed them in, and he and Najee strolled into the lobby with authoritative swagger.

Najee chanted bullshit police codes into his walkie-talkie while Detective Brooks did his thing.

"Who's in charge?" Detective Brooks questioned like a military drill sergeant.

The four-armed security guards loitering around the lobby desk stiffened their backs.

"I'm in charge, sir!" A fifteen dollar an hour African American rent-a-cop spoke up.

Detective Brooks knew he had to get the guards away from the lobby desk and security cameras. He puffed out his chest and said, "Listen up, *Mr. I'm In Charge*, stay out of our way and position your men near the bank and the jewelry store. If this is some sort of trick to distract us, the assailants will be going after this building's most valuable assets. You got that?"

The rent-a-cop acknowledged the order with a head nod, and Detective Brooks kept laying it on thick.

"This may be the work of some nut case who gets his rocks off by making prank calls, in which case we'll be out of your way in a matter of minutes. But if this is a real ten-eighty, we may need to evacuate the building."

The rent-a-cop had no idea what a ten-eighty was, but it sounded official. He ordered his men to take post by the bank and jewelry store. Having the security guards preoccupied, Najee and Detective Brooks sprang into action. The steps were on the left. The regular elevator was in the middle, and the freight elevator was to the right.

"Take the freight elevator," Najee suggested. "And I'll take the steps."

"Good idea," Detective Brooks agreed. He had something else to say but now was not the time. Both of their heads needed to be in the game.

Inside the freight elevator, Detective Brooks calmly whistled *Amazing Grace* while screwing a silencer onto his nickel-finished Smith and Wesson.

Chino and Shadow posted up on opposite ends of the long hall-way outside the penthouse. They leaned against the wall and day-dreamed about guns, dope, the Bible, or whatever cartel operatives thought about when they were bored.

The freight elevator slid open on the penthouse level, but no one got out. Chino peeled himself off the wall and went to investigate.

"Psst, check this out, dog!" he called to Shadow and slowly stuck his head inside the elevator.

Detective Brooks greeted him with the barrel of a .45.

"Police, drop your fuckin' gun!" he demanded.

Chino dropped his gun.

Detective Brooks shot him anyway. The silencer suppressed the report of gunfire. Chino fell face forward, and Detective Brooks grabbed both of his wrists and dragged him inside the elevator. The door closed, and he continued whistling Amazing Grace.

Najee trotted up the long flight of steps and approached a door with the letters PH painted in red on the outside. He assumed it stood for penthouse. He extended the SIG Sauer and gently opened the door. He saw Shadow moving cautiously toward the freight elevator. Najee crept up behind him, and when he got close enough, he jammed the strap against Shadow's spine.

"On your knees!" Najee ordered.

Shadow refused, but slugs have a way of making a stubborn man comply. Najee blasted him in the back of his kneecaps. Shadow screamed in pain and dropped to his knees. Najee searched him for a key card.

He didn't find one, so he pressed the barrel against the side of Shadow's neck and asked, "How many people are inside the casa?"

"Fuck you, mayate! I ain't tellin' you nada!" Shadow yelled.

Even on his knees, he remained a stand-up soldier who had no delusions about the game. He bent over, touched his forehead to the floor, and prayed.

The Deacon's words tumbled in Najee's heart. He stood over Shadow with the blicky in his right hand, the hand that had sent so many bad men to meet their maker.

He pressed the SIG flush against the skin and said, "Why pray to God when you can meet Him in person." Najee squinted his eyes and shot him four times, a bullet for his hate, a bullet for his pain, a bullet for his rage, and a bullet for the fuck of it.

Shadow's body jerked violently; blood splatter stained the toe of Najee's Chuck Taylors. He grabbed Shadow by both ankles and dragged his dead body into the stairwell.

El Feo heard Shadow's initial scream and ran to the surveillance monitors. He zoomed in on the hallway, everything looked gravy, but that's what bothered him.

"Torres, get your fuckin' boots off my table and come check this out."

Torres stood next to El Feo and stared at the empty hallway.

"What do you see!" El Feo asked.

Torres shrugged his shoulders.

"Nothing."

"That's the problem! Where the fuck are Chino and Shadow? It's a setup." El Feo quickly walked onto the terrace, looked over the rail, and saw flashing red and blue lights. "Policia!" he yelled and ran back into the living room.

He snatched the cushions off the leather sofa and pulled out a .9mm and an AK-47. He tucked the Nina in his waistband and chambered a slug into the AK. He wasn't going out easy. He'd rather push up flowers than share prison showers.

Thinking the police were his only threat, he turned to Torres and said, "Make the call!"

Torres made the call. The squad of young killers El Feo kept in a condo on the tenth floor were tired of drinking beer and playing video games. They were hungry dogs salivating for drama and waiting to be unleashed. The three of them strapped up and moved out.

Najee heard a door open and close below him. He stuffed the SIG in the small of his back, slung the illegally modified AR-15 off his shoulder, and flicked the switch. Another door opened and closed. His heartbeat faster. He could hear shoes urgently scrambling up the steps.

"Damn, is this a resident, or is Niko's intel incorrect?"

The footsteps got closer. Someone twisted the doorknob. Najee pointed the AR.

"¿Quien es?" he asked. "Who's there?" in Spanish.

A voice came from the other side of the door.

"¿Está bien El Feo?" They wanted to know if El Feo is straight.

"Si," Najee replied, opened the door, and shot the Nogales Cartel goon in the mouth. He never saw it coming.

Detective Brooks heard the clap of gunfire and knew the show had begun. He reached for the button to open the door on the penthouse level, but the freight elevator suddenly started moving down. Detective Brooks looked up. The row of lights indicated the elevator was headed to the tenth floor. Could be a resident, could be the opposition. Detective Brooks was not sure, so he moved to the back corner of the elevator with his pistol concealed behind his back.

The freight elevator door squeaked open on ten. A Nogales Cartel goon heard someone whistling Amazing Grace, so he stuck his head inside. Detective Brooks blew it off his shoulders. The game was unapologetic. His body landed in the archway keeping the door from closing.

Detective Brooks reached down to roll the heavy body out of the doorway, but he got struck by bullets. The sizzling lead stung. It felt like he'd been hit repeatedly with a nail gun.

The third Nogales Cartel reinforcement goon stood by the resident's elevator with sparks and brass shells ejecting from his FN. Detective Brooks' bulletproof vest and Kevlar helmet ate most of the slugs, but blood dripped onto the floor. He was hit, but he didn't know where. Everything burned, everything hurt. He fell into the elevator and used his feet to kick and shove the dead body out of the archway. The freight elevator closed as the third goon ran up with his chopper blasting. The bullets missed and ricocheted off the metal door. *Amazing Grace!*

Detective Brooks' body went numb, but he knew he was still alive because his ears were ringing. He struggled to reach for the elevator panel and managed to hit the letter P. He smeared blood on the button in the process. The elevator descended and opened to the underground parking lot. Parker and Tank were there with their service weapons drawn. They didn't recognize Detective Brooks. All they saw was blood and an officer down.

"Hold tight, cowboy. I'll call the paramedics," Parker volunteered.

Tank kneeled next to Detective Brooks, held one of his eyes open, and pointed a flashlight at his pupil.

"Where you hit?"

"Geez, get that damn light out of my face, man. I took a slug, but I'm vested up," Detective Brooks grunted. "That's not my blood. It belongs to him." He told half the truth and pointed to the body of the first goon he shot and dragged onto the elevator. "There's more bad guys on the tenth floor." He purposely diverted them away from the penthouse level.

Parker and Tank decided that the elevators were a mobile death trap and opted to take the steps instead. On the tenth floor, they found residents with cell phones live streaming the bloody body of the dead Nogales Cartel thug. Parker ordered everyone back inside their homes, and he and Tank advanced toward the sound of gun-shots.

On the twelfth floor, tragedy struck. The stairwell door swung open. Citizen or combatant? In the split second it took Tank to decide, the third Nogales Cartel soldier stood at the top of the steps and greeted them with a hail of slugs. Tank caught heat from the neck up. The big man's legs gave out, and just like that, it was a wrap.

Parker rolled to his left, dropped to one knee, aimed, and fired. His shot missed. The Nogales Cartel soldier clapped back. Parker dived away from the muzzle flash, landed on his back, pointed his gun, and shot. The Nogales Cartel soldier took a hit to the thigh, tumbled down the steps, and broke his neck. Parker drilled him between the eyebrows for Tank and kept moving toward the penthouse level.

Inside the penthouse, El Feo stalked back and forth spewing drunken profanities in Spanish. He stopped ranting long enough to sniff another line of white girl and stepped onto the terrace.

"Come get me, motherfuckers!" he howled at the moon like a mad man and marched back inside.

Torres quickly realized the life of an outlaw wasn't as poetic as they made it seem in the movies. Hell, it was only his first day on the job, and things had already gone from sugar to shit. He rushed to the surveillance monitors, clicked through the camera angles, and caught Najee emerging from the stairwell.

"El Feo, come check this out!"

El Feo stood next to Torres and pointed his AK at the monitor.

"He's a dead motherfucker, homes!

Najee's walkie-talkie crackled. It was Detective Brooks. He was ok, he'd wait at the rendezvous spot for ten minutes, then Najee was on his own. Najee looked at his watch, placed his back against the penthouse door, and took a deep breath. It was do or die. Turning slightly to his left, he aimed the AR at the lock and blew it to smithereens. The door swung open. Najee jumped to the side and waited for gunfire.

Torres wisely fell back, but El Feo let the AK-47 rip and yelled, "¡Vamos, cabrón! Come get me!" He clicked off until the fifty-round magazine was depleted.

He dropped the chopper, upped the nine, saw a silver canister roll into the penthouse, and ran for cover.

Najee tossed a second flashbang grenade into the penthouse, put his back against the wall, and braced himself for two loud booms. The flashbang grenades detonated with a burst of sparks and a deafening roar, disorientating Torres and El Feo.

Najee swung his assault rifle into the living room, held the stick at his hip, and swept the barrel from left to right, torching everything—couch, coffee table, windows, pictures on the wall, eighty-gallon fish tank. Feathers flew from the couch cushions, and an expensive blue queen angelfish flopped on the marble floor, its puckered lips sucked air, its azure scales shimmered in the light.

Torres came over the kitchen island holding the butt of his gun firmly in both hands just as he practiced at the shooting range. He laid down cover fire, ducked, and moved positions.

Najee honed in on Torres' last location, aimed in the general direction, and pulled the trigger.

Torres wormed forward on his belly, reached his gun hand around the corner of the island, and popped off four more rounds. Two of them slammed into the trauma plate in Najee's vest and threw him against the wall. Najee felt pain in his ribcage. The AR fell out of his hands, and he clutched his right side. He slowly rolled over onto his knees and crawled into the hallway.

Torres stalked him like a lion hunting a wounded gazelle and drove a boot into Najee's ribs.

"Where do you think you're goin'?" Najee fell flat on his stomach. Torres stomped on his back. "We're just getting started," he taunted with a steel toe to the back of the head.

El Feo stumbled down the steps, holding his gun to Angela's head.

"What are you waiting for? Shoot that puto!"

Torres lifted his heavy boot and brought it down hard on Najee's spine. Najee groaned and slithered on his stomach trying to escape. Torres stepped on Najee's hand and aimed the tool at the crown of his head.

Parker exploded through the stairwell door, spotted an armed assailant, and screamed, "Police! Drop your weapon!"

It all happened so fast. There's no time to think in the midst of combat, only moments to react. Reflexes, muscle memory, eliminate the threat. That's what they taught in the academy.

Torres started to raise his gun.

"Don't move!" Parker warned. "Don't you fuckin' move!"

Torres recognized Parker's voice but made the mistake of turning around before lowering his gun.

Reflexes, muscle memory, Parker fired first to eliminate the threat. It's a textbook shot. Single slug center mass. Torres slid down the wall, looked at the blood trickling from his gut, and looked up at Parker with shame in his eyes.

"Oh, shit!" Parker realized it was Torres and rushed to his partner's aid. "What the fuck are you doing here, Torres?" he asked as he applied pressure to the wound.

Blood gushed from Torres' mouth, trickled down his chin, and soaked the collar of his shirt.

"It wasn't supposed to be like this, man," he moaned in agony. "I was supposed to collect five gees a week to look the other way and live happily ever after."

Parker cradled his partner's head in his arms.

"Come on, dude, that's not how we're built. What were you thinking?"

"The Agency doesn't give a shit about us, man. All the blood, all the sacrifices, all the time away from our families, and for what, a measly paper certificate when it's all over with?"

Parker pressed harder on the wound to stop the bleeding. It wasn't working.

"What do you expect? We're door kickers, bro. It's what we signed up for. It's who we are. We do all the dirty work to keep the streets clean."

Torres didn't respond, the light in his eyes dimmed.

The distraction allowed El Feo to ease out of the penthouse and inch his way to the resident's elevator. He held Angela in a choke-hold and kept his .9mm jammed against her temple.

Najee struggled to his feet and pulled the SIG Sauer from the small of his back.

"Let her go, El Feo!" he demanded.

El Feo gripped Angela tighter and hit the down button. "Fall back or I'm gonna blow this cunt's brains out!"

The elevator door opened.

Najee aimed the SIG at El Feo's head. He couldn't allow him to get away. Not this time.

Angela and Najee made eye contact. She knew what Najee had in mind, but she was afraid his shot wasn't accurate enough. She saw his eyes squint. She saw his trigger finger twitch. He was gonna shoot.

She closed her eyes and screamed, "Don't do it! Don't do it!"

Najee did it, he readjusted his aim and pumped the trigger. Angela yelled and fell.

El Feo reached down to pull her back into his grip. It was the window Najee needed. He turned the strap sideways and dumped. El Feo was blown back and stumbled into the elevator.

Najee ran up and got off again before the door closed.

Angela's groans snapped Najee out of his zone.

"Damn, papi, you shot me in the foot!" she complained.

"You're lucky, I was aiming for your head!" Najee kneeled, put Angela's arm over his shoulder, and helped her stand up. He supported her weight, and they limped to the resident's elevator.

Parker had the drop on Najee and Angela. This was his moment. It was the bust of his career, a wanted fugitive, a female cartel assassin, and a dead drug lord in the elevator. His partner would be a hero, too. The report would say Torres was gunned down in the line of duty. The footage of the bullet-riddled penthouse would look sensational on the five-o'clock news, and his face would grace the front page of the Los Angeles Times. The best part would be watching that prick Schwartz pucker up and kiss his ass at the retirement party.

Parker knew what he had to do. It was the right thing to do, but he didn't do it. He pulled the fire alarm instead, and said, "Keep your eyes low and blend in with the other residents evacuating the building. If you leave now, you can catch up with Detective Brooks."

Najee turned to Parker. They have a mutual understanding.

"Good looking out!" Najee expressed his gratitude and hit the elevator's down button.

"Don't thank me yet. You owe me one."

"Nah, we even, homie. When you get back to your office, look on page fifty-two of that book, *To Catch a Thief*. I left you a message."

The elevator door opened, but El Feo's body was not inside. Najee thought it was over, but the war had just begun.

As Najee, Angela, and Detective Brooks sped away from the crime scene, Najee's cell phone rang. The number was blocked, Najee answered anyway.

"You fucked up, nino!" the voice on the other end threatened.

"It is what it is," Najee said defiantly. "What do you suggest I do?"

"I suggest you run! Run fast! Run far!"

To Be Continued…
The Streets Made Me 4
Coming Soon

Submission Guideline

Submit the first three chapters of your completed manuscript to ldpsubmissions@gmail.com, subject line: Your book's title. The manuscript must be in a .doc file and sent as an attachment. Document should be in Times New Roman, double spaced and in size 12 font. Also, provide your synopsis and full contact information. If sending multiple submissions, they must each be in a separate email.

Have a story but no way to send it electronically? You can still submit to LDP/Ca$h Presents. Send in the first three chapters, written or typed, of your completed manuscript to:

LDP: Submissions Dept
Po Box 944
Stockbridge, Ga 30281

DO NOT send original manuscript. Must be a duplicate.

Provide your synopsis and a cover letter containing your full contact information.

Thanks for considering LDP and Ca$h Presents.

NEW RELEASES

FRIEND OR FOE 3 by MIMI
A GANGSTA'S KARMA by FLAME
NIGHTMARE ON SILENT AVE by CHRIS
GREEN
THE STREETS MADE ME 3 by LARRY D.
WRIGHT

<u>Coming Soon from Lock Down Publications/Ca$h Presents</u>

BLOOD OF A BOSS **VI**

SHADOWS OF THE GAME II

TRAP BASTARD II

By **Askari**

LOYAL TO THE GAME **IV**

By **T.J. & Jelissa**

IF TRUE SAVAGE **VIII**

MIDNIGHT CARTEL IV

DOPE BOY MAGIC IV

CITY OF KINGZ III

NIGHTMARE ON SILENT AVE II

By **Chris Green**

BLAST FOR ME **III**

A SAVAGE DOPEBOY III

CUTTHROAT MAFIA III

DUFFLE BAG CARTEL VII

HEARTLESS GOON VI

By **Ghost**

A HUSTLER'S DECEIT III

KILL ZONE II

BAE BELONGS TO ME III

A DOPE BOY'S QUEEN III

By **Aryanna**

COKE KINGS V

KING OF THE TRAP III

By **T.J. Edwards**

GORILLAZ IN THE BAY V

3X KRAZY III

De'Kari

Larry D. Wright

KINGPIN KILLAZ IV

STREET KINGS III

PAID IN BLOOD III

CARTEL KILLAZ IV

DOPE GODS III

Hood Rich

SINS OF A HUSTLA II

ASAD

RICH $AVAGE II

By Troublesome

YAYO V

Bred In The Game 2

S. Allen

CREAM III

By Yolanda Moore

SON OF A DOPE FIEND III

HEAVEN GOT A GHETTO II

By Renta

LOYALTY AIN'T PROMISED III

By Keith Williams

I'M NOTHING WITHOUT HIS LOVE II

SINS OF A THUG II

TO THE THUG I LOVED BEFORE II

By Monet Dragun

QUIET MONEY IV

EXTENDED CLIP III

THUG LIFE IV

By **Trai'Quan**

THE STREETS MADE ME IV

By **Larry D. Wright**

IF YOU CROSS ME ONCE II
By **Anthony Fields**
THE STREETS WILL NEVER CLOSE II
By **K'ajji**
HARD AND RUTHLESS III
Von Diesel
KILLA KOUNTY II
By **Khufu**
MOBBED UP III
By **King Rio**
MONEY GAME II
By **Smoove Dolla**
A GANGSTA'S KARMA II
By **FLAME**

<u>Available Now</u>

RESTRAINING ORDER **I & II**
By **CA$H & Coffee**
LOVE KNOWS NO BOUNDARIES **I II & III**
By **Coffee**
RAISED AS A GOON I, II, III & IV
BRED BY THE SLUMS I, II, III
BLAST FOR ME I & II
ROTTEN TO THE CORE I II III
A BRONX TALE I, II, III
DUFFLE BAG CARTEL I II III IV V VI
HEARTLESS GOON I II III IV V
A SAVAGE DOPEBOY I II

Larry D. Wright

DRUG LORDS I II III
CUTTHROAT MAFIA I II
KING OF THE TRENCHES
By **Ghost**
LAY IT DOWN **I & II**
LAST OF A DYING BREED I II
BLOOD STAINS OF A SHOTTA I & II III
By **Jamaica**
LOYAL TO THE GAME I II III
LIFE OF SIN I, II III
By **TJ & Jelissa**
BLOODY COMMAS I & II
SKI MASK CARTEL I II & III
KING OF NEW YORK I II,III IV V
RISE TO POWER I II III
COKE KINGS I II III IV
BORN HEARTLESS I II III IV
KING OF THE TRAP I II
By **T.J. Edwards**
IF LOVING HIM IS WRONG…I & II
LOVE ME EVEN WHEN IT HURTS I II III
By **Jelissa**
WHEN THE STREETS CLAP BACK I & II III
THE HEART OF A SAVAGE I II III
By **Jibril Williams**
A DISTINGUISHED THUG STOLE MY HEART I II & III
LOVE SHOULDN'T HURT I II III IV
RENEGADE BOYS I II III IV
PAID IN KARMA I II III
SAVAGE STORMS I II

284

AN UNFORESEEN LOVE

By **Meesha**

A GANGSTER'S CODE I &, II III

A GANGSTER'S SYN I II III

THE SAVAGE LIFE I II III

CHAINED TO THE STREETS I II III

BLOOD ON THE MONEY I II III

By J-Blunt

PUSH IT TO THE LIMIT

By **Bre' Hayes**

BLOOD OF A BOSS **I, II, III, IV, V**

SHADOWS OF THE GAME

TRAP BASTARD

By **Askari**

THE STREETS BLEED MURDER **I, II & III**

THE HEART OF A GANGSTA I II& III

By **Jerry Jackson**

CUM FOR ME I II III IV V VI VII

An **LDP Erotica Collaboration**

BRIDE OF A HUSTLA **I II & II**

THE FETTI GIRLS **I, II& III**

CORRUPTED BY A GANGSTA I, II III, IV

BLINDED BY HIS LOVE

THE PRICE YOU PAY FOR LOVE I, II ,III

DOPE GIRL MAGIC I II III

By **Destiny Skai**

WHEN A GOOD GIRL GOES BAD

By **Adrienne**

THE COST OF LOYALTY I II III

By Kweli

Larry D. Wright

A GANGSTER'S REVENGE **I II III & IV**

THE BOSS MAN'S DAUGHTERS I II III IV V

A SAVAGE LOVE **I & II**

BAE BELONGS TO ME I II

A HUSTLER'S DECEIT I, II, III

WHAT BAD BITCHES DO I, II, III

SOUL OF A MONSTER I II III

KILL ZONE

A DOPE BOY'S QUEEN I II

By **Aryanna**

A KINGPIN'S AMBITON

A KINGPIN'S AMBITION **II**

I MURDER FOR THE DOUGH

By **Ambitious**

TRUE SAVAGE I II III IV V VI VII

DOPE BOY MAGIC I, II, III

MIDNIGHT CARTEL I II III

CITY OF KINGZ I II

NIGHTMARE ON SILENT AVE

By **Chris Green**

A DOPEBOY'S PRAYER

By **Eddie "Wolf" Lee**

THE KING CARTEL **I, II & III**

By **Frank Gresham**

THESE NIGGAS AIN'T LOYAL **I, II & III**

By **Nikki Tee**

GANGSTA SHYT **I II &III**

By **CATO**

THE ULTIMATE BETRAYAL

By **Phoenix**

BOSS'N UP **I , II & III**

By **Royal Nicole**

I LOVE YOU TO DEATH

By **Destiny J**

I RIDE FOR MY HITTA

I STILL RIDE FOR MY HITTA

By **Misty Holt**

LOVE & CHASIN' PAPER

By **Qay Crockett**

TO DIE IN VAIN

SINS OF A HUSTLA

By **ASAD**

BROOKLYN HUSTLAZ

By **Boogsy Morina**

BROOKLYN ON LOCK I & II

By **Sonovia**

GANGSTA CITY

By **Teddy Duke**

A DRUG KING AND HIS DIAMOND I & II III

A DOPEMAN'S RICHES

HER MAN, MINE'S TOO I, II

CASH MONEY HO'S

THE WIFEY I USED TO BE I II

By Nicole Goosby

TRAPHOUSE KING **I II & III**

KINGPIN KILLAZ I II III

STREET KINGS I II

PAID IN BLOOD **I II**

CARTEL KILLAZ I II III

DOPE GODS I II

Larry D. Wright

By **Hood Rich**
LIPSTICK KILLAH **I, II, III**
CRIME OF PASSION I II & III
FRIEND OR FOE I II III
By **Mimi**
STEADY MOBBN' **I, II, III**
THE STREETS STAINED MY SOUL I II
By **Marcellus Allen**
WHO SHOT YA **I, II, III**
SON OF A DOPE FIEND I II
HEAVEN GOT A GHETTO
Renta
GORILLAZ IN THE BAY **I II III IV**
TEARS OF A GANGSTA I II
3X KRAZY I II
DE'KARI
TRIGGADALE I II III
Elijah R. Freeman
GOD BLESS THE TRAPPERS I, II, III
THESE SCANDALOUS STREETS I, II, III
FEAR MY GANGSTA I, II, III IV, V
THESE STREETS DON'T LOVE NOBODY I, II
BURY ME A G I, II, III, IV, V
A GANGSTA'S EMPIRE I, II, III, IV
THE DOPEMAN'S BODYGAURD I II
THE REALEST KILLAZ I II III
THE LAST OF THE OGS I II III
Tranay Adams
THE STREETS ARE CALLING
Duquie Wilson

288

MARRIED TO A BOSS I II III
By Destiny Skai & Chris Green
KINGZ OF THE GAME I II III IV V
Playa Ray
SLAUGHTER GANG I II III
RUTHLESS HEART I II III
By Willie Slaughter
FUK SHYT
By Blakk Diamond
DON'T F#CK WITH MY HEART I II
By Linnea
ADDICTED TO THE DRAMA I II III
IN THE ARM OF HIS BOSS II
By Jamila
YAYO I II III IV
A SHOOTER'S AMBITION I II
BRED IN THE GAME
By S. Allen
TRAP GOD I II III
RICH $AVAGE
By Troublesome
FOREVER GANGSTA
GLOCKS ON SATIN SHEETS I II
By Adrian Dulan
TOE TAGZ I II III
LEVELS TO THIS SHYT I II
By Ah'Million
KINGPIN DREAMS I II III
By Paper Boi Rari
CONFESSIONS OF A GANGSTA I II III

Larry D. Wright

By Nicholas Lock
I'M NOTHING WITHOUT HIS LOVE
SINS OF A THUG
TO THE THUG I LOVED BEFORE
By Monet Dragun
CAUGHT UP IN THE LIFE I II III
By Robert Baptiste
NEW TO THE GAME I II III
MONEY, MURDER & MEMORIES I II III
By **Malik D. Rice**
LIFE OF A SAVAGE I II III
A GANGSTA'S QUR'AN I II III
MURDA SEASON I II III
GANGLAND CARTEL I II III
CHI'RAQ GANGSTAS I II III
KILLERS ON ELM STREET I II III
JACK BOYZ N DA BRONX I II III
A DOPEBOY'S DREAM
By **Romell Tukes**
LOYALTY AIN'T PROMISED I II
By Keith Williams
QUIET MONEY I II III
THUG LIFE I II III
EXTENDED CLIP I II
By **Trai'Quan**
THE STREETS MADE ME I II III
By **Larry D. Wright**
THE ULTIMATE SACRIFICE I, II, III, IV, V, VI
KHADIFI

IF YOU CROSS ME ONCE
ANGEL I II
IN THE BLINK OF AN EYE
By **Anthony Fields**
THE LIFE OF A HOOD STAR
By **Ca$h & Rashia Wilson**
THE STREETS WILL NEVER CLOSE
By K'ajji
CREAM I II
By Yolanda Moore
NIGHTMARES OF A HUSTLA I II III
By King Dream
CONCRETE KILLA I II
By Kingpen
HARD AND RUTHLESS I II
MOB TOWN 251
By Von Diesel
GHOST MOB
Stilloan Robinson
MOB TIES I II
By SayNoMore
BODYMORE MURDERLAND I II III
By Delmont Player
FOR THE LOVE OF A BOSS
By C. D. Blue
MOBBED UP I II
By King Rio
KILLA KOUNTY
By Khufu
MONEY GAME

Larry D. Wright

By Smoove Dolla
A GANGSTA'S KARMA
By FLAME

BOOKS BY LDP'S CEO, CA$H

TRUST IN NO MAN

TRUST IN NO MAN 2

TRUST IN NO MAN 3

BONDED BY BLOOD

SHORTY GOT A THUG

THUGS CRY

THUGS CRY 2

THUGS CRY 3

TRUST NO BITCH

TRUST NO BITCH 2

TRUST NO BITCH 3

TIL MY CASKET DROPS

RESTRAINING ORDER

RESTRAINING ORDER 2

IN LOVE WITH A CONVICT

LIFE OF A HOOD STAR

Larry D. Wright

www.ingramcontent.com/pod-product-compliance
Lightning Source LLC
Chambersburg PA
CBHW070601260626
47161CB00002B/677